"A must read for anyone who ever touched a baseball."
—Houston Sun Times

"Adorable ... insightful, warm and fun loving —a must read."
—*Atlantic Journal*

"This book is better than the Mariners have ever been—and might ever be."
—Bart Giamoni

"This book will always be out—what a read!"
—Rudy A'Bramauitz
Library of Congress

"It's the last book I read—it's the last book I'll ever read."
—Carl Chessman
San Francisco Bee

"*The Thirty Hit Season* makes *Field of Dreams* seem like a book on bowling."
—*Publishers Monthly*

"If Tomkins doesn't write another book it will be a tragedy of immense proportions on the scale of the Titanic."
—*Orlando Times Sentinel*

"This book is similar to Bobby Thompson's home run—majestic, timely—perfect. A must read."
—*Entertainment Today*

"Funny and warm best describes this fantasy baseball book that can be read by ages 9-90."
—*Seattle Monthly*

"A Hall of Fame book written by an All Star writer for the fan of the '90s."
—*Los Angeles Intelligencer*

"This book almost drove me crazy. You'll like it."
—Jimmy Piersall

"Well plotted and well written ... again Tomkins demonstrates that he is both a knowledgeable student of the law, baseball and human nature.
—*Book Review Ltd.*

"Tomkins has condemned another summer of readers to addictive page turning .... A tale that could have, maybe should have, happened.
—*The Zimbabwe Register*

"Tomkins is utterly convincing in the picture he paints .... His quick intimate word pictures are a pleasure to read."
—*Arizona Daily News*

"David Pasteur is every man who ever had a dream and the luck and guile to pull it off."
—*The State*

"Tomkins' prose is clear, his dialogue real and his people lively and funny."
—*Chicago News*

"The most entertaining baseball story I've ever read."
—Irv Krassler
Baseball World

"David Pasteur can both hit, talk, and tell a great story."
—*World Series Digest*

Between a dream and reality is...

THE 30 HIT SEASON

A NOVEL

D. MICHAEL TOMKINS

PEANUT BUTTER PUBLISHING

226 Second Avenue West, Seattle, WA 98119 • 206-281-5965

ISBN # 0-89716-523-3

Cover design by Robert Dietz
Typesetting by Packard Productions

Printed in the United States of America
First printing, February 1995
10 9 8 7 6 5 4 3 2 1
410.025

PEANUT BUTTER PUBLISHING

Published by

Peanut Butter Publishing
226 Second Avenue West
Seattle, WA 98109
(206) 281-5965

Dedication

This book is dedicated to Mrs. Mahan, who recognized dyslexia before it was even a word; to Michael Hermes who taught me not to make excuses; and to Ida Singer, who put her money where her heart was to make it all possible.

They keep saying that what really matters is not whether you win or lose, but how you played the game. The trouble is that the best way to determine how you played the game is whether you won or lost.

—*William Hazlitt*

There ain't no man can avoid being born average. But there ain't no man got to be common.

—*Satchel Paige*

1

David Pasteur—no relation to the milk guy in France—was driving his 1976 two-door white Jaguar, with a Chevy engine under the hood, down a narrow, wet, busy street in Seattle. He drove the same route to work every day so he could see his billboard as he passed the corner tavern where he often had lunch. The billboard read, "If you were hurt in an accident someone owes you money." Not legally true of course, but catchy, very catchy. His radio ads reflected a similar sentiment.

David was an ambulance chasing litigator, a personal injury attorney, who specialized in clients who called his number. David did all he could to get people to call *his* number, rather than the number of one of the other 250,000 attorneys in the area. Not that all personal injury attorneys were the same, but how would a client know the difference without calling David's number to find out? Hence the billboard and the radio ads.

David thought about his current case, a case which was taking much time and much cash from his too-small bank account. He was emotionally drained and economically depleted. David had developed an accounting theory and philosophy that his office staff called the Jewish accrual system. Simply stated, if David could have earned a fee of say $25,000, but the jury awarded $15,000, then David felt that he had lost a cool $10,000 in that one case alone.

It drove his wife, who loved David in spite of his peculiar ways, crazy. Her name was Casey Carr. She was 37 and quite fetching, in a cheerleader sort of way. She tended to smile a lot, especially at her two little girls. David and Casey lived in a rambling 4,000-square-foot house overlooking Puget Sound. Two cats and a 90-pound sheepdog completed the family, but only time would complete this trial, and time was running out.

That morning David rehearsed his closing argument for the seventy-third time. With less than two hours before delivering it to the jury and press, he polished it in front of the mirror in his own private chambers, the black and white bathroom of his almost-paid-for home.

He picked this particular jury because he felt that this group would be sympathetic to his case and not dislike his personality, which had been described by court watchers as humorously irreverent and ambitiously creative. He was clearly no downtown law firm cookie-cutter "mechanic" who knew the law well and presented the evidence dispassionately to a trier of fact. David built his cases one fact piled onto another, one piece of evidence at a time, until a picture of reality—*his* reality and coincidentally the reality most favorable to his client—became crystal clear to the jury, who then dutifully awarded his client cash. Sometimes lots of cash. Sometimes none.

David hated this part of the day. He stood with a fluffy towel wrapped around his thickening waist. At 43 he was, well, 43—a desk jockey whose metabolic system had met in secret four years earlier and decided to retire en masse. No more calorie burning, it was declared. No more weight reduction, no more assisting the infrequent exercise program. His metabolism just flat quit. Of course it took several years before David's brain got the message, and by that time new suits and shirts were in order. Twenty extra pounds will do that to a middle-aged sedentary person, whose exercise program consisted of rolling down the electric car window to order at McDonald's.

"What are you doing, David?" came a muffled moan from the bedroom.

"Watching my belly get huge and my bank account shrink!" David answered, while toweling off his dark, wispy, thinning hair.

"Oh, Honey, you'll do just fine. What time is your closing today?"

"Ten A.M., or whenever the fat guy takes the bench."

"I think I'll keep Lindsey out of school and bring her so she can see Daddy wow the jury," Casey said while fluffing a pillow.

"Have her wear the T-shirt that says 'My daddy is the one that's winning' and make sure the jury knows I'm the daddy."

David began to pace in front of the king-sized bed, where his wife of ten years lay with two large, indolent cats perched on her trim, hard belly, the felines sleeping the sleep of cats who never worked and never rose before nine.

"David," Casey inquired, while stroking the fat cat named Ruth, as in Babe Ruth, his daughter's second favorite fat guy.

"What?" David snapped.

"Go ahead, Honey, just do it. I haven't heard it for three days, and it's good luck anyway. Besides, the cats need the sound of your voice to soothe them back to cat sleep."

David began to pace in front of the bed, back and forth from the large picture window overlooking Puget Sound and the snow-capped peaks beyond, to the closet full of lawyer clothes David wore only during trial. The rest of the time David went to work in jeans, shorts or sweats, depending on his mood and the fickle weather. You can do that when you're the senior partner of a one-man firm.

"Ladies and gentlemen of the jury," he began, waving his hands like a pushcart vendor showing off melons.

"You have heard testimony from many people over the last three weeks. Doctors, baseball coaches, big league scouts, policemen, ambulance drivers, and teammates. You have heard that a promising career in professional baseball has been taken from Ms. Rodriquez, due to the negligent driving of Mr. Harms, an employee of Mountain Beer Company of Golden Colorado. It is ironic and sad that a beer company, whose employee delivers intoxicating spirits to taverns, now asks you to punish Ms. Rodriquez for using its product prior to their truck striking her in a crosswalk."

"Daddy," a sleepy little girl came through the closed door wearing her Tampa Bay Mariner oversized T-shirt and rubbing her blue eyes with a small soft fist.

"Hi, Honey," David said, grabbing a robe from the closet and picking up his oldest girl in one smooth move.

"How did you sleep?"

"Are you doing closing?"

"Why do you ask, Lindsey Joy?" he inquired, knowing her answer.

"Because you're naked and walking back and forth in front of Mommy."

"Good guess!" David said laughing and tossing her on the bed beside her mom, scattering the cats.

"It's not like we're dating, Lindsey. Besides it's called strolling to the thoughts of justice, not walking back and forth in front of Mommy."

"Naked," added Lindsey, snuggling in beside Casey as if she was a second skin, giggling.

"Go ahead, Honey, I'm still listening,"

said Casey.

"No, I've lost the momentum. I'll save it for later this morning, when it just may count."

David went downstairs to put out the dog, get the paper and continue to worry about the case that he could very well lose in front of a whole bunch of people watching the outcome across the country—if you count ESPN viewers as the country.

The facts were routine enough: A professional truck driver was coming back from a long day of tavern and bar deliveries, around 11 p.m., in downtown Seattle. He failed to see a 21-year-old college student enter the crosswalk in front of him on a blinking "Don't Walk" sign. She was halfway across the street when he first saw her in her light-colored clothing, and by then it was too late to stop. The truck struck her right leg with its front bumper, shattering her ankle and breaking her leg. A good recovery followed almost two full years of rehabilitation. Medical billings of $30,000 were undisputed by the insurance company. The small lump on her leg would reappear when she was tired, the scar being no worse than she might have gotten after a routine ski accident surgery. The pain would return, especially with inclement weather, but all in all she was a very lucky young woman who had achieved an excellent recovery, through hard work and perseverance.

The problem was that her dream, her life's goal, had been taken from her on the operating table. Maria was a baseball player—a real, honest-to-goodness professional baseball prospect who could throw an 88-to-90-mile-per-hour fastball with good movement and pin-point control. She was a Mexican-American college student attending Washington State University, majoring in coaching and physical education. Her grades were average, her looks were better.

Her parents were retired field workers from the Yakima Valley and lived in a small airless shack along a dusty orchard road. They had worked in the blazing sun, picking berries and fruit for 35 years while they doted on their only child at the end of their 14-hour days.

A Little League coach had spotted Maria throwing rocks with uncanny accuracy and speed, and lobbied the provincial rulers of the league to allow her to play. Thus began a slow rise to medium celebrity. By college, she had already been on the cover of several sports magazines and had appeared on local and regional talk shows. She was shy, articulate, and loved to play baseball in the heat of Eastern

Washington, striking out her male opponents with the ease of a much more experienced male pitcher.

She was a 5-foot 9-inch, 155-pound throwing machine. And therein lay the rub. She had been the first for-real female college baseball pro prospect, and now she would never be able to pursue her dream. Her ankle would be usable for 97 percent of life's functions and duties. But pitching in college, let alone at any higher level, was in that forever out-of-reach three percent. Her cutting-edge career was permanently dulled.

David let himself into his office. It was usually a quiet place at 7:30 A.M., but today the phone was ringing when he entered the deeply carpeted lobby. He reached for the phone, with its many buttons on the mahogany desk of his secretary Catherine "I run this place" Daniels.

"Pasteur and Associates, where justice never sleeps," he answered.

"David?"

"Yes?"

"Parker, *Seattle Times*. Got a minute?"

"No, I'm a lawyer, a very uptight lawyer. One who's about to beg for two and a half million dollars for Maria Rodriquez, hoping that sexist pig Judge Burns gets out of my way and lets me close like the guys on *L.A. Law* get to do." David dropped his briefcase on the reception area couch and leaned on Catherine's otherwise unoccupied desk.

"I noticed that, too, Dave. How come he hates you?" inquired the smoky, gravely voice from the other end of the phone.

"Me, he just dislikes. It's my case that he hates. He thinks that Maria should still be out in the field—that's lettuce, not playing. He's made it clear that she should be content with a college education, a little fame and a modest verdict. He's a misogynist pig."

"So the judge doesn't buy your argument that she lost huge money because of this accident. No more competitive baseball, no possibility of the majors, huh?"

"Right. Way too speculative. Burns does everything he can to let the jury know that he thinks I'm an overreaching, money grubbing, little, Jewish guy who's looking for headlines, and who should have settled this case long ago, rather than waste his precious time in court."

"And?"

"Guilty, except for the settling part, but so what? I think the jury likes my deal. They like Maria, and I'm going to make those twelve strangers laugh, cry, and do the hokey-pokey while they reach into Continental Insurance Company's pocket and squeeze until Ben Franklin's head explodes into our bank account."

"Can I quote you on that?" The reporter laughed, as he slurped his coffee. "Pretty colorful, even for you."

"Go write an obituary. I'm busy."

"Good luck, Dave. I'll be there this morning. Which tie are you going to wear for TV?"

"The one you gave me, Parker. You know, the hula girl on a background of waving palm trees. The power tie."

"Good choice. Don't stutter," Parker said with amusement, and hung up.

"Goodbye," David said to no one in particular. He hung up the phone and picked up his briefcase. As he turned toward the office door, Maria walked in, tense, frowning, and scared.

"Hi, Coach," David said lightly.

"Hi, David. How are you?" she said. David had always found her faint Spanish accent appealing.

"Fine," he lied. "I'm just getting psyched up to dazzle the media, the jury and, of course, you. Coffee?"

"One cup. I couldn't sleep. I can't eat. This is worse than ..." she trailed off, looking down at the new Reebok high tops she had worn all through the trial. There had been much discussion about what she should wear in the courtroom. It was decided, after much argument, that she should dress like who she was, a jock. A female jock to be sure, but a jock nonetheless. No dresses or frilly blouses just for court. No. Nice athletic clothes which were feminine, but clearly sent a subtle message—I am an athlete, regardless of my gender.

They went back to David's eccentric office, which boasted a dart board on one wall with a fee schedule sign above, a full-size skeleton that his daughter had named Bones, and a very neat desk with a formal wooden sign in front which read, in fancy letters, "No Whining."

Maria sat in the red, fake leather wingback client chair across from the desk sign, looking into her coffee cup.

"Well," she said blowing on the coffee and smiling through her very white teeth.

"Well what?" Dave asked, smiling back at his client, whom he liked very much.

"One last time, give me those jerks' best argument for screwing me."

"Well, Maria, are we a little uptight today?"

"Damn right I am. This is it, bottom of the ninth and all that stuff, and I can't do squat about it, just sit and listen. That's hard, real hard, especially when they just get to, you know, distort the facts. I don't know. Boy, what a system.

"I need this money. Not *need* need, maybe. Not like I need oxygen, but I was in line for a lot of ... oh, a lot of what?" She sipped her coffee and thought for a moment. "Security, I guess. I promised my dad. I promised him that he gets to move into a real house, go to a real doctor for his back. Live, finally live. I promised him, and those two-faced sleazeballs aren't going to take this away from him. Are they, David?"

"Not a chance, but let me ask you this. I've never asked you before because the insurance company's offer has been only $100,000 including medical bills. But tell me right now, what would you take this morning, net in your pocket, to walk away after I'm paid, the medical bills are paid, all costs paid, tax-free to you. How much?"

"I don't know," she sighed, gazing off.

"Bad answer. I want a number," David demanded.

"I want to pitch," she responded.

"You can't".

"Yeah, I know."

"So, how much?"

A long silence followed, while she wiggled in her chair and began to rub her bad ankle, a habit she started during trial, and one that David subtly encouraged. Every little bit helps.

"What's the lowest we get?"

David picked up a pencil and began twirling it like a bad majorette.

"Always zero. We can always get zero, but for a realistic low number, $75,000."

"I'd take $250,000," she whispered.

David wouldn't. Not that he had the choice. The law firm of Nelson, Nelson and Paggett had fought this case with a ton of their client's money, two partners' time, and three associates. Their client the beer company, and the beer company's insurance carrier had drawn a line in the sand early on, having decided very little money would ever be offered, and had stuck with that philosophy throughout the proceedings.

"Is that too high?" she asked uncertainly.

"No. We'll do better. I hope," he said, "But we have our problems too, as you well know."

"Sometimes I'm sorry I worked so damn hard to get my leg back right. Now, as I hear those slimy corporate drones tell it, I sprained my ankle, the baseball was a publicity stunt by the college, and I'm a drunken whore who kills babies and deserves to be run over."

"Taking away all that fancy lawyer talk you've heard in court, yes, that sums up their case nicely. Ever think of going to law school?"

"How did this happen? How come I'm on trial for getting hit by *their* truck?"

"I have to admit Maria, I never guessed it would get this dirty and this mean-spirited, but it has and, well, we did what we could to counter it. The defense has taken a big gamble—they went after you personally, brought up the abortion you had when you were 16, pounded the fact that you were legally intoxicated and in the company of seven men, who were also drunk, when you were struck walking in the crosswalk."

"I had four beers on an empty stomach, had pitched seven innings in 90-degree weather, and had gone out to celebrate with my teammates."

"And you explained all that on the stand very well, even when Nelson tried to rattle you about your drinking that night."

"I know, I know, but that jerk attorney pissed me off. I ...."

"I know, and I don't think the jury minded you suggesting to him that he might play checkers, but that didn't make it a sport. It was rather funny. The jury likes you."

"Do they?"

"That, my sweet Hispanic fast-ball pitcher, is the big home run, put-some-money-in-our-jeans question, isn't it?"

"What does Casey think? She's smart, and she goes to all your trials. You said she can read people."

"Casey likes you too much. She doesn't count." David stood up to put his closing notes in his favorite good-luck briefcase. It looked like it had been made in 1920 by a bootlegger who drank bathtub gin and had gone blind. "But to answer your question, Casey's scared as hell about that abortion issue. A jury can crucify people for the damnedest things, and an abortion isn't trivial, so ...." David trailed off, fiddling with the briefcase latch.

Maria shrunk into herself, as if trying to become part of the chair. She worried her ankle with her left hand more vigorously, and stared into the distance.

"I know. I'm not sure I wouldn't punish me, too," she said softly, as if to herself.

David wanted to come around the desk and hug her, but this was too personal. Too female. He had to get centered on the next four hours, which would at least end her nightmare, win or lose.

"Maria, I'm not going to talk about that on closing. But now I want to hear you tell me about baseball."

She smiled like a seven-year-old looking at her first baseball glove.

"But we've talked about this a lot before."

"I'm the lawyer, your mouthpiece as it were, which is an old but accurate description of my function in this trial. So tell me this. When you're warming up on the sideline before a game, what are you feeling?"

Maria rose from her chair, placing her empty mug on the polished desk. She walked to the window of David's office and stood still, pensive. She remembered the last time she stood on the mound, 22 months ago, on the day of the accident. She had pitched a two-hitter in front of 15,000 fans at the PAC-10 finals at the Kingdome where the pros play, and where she never would again.

"It feels free. Independent. Powerful. No sexist stuff, no racial stuff," she answered, looking David straight in the eyes.

She continued. "It's just me, a white ball and a batter. Everyone can see the results. It's the best feeling a person can have. If you're better, everyone knows it. If you're not, everyone knows it. No one thinks I'm a Mexican woman in a man's game when I'm on the mound. Not after I throw some heat at their heads they don't. Or they didn't." She closed her eyes, clenching her fists.

"It's total freedom. Freedom to win or lose on your own merits. There are a lot of agendas in other parts of life, but on the field it's, well, it's pure. Earn it or not. If you do, it's the best. If you don't, it's still great." Maria looked back up at David.

"I wish I could have experienced something like that, Maria."

"I wish everybody could because if you get that feeling just once, it can really change you, and I think it can change people so that they, ... well, respect each other more, based on their abilities alone. We all need more of that, don't we?"

"Except for that jerk, Nelson?" David laughed.

"Yeah, he should get one stuck in his ear."

David looked at his watch and finished packing up for court.

2

They were all sitting in a restaurant across the street from the courthouse—Casey, Lindsey, Maria, David and Catherine, David's secretary of twenty years.

Lindsey was chomping on a hamburger trying to understand the tension she felt around her. "Daddy," she finally asked between bites of catsup-dripping french fries, "how come you got to talk two times and the old man only one time?"

"Lindsey," Casey interrupted, "his name is Mr. Nelson, not 'the old man.' That's not polite."

"Well, he made fun of Daddy. I didn't understand a lot of it, but he doesn't like

Daddy or Maria, does he?"

"Yeah, she's right," Maria opined. "He didn't like us, did he Lindsey?"

David cut in after swallowing a big gulp of scotch and water, his third in an hour. "We don't care about that pompous ass. We care who they elect as a jury foreman, because if it's number seven, with those expensive suits and that superior look, we're toast. He looks like he'd evict his mother for late rental payments."

"What does he do?" Maria asked.

"Number seven, in the front row, is an accountant for the State of Washington. He's single, superior, and probably hates Caesar Chavez," said Casey. "Remember, we couldn't get him off the jury because the next person in line was Hitler."

"I think number seven liked your closing. He laughed when he was supposed to," Maria offered.

David smiled at Maria and said, "Accountants are not to be trusted with other people's money. On the other hand, they are generally not frightened by big numbers and are comfortable with lots of zeros, rates of inflation, and discount rates, things which put most people to sleep."

Casey asked, "Well, three million never put me to sleep. And by the way, how come you came up with that figure at the end of closing?"

"It just felt right."

"All your education, training and experience, and 'it just felt right' is your insightful answer? Boy, what a businessman."

Seventy-two hours later the jury was still out. To David, it was worse than waiting for the birth of his first child. In labor, you knew something would happen, just not exactly when. But waiting for a verdict was worse. First of all, there may not be one. A hung jury is nine to three in favor of or against a party, and it doesn't count. Instead, you do it all over again. The jury in a civil case needs at least ten to two in favor of someone to get a verdict. A dollar amount needs to be agreed upon, even if that amount is zero.

David's office was beyond inefficient during this waiting time. Every phone call, and there were many during the average day, sent a shiver of expectation through the staff, awaiting the call from the bailiff, who would say, "We have a verdict." It still had not come after 24 hours of deliberation.

"Is the longer they're out good, bad, or who knows?" asked Maria by phone, each day the waiting continued.

"I have not the slightest idea," David answered, reaching for yet another Tums. "I'll call when we hear."

Casey came into the office with both girls who promptly took their places on the floor with their equipment in hand. They began to do the most bizarre things with stick-ons, scissors, colored pens, and staplers.

"Well?" Casey asked. She took a seat in one of the client chairs, slinging her legs over the chair arm.

"Well, what? I hate this part."

"Okay, lets talk about after your big win. What's next in the fun-filled life of our little family unit?"

"I was thinking," David said, looking out the window at a rainy, late February Seattle afternoon. "Let's go to spring training in Arizona. Just pack shorts, lotion, see the sun, drown our sorrows or rejoice in justice, and 'just do it', like Bo says."

"I could call Saint Esther, see if she can

watch the monsters while we're gone. I'd love to go. Can we?"

Esther, Casey's mom, was one of those old-fashioned mothers. She had all the skills of the traditional models from the 1920s to the 1950s sewing, cooking, cleaning, caring, and she even liked it. She also was educated, sensitive, and just plain nice like the dictionary describes. Saint Esther loved her grandchildren almost as much as she loved baseball. Casey and Esther had never been to spring training. Neither had David. They had all talked about going to observe the rites of spring, eternal hope, and the green Arizona grass, but something always got in the way to prevent it.

One time, several years before, Casey and David were packed, in the car, literally on the way to the airport in hopes of finally going to spring training, when the car phone rang. Instead of turning off the phone, David picked it up. The next thing they knew, the car and the luggage were parked at a hospital lot where, inside, a 19-year-old college girl was coming out of surgery. That was as close as they had ever come.

"Spring training," Casey wistfully imagined, "I'd like that. Could we go win, lose or draw, and turn off the car phone this time?"

"Why not? We win, I treat us like

royalty. We lose, well, we're in Arizona watching young men do what I could be doing if I wasn't, well, 43 ...."

"—and could throw, hit and catch," Casey interrupted, digging in her purse for their travel agent's number. "When can we leave?"

"We leave when, and if, the damn jury ever comes back. What could they be doing? Besides eating lunch at the taxpayers' expense, it isn't even great food, but ...." The phone rang. The jury had a verdict, and David had a problem.

3

"Please fasten your seatbelts," the breathy stewardess commanded. "We will be landing at Sky Harbor Airport in approximately 20 minutes. The temperature on the ground is currently 84 degrees, with blue skies, and winds at 10 miles per hour."

Casey and David were sitting in the middle of the plane, holding hands and thinking their independent, though somewhat related, thoughts. It had been an interesting ten days since the verdict was returned. The foreman, number seven, that wonderful insightful, sensitive, brilliant state employee, had seen through the beer company's personal attacks on Maria. He had led the jury to the reasonable and fair conclusion that Maria Alicia Rodriquez, the first female baseball player to have a legitimate shot at the Show, was to be compensated by the same standards as a male ballplayer with similar talent. The foreman convinced two of the women on the jury to disregard the fact that Maria had terminated a pregnancy; it having nothing to do with the legal issues presented to them by the court and counsel. He further argued in the jury room that a 21-year-old is allowed to drink beer then walk across the street to go home, and further, Maria was not comparatively negligent, as the beer company had maintained.

The award, after all the bickering and arguments about outlandish professional sports salaries and the actual likelihood of a female succeeding in organized baseball, came down to this: 1.725 million dollars. A home run on anyone's verdict scorecard. David and Maria were ecstatic. Nelson and Nelson went ballistic, which was no surprise. They immediately began to file post-trial motions, asking the trial judge to overturn the verdict, grant a new trial, or reduce the verdict to a reasonable amount that was supported by the evidence, and not the passion and prejudice of a runaway jury, egged on by Plaintiff's attorney's speculative and bizarre analysis of future lost earnings. "My God," they argued to the judge, "Plaintiff is an Hispanic female college student with one aching ankle and two great legs. That just isn't worth what the jury awarded to her."

All of which were the routine ramblings of a defeated downtown law firm who had just lost a highly visible case after assuring their insurance company client not to worry about the outcome.

It was all very much routine, until the trial judge, the Honorable Leonard W. Burns, a man of 68 years, and with little respect for the jury system unless he happened to agree with the result, began to consider Nelson and Nelson's post-trial motion seriously.

"I'm inclined to agree with Mr. Nelson's motions Mr. Pasteur. I do feel that this verdict is not supported by the trial evidence and, therefore, I am compelled to look very closely at this jury award. I have before me, Counsel, a Motion for Remittitur asking me to reduce the award by my own order; not substituting my judgment for that of the jury, but reducing the monetary award to conform with the evidence as presented by the parties throughout the trial."

"Your Honor," David began, stunned at how this routine hearing was suddenly turning into a serious threat to his verdict, "with all due respect, what *you* feel is fair, what *you* think is adequate is interesting, but not legally relevant. The jury has listened, discussed and then spoken. Just because *you* don't agree with what the jury has awarded is not a legal reason to demand that Plaintiff take less money. We won't. Period."

Judge Burns had a background in insurance defense work prior to ascending the bench. He was pompous as a lawyer, and arrogant on the bench. This arrogance had grown every year, along with his belly. He now weighed close to 300 pounds and perspired constantly even though his courtroom temperature was kept at that of a meat locker.

"Well, Mr. Pasteur, that's too bad," said the Judge, as he wiped his dripping forehead, which looked like it hadn't seen sunlight since the Eisenhower Administration, "because *I* think we have experienced a runaway jury. And I am empowered, nay, *mandated* to fix this miscarriage of justice.

"Now, another three-week trial is not cheap, so rather than retry the entire case, I will award to Plaintiff the sum of $200,000 inclusive of all medical billings. You will accept this amount or I will order a new trial in this court room to begin within six months, or whenever my calendar first permits."

"You're kidding!" David shouted. "On what grounds?"

"My grounds, Counselor. I just told you. The evidence does not support this dollar award. I have ruled. I am the judge."

So David had won big, lost bigger and was now in that uncomfortable place called legal limbo. He was out of pocket $34,000 for the costs and expenses of the trial. He would receive no fee. Maria still had no money. More time and much money would be needed to appeal the court's ruling. David wanted to get drunk and stay drunk until much later in life, when this nightmare would be over.

"It's sunny, David. That's nice isn't it?" Casey said in a little girl's voice which mimicked their youngest daughter, Lauren, and usually made David laugh. Not this time.

"Yeah, that's nice, but I just lost a million dollars, one *million*. I can't even count that high. A million dollars gone. It was right here, in my hand." He showed his wife his soft, white palm.

"I've never known a man who lost a million dollars before. Jeez, I'm blessed. C'mon, David, lighten up. If you're not going to have fun down here in Arizona then why did we even come? Besides, you didn't *lose* it, it's just on loan until we can bring it home to a new and better place to stay. Much better than that mean old insurance company where it now resides."

David smiled. "Deal. We talk baseball, think sun, and never again mention that fat, brain-dead, misogynist judge who wouldn't know a fungo from a Frango."

"Deal," said Casey. They shook on it. He ordered another scotch, and worried.

That night they drove their rented red convertible to see their first spring training game. It was an evening event between the beloved, perennially inept, step-children of Major League Baseball—the Seattle Mariners—and the San Francisco Giants, at the new Scottsdale Stadium in downtown Scottsdale. The night was clear, warm and perfect. The trial memories were put in the back of David's head for five luxurious hours, while balls and strikes were counted by men in blue for the benefit of boys in white.

The Seattle Mariners, who had finished in the cellar the last three years, had changed uniforms, owners, coaches and managers but remained talent-starved and fan-discontented. The team was also on its lips financially due to the above. But this year, this year would be different. This year the newest of the new owners in baseball had decreed to the world that he alone would change things for this sorry organization, by his iron will to start with, and by whatever else it took thereafter.

The new majority owner was a 72-year-old, idiosyncratic, undereducated business genius. He was reportedly worth several hundred million dollars, all made within the last twenty years. A native of Seattle, he was a widower with one daughter and one grandchild, on whom he doted. His name was Cyrus, and he didn't understand the game of baseball, but he understood the dynamics of people. People played this game. He understood people, ergo, he would make this particular project, the new Mariners, a success, as he had with other organizations several times in the past two decades, by applying the old Cyrus magic. His often quoted reason for success was "listen with your heart, react with your gut, and for damn sake take some chances."

By purchasing the ball club for an obscene amount of money, Cyrus had certainly taken a chance. The sale had been finalized mere weeks before spring training began. David was only peripherally aware of the sale, as he had been immersed in his own business problems, namely the Rodriquez trial. The product that David and Casey saw that first spring night looked much less than promising, and similar to years past. The pitching was young, therefore untried and untested. No strong, consistent hitter was on the roster as the spring opened, and the manager, Lou Piniella, was deeply troubled by the lack of speed throughout the team. The old, hackneyed sports phrase "we're small but slow" came to David's mind, watching the team lose their seventh spring training game in ten tries.

"Another ugly start to an ugly season," Casey remarked, while polishing off her second bratwurst in as many innings.

"Who's number 17?" asked the college student sitting next to David, pointing toward a surly looking black youth.

"Not in my program. Oh, here he is, a pitcher from Jacksonville Double A ball, 20 innings pitched last year. He looks like he's 12, ERA of 4.17."

"Sounds like a prospect to me," said the student. "With those stats, he could start for the Mariners."

David gazed out onto the green lushness of the baseball diamond, watching the frolicking youths of many colors. Baseball was truly an international and cross-cultural sport. He spotted a strapping youth who looked, well, not out of place, for he had a perfect athlete's body, but something was very different. David stared and analyzed, attempting to identify the difference. It suddenly dawned on him, and he blushed. Number 96, a young man closer to 19 than 20, was Japanese. This youth was followed around by another Japanese individual considerably older than the player. Maybe his dad? Maybe his agent? Maybe his Yakuzi boss? "What's with the Asian twins?" David inquired of his mustard dripping wife.

Casey licked her fingers like a cat. "That, my little litigator, is Mac Suzuki, an eighteen-year-old born and bred Japanese phenom from Kobe. He quit high school, came to these great baseball shores and labored in the Minor Leagues for two and a half hours and is now in camp trying to stick with a fabulous fastball, great curve, and a good change. He also speaks absolutely no English—the shadow is his translator."

"How do you know all this current baseball lore?"

"I read, I study, I know."

"So does he make the club?"

"David, he's only eighteen, never been

near a big league team, never faced a real Major League hitter, and you ask if he can pitch for our beloved Mariners this season with our depth?"

Indeed, another season like all the rest, David thought. But hell, it's baseball, and if you are lucky enough to get to have Major League Baseball in your geographic area, then you are blessed. Maybe not as blessed as some pimply-faced youth, who can leverage generally useless talent into huge, multi-year contracts, but blessed nonetheless.

The truth is, David pondered on the way back home from the game, every single Major League player would play the game for one-tenth of their current salary, regardless of that particular figure. Who in their right mind wouldn't want to play this child's game out in the summer sun, in front of your friends for six months of the year, garner respect and attention from people in all walks of life, only because you can perform the somewhat specialized, if unimportant, skill of hitting a white ball a long distance with a round piece of polished wood one out of four times? So, David wondered, why in the hell pay these lucky individuals millions of dollars when they would play and perform for much, much less?

"Casey, Sweetie?"

"What, Honey?"

"I've been thinking. I've decided I should be the new Commissioner of Baseball and restore order, both economic and social, to this great pastime. How do I apply for the post?"

"Feeling better, are we?" she said while putting her arm around his shoulder, letting the desert air caress her sunburned arm as they made their way back to their hotel.

"Yeah, I'm feeling better."

"Good, because we don't have seats for tomorrow's game, and we are going, no matter what."

"Yes, Dear."

"So find us some tickets."

"Yes, Dear."

4

They rose at 8:30 to a brilliant day in the Valley of the Sun. Casey retreated to the balcony overlooking the pool. Relaxed, with a cup of tea in her hands, she looked peaceful, pretty, and tan.

"Hi." She smiled as David padded out to a comfortable chair beside her.

"What's on tap for this glorious day, this day of sun, no clients, baseball, and warm, desert air?"

"My, we slept well, didn't we, Mr. Pasteur?"

David looked at his wife with her long, luxurious black hair hanging down her back, as she sipped tea in the morning sun, and became frisky.

"I slept well, yes, but I also have morning needs that require some exploring in the bedroom, where I can lie down and talk about these cravings to someone sympathetic."

Casey looked at her husband, amused. "What will you give me if I let you have your sick way with me?"

"A bratwurst? You like those."

He pulled her to her feet, wrapped his arms around her trim waist and led her to the room where people rested after a tiring day. But they weren't tired.

In the middle of their lovemaking, which was noisy and athletic, the phone rang.

"Let it ring. Someone will take a message. No dog, no kids, forget the phone," David pleaded, attempting to concentrate on the pleasurable task at hand.

"I'm not answering it," Casey said with a giggle—the giggle that killed. David often thought that if females carried a tape recorder containing a laugh track, a good many sexual assaults could be thwarted in mid-act. A laugh, regardless of how it was intended, was devastating to men in general. Not to men themselves, but to their aroused equipment. The only reason David had not pursued this line of inquiry and turned this observation into a business opportunity was that he didn't know if it was true for any other males or just him. After all, he had never seen another man naked and excited, up close and personal, and if he had, a laugh or a giggle would not have been either appropriate or appreciated.

The phone rang two more times before it became apparent that it might as well be answered, as the giggle had done its work.

"Hello. This better be good."

"Judge Burns here, and it is good, Mr. Pasteur, or at least I deem it so."

"Oh, Judge, nice to hear from you. Missed your voice these last two days. Truly a pleasure."

As Casey pulled up the sheet to cover herself, David gave her a very disappointed look. At the same time little beads of perspiration sprang into life on his sunburned brow. This call was not expected. He hated phone call surprises.

"I got your number from your office. They said you had flown off to Arizona, very disturbed. Very disturbed indeed."

"Well, you did pick my client's pocket for a substantial amount of money, Your Honor. I didn't trust myself to speak, how would you say, appropriately."

"Pretty pissed are you, David?"

"Very astute, Your Honor. Pissed is a mild word."

"Well," the judge cleared his throat and continued, "I am calling due to the defense motion which I orally granted and which is to be presented today in order form, granting a new trial. I understand that no one from your office is going to be in attendance for the presentation of the order granting said motion."

David sat still, then turned toward Casey and slowly pulled down the hotel sheet until he was able to see her as no one else would. Or so he hoped.

"Counselor?" Burns queried.

"I'm here," David finally allowed.

"Well ...."

"Well, what?"

"Well, are you coming to the presentation of the order?"

"I have a question, Judge. Did you dial this call yourself, Your Honor?" David asked, his voice edged with sarcasm.

"Yes," the judge exclaimed.

"Well, area code 602 is not in Western Washington. So what is your best guess, uh, your Judgeship?" David said softly into the phone.

A pause emanated from the Great Northwest, specifically from King County Courtroom number 1103, a room with bad fluorescent lights, a meat locker temperature, and an ugly bailiff.

"I will sign the order that Mr. Nelson presents to this court, with or without your personal presence, make no mistake about that."

"Which is exactly why I didn't stay in Seattle for this legal ceremony."

"The signing of a court order is not a 'ceremony,' Mr. Pasteur, and your attitude, tone of voice and personality have made this court, uh, will make this court's, uh, job much more, uh, well, quite literally not easy."

"Your Honor, *my* job is not to make your job easy, but to represent my client. Your current decision is dead wrong. You were incorrect in almost all of your trial rulings, and I tried my damnedest to demonstrate that to you throughout, but I couldn't. The appellate court will review your errors. You *will* be reversed. For me to stay in Seattle for you to do to me what your call interrupted me doing to my wife is and would be a waste of both my time, and the court's time. So I'm in Arizona getting laid while you're in Seattle doing ... whatever. But thanks for the call."

"I will now put on the record that your client is unopposed to the signing of the order JNOV," said Judge Burns, his voice quivering with anger.

"No, you will not. You can sign the order noting that Plaintiff's counsel did not appear. Period."

A long silence ensued.

"Hello?" David said finally.

"I will sign the order as presented."

"That's what you said you would do before I left. That's what you intend to do now. So why call me here? If you are telling me you will entertain further argument ...."

"Absolutely not. I've ruled," he said authoritatively, "and it stands."

"Okay, Your Honor, thanks for the call.

Sign the order and read the advance sheets." David hung up quietly with an exaggerated abundance of small muscle control.

He sat naked on the edge of the bed. David shook his slightly balding head as he sat there for a while thinking, adrenaline charging through his bloodstream; unexpected combat in the civilized 1990s. Had he just cursed at a judge? He *did* need a rest, he thought.

"Hello?" Casey said, running her hand over David's back, her dark eyes concerned, but even more curious.

"He's a dick," David answered staring at the beige carpet at his feet, breathing deeply.

"So what's the sweating one want with you now?"

"He called here just to screw with me. There was no need for that call, except to play with my head."

"Did it work?"

"I guess it did. Just look at me, fat, 43, foolish and flaccid."

"Not for long, you big barrister you," she said as she reached for him.

That night, David crawled into bed at 1:00 A.M., sunburned, stomach full, and slightly buzzed from three Black Russians. He slept in one of the two beds in their spacious Holiday Inn room, the one his wife was not occupying. Casey had gone to bed an hour earlier, while David sipped his drink on the balcony overlooking the large, well-lit pool. It had been a most delightful evening, grabbing a late-night snack after their second baseball game of the spring.

He slept well. He dreamed better. It was one of those all-time great dreams—vivid, clear, and upon waking, absolutely real.

Despite the early hour, David felt refreshed. He sat up in bed, watching the sun come up over the desert city, attempting to determine if the dream he had just experienced was only a dream or ... a vision. What the hell am I thinking, he asked himself. A vision? David didn't even use that kind of word in college during the '60s, when people were experimenting with many different vision-producing consumables. Why, he wondered, would he now think of a simple dream in New Age terms?

Because, Stupid, this dream was *so* real, so right, that *not* to believe in it would be illogical. Like *that* thought made any sense.

The dream was clear: David Pasteur was apparently capable, only now capable, beginning last night, of hitting Major League pitching. Thirty total hits. In a row. Pitched by a professional baseball player. The dream continued, showing David examples of his new-found ability in action. Driving in base runners in clutch situations throughout a glorious season, leading his team to new heights, successfully competing in the Show. Then he awoke to be confronted with reality—his pretty, sleeping wife, their moderately priced hotel room, not to mention the recent loss of a big public trial, and of course his 43-year-old body. Certainly this was not the stuff of dreams—maybe nightmares, but not dreams.

He stared at the dull gray eye of the TV, pondering his past sleeping hours of stardom.

"Did you have a stroke, Honey?"

"Huh? What?"

"You're so still. You haven't moved. You always move and squirm. Are you okay?"

"I'm just thinking of a dream I had last night. Very spooky."

"How young was she, and could she put her feet behind her head?" Casey asked, stretching her arms toward the ceiling.

"It wasn't that kind of dream. It was a real dream. I mean, it was a message. No, not a message ... more like ... a premonition. No, premonitions are bad, aren't they? This was a .... Oh, it doesn't matter."

"David, what's going on?" asked Casey, now a bit concerned for the first time, reacting to David's voice a mix of otherworldly tones and lawyer certainty.

"I think I've just discovered a gift—a certain athletic excellence. I think I can hit Major League pitching."

"Jeez, I didn't think you got *that* much sun, yesterday," Casey chided.

"I think I can. I was told I could. I was shown I could."

"Oh, brother." Casey looked at David sitting calmly in bed, his back rigid against the headboard, appearing very peaceful. Very pensive. Very scary.

"David, how about sharing with your best friend what happened last night in the privacy of your own head?" Casey asked as she walked to David's bed. She slid in beside him, snuggling. He didn't feel feverish. It wasn't malaria.

He told her, attempting to convey to his

wife the realness of the dream. When he finished repeating what he remembered about the night movie his head had run, Casey lay still, lost in her own thoughts.

"So what do you think, Casey? Can it be true?"

"I think you took way too many street drugs in your misguided youth, and it's all coming back to haunt you."

"It wasn't a *dream*, Casey—it was a *vision*. I've been given this opportunity, and I need to follow through with it."

"Well, you certainly had a very interesting evening in your own little bed. Apparently I can't leave you alone even for one night. Look, Honey, you're just tired. You've been working your tail off, lost a big trial, saw a spring training game and had a wonderful dream about the on-field success of someone who resembled you in your youth. Way in your youth."

"I would agree that, on the surface, it appears to be just a dream, but I really don't think it was. There's more to it, I think."

"Well, it doesn't really matter anyway, does it? You can't do anything about it, can you? There must be millions of people in the world who have talents, gifts, abilities, who, for whatever reason, haven't been able to maximize them. I bet there are a ton of people who can throw a football as well as Joe Montana, hit as well as Dave Winfield, or play the piano like Jerry Lee Lewis, but for whatever reason—kids, job, dropped out of school, bad luck, anything—will never be able to prove they could perform as well as they know they could."

"That's true," David said, continuing to sit very still, as though movement would break his contact with the night movie.

"So I suggest you enjoy last night's dream, take me to breakfast, whisk me to a baseball game, and buy me a romantic dinner, after which I will give you something that most people can only dream about."

The couple did as Casey suggested.

5

One cannot drive in Arizona in anything but a roofless automobile, particularly if one resides in the great wet Northwest, David thought as he drove to the Peoria Sports Complex for the game between the California Angels and the Seattle Mariners. The top was down; the sun was up. The radio was on a country western station. When Casey and David first met, she was astounded and intrigued that David's car radio was tuned to a country music station. "Aren't you Jewish?" she asked on one of their first nights together.

"No, but three of my good friends are, and I observed their ways. So your question is not unexpected."

"What friends?"

"Mom, Dad, and my brother Maurice."

"Maurice. You have a sibling named Maurice?"

"Yes, I do."

"Like Chevalier? The French Robert Goulet?"

"Who?"

"Chevalier. Maurice Chevalier."

"Yeah, okay. Maurice. That's my brother Maurice Chevalier Pasteur."

"Are you related to ... Louis?"

"No, but I like milk, and I fully understand pasteurization and endorse it as a societal good. And you?"

"I like milk, too," Casey said. "You're nuts."

"No, I'm not nuts. I'm driven by forces that speak to me, and those forces have been very chatty lately."

"And they say?" Casey inquired.

"Beware of black-haired, black-eyed women who crave Jewish men with sheepdogs."

"I like sheepdogs," Casey said, looking into the back seat of David's car, where Cardozo slept and drooled onto his big furry sheepdog paws.

"I like you," David said, watching Casey look at Cardozo.

"I know," Casey said.

"How do you know? I may have lots of female companions who are fond of sheepdogs, attorneys, and sun," David noted.

"I like Cardozo."

"How do you know? You only saw him one time before, when I was jogging around Greenlake with him in tow, when we first met."

"You mean *walking* at Greenlake."

"Well, maybe that was my jog."

"Maybe you need a real workout."

"Is that an offer?" David replied.

"No, an observation."

Greenlake was a large man made lake in the middle of Seattle. Here David pretended to exercise, joining the hordes of the truly athletic during their daily cardiovascular ritual. Cardozo often accompanied him. He was David's sheepdog, of no important parentage, but he possessed a winning personality and big paws, a lot of hair, and eyes like Liz Taylor's without the lashes. One day, while strenuously trying to keep up with a woman pushing a stroller, David had noticed Casey feeding ducks next to a "Don't Feed The Ducks" sign and stopped to chat. Later that week they had gone to a houseboat party where Cardozo swam in another lake, called Union. Held every August 25, the party had an unusual theme. It was in observation of the hosts' divorce 12 years earlier. The owners still lived with each other, but dated other people. They both credited David's sensitivity and professionalism for keeping the divorce businesslike, friendly, and fair. The couple jokingly advised Casey to keep Cardozo and lose the attorney. Casey kept both. It had worked out.

David and Casey arrived at the Mariners' home field at 11 A.M. They had purchased tickets on the sidewalk near the entrance to the stadium from a spring training scalper. During spring training, scalpers can demand as much as 50 cents over the face value of a ticket. Now that's a business—stand out in the hot sun, flagging down a stream of passing cars, inhaling noxious fumes, waving thick pieces of paper at drivers as if they were movie star maps, for a profit margin of nearly nothing. David liked his side of the transaction better.

The couple approached the steel gates, reading the red lettered signs that declared what was and was not allowed beyond the turnstiles. The many signs stated "No coolers, bottles, cans, thermoses, liquor, juice, water or food. Strictly enforced."

"I think we're about to be strip searched," observed David.

"I've never been strip searched before. Is it fun?" asked Casey.

"Like anything else, it's what you make of the opportunity."

A tottering ticket taker, who looked not a day under 107 years old, peered at Casey's large purse, eyeing it for all the potential contraband described on the wall. Casey's purse was large enough to hide Cardozo within its confines.

"Ma'am, is there anything in your purse?"

"No. Would you like to take a look?" Casey asked, smiling. She handed him two tickets while David hung back behind her, not unlike a wayward child.

"Okay. Have a nice ball game," the ticket taker encouraged, pointing to their seats in the distance.

"Now *that's* security," said David, checking on his iced bottle of wine nestled nicely in the bottom of Casey's purse, now safe from old prying eyes which would keep him and the object of his thirst apart.

"This is so cute," exclaimed Casey, looking at the numerous concession stands at the top of the miniature stadium. The seats were close to the field, with a feel of an upscale minor league park. The crowd assembled leisurely, as both teams warmed up along their respective sidelines, pestered by young fans calling for the players' attention and autographs.

The thing that struck both David and Casey was that the seats were positioned directly on top of the rich green, grassy field. Not a bad seat in the entire park. A cute stadium indeed.

They wandered around the stadium, eyeing the venue. They found their seats with ease, thanks to a series of elderly men who volunteered on behalf of the Boys and Girls Clubs of Arizona. The ushers were friendly and gentlemanly, but could not help but stare at Casey's long, tanned legs, which disappeared into tight shorts, as she found her seat in the very front row along the third base line.

"These are fantastic seats," Casey observed as she checked her ticket for accuracy. "I like scalpers."

"I am in the process of re-evaluating the entire industry of scalping," David said. "I have never sat in such great seats, including Little League games. We're practically in the dug-out."

"I like Arizona, David. Can we buy a baseball team if we win the appeal?" she teased, settling into her space. She plopped down her purse as if it were an overstuffed suitcase and immediately extracted David's bottle of 1994 Chablis with twist-off cap.

The sun climbed into the cloudless sky as the grounds crew watered the infield, after grooming the grass like an expensive barber. The playing field was immaculate.

"I want that guy's job," David said, pointing to a young man holding a small section of a large garden hose, while another person—the head hose guy—sprayed water on the infield, utilizing the brass spray nozzle as would an artist.

Casey smiled. "Looks like a two-man job to me. Good union."

"I wonder how one applies for the assistant hose guy's job? Not too much pressure, like the spray guy. Don't want his job. Way too many decisions–how wet to get the dirt, what kind of pattern to make with the water, dirt to dust ratio. Now, that's pressure."

"What are you babbling about?" Casey laughed, eyeing the concession stand on the top row of the stadium, not too distant from their fabulous seats, another reason Casey thought the seats were so great.

David looked down his row, which was beginning to fill as game time approached. A mother and daughter started to snake their way toward David as the hose guys finished their watering. A job well done. Obviously time for a beer.

"Excuse me," said the polite little girl to David, as she squeezed by to plop down on his immediate left. She was followed closely by her mom, who was loaded down with a purse, a cardboard tray full of food, and a large infielder's glove which dangled from her little finger.

"I feel like a pack mule," said the mom, a redhead with blue eyes, as she unloaded her equipment on the seats next to her and her daughter.

"You don't look like a pack mule," said David, assisting her with the unloading process as she handed her cardboard tray of hot dogs to her little girl.

"Whew. Thanks. I should hire a bellboy. Who knew getting to the ballpark with just one child would be so complicated?"

"I knew. I have two girls at home," said Casey, "and the equipment equation gets worse the older they get."

"Ain't that the truth. Hi, I'm Susan Snide, as in Snidely Whiplash," she smiled, shaking hands with David and Casey while her daughter devoured a hot dog with both hands, relish dripping.

"I love that word," David observed.

"Excuse me?"

"Whiplash. I love how it sounds."

"You a lawyer?" She smiled, blue eyes twinkling.

"Ambulance chaser, really. I like to think I don't have to chase them anymore, but am now able to meet them at the scene."

"That's funny," Susan said.

Casey was rolling her eyes, having heard

this particular stupid line countless times in the past.

"Susan, listen," Casey said, "we can change seats so you don't have to listen to his nonsense. He's not a well man. Never has been really, but the kids, I stay for the kids."

Susan turned to her daughter. "Denise, say hello to the nice people from ...."

"Seattle," supplied Casey. "That's near the North Pole, where the weather is different."

"Us too."

"Oh? Where?"

"Near Carkeek Park."

"Us too."

"Hi," David said to the pigtailed eight-year-old. She was missing a front tooth and had a deep tan, unlike her redheaded mother, who was sunburned and lightly freckled.

"Hi. I'm Denise Snide. I'm eight-and-a-half."

"Nice to meet you. I'm David, and this is Casey. I'm 43 and she's 16. *We* have all our teeth."

Denise scrutinized Casey closely. "You're big for sixteen."

"Don't believe anything he says," Casey advised. "I'm closer to 20, and David is missing teeth, just like you, except they're in the back."

Denise giggled.

The lineups were announced as the four Northwesterners settled in for a day in the sun.

It was a great five innings. The game was good, the conversation great, and the weather perfect. Casey continued to be amazed at how close they were to the action, literally less than 80 feet from the batter's box. One could see the beads of sweat on the foreheads of the players as they stood at the plate, attempting to impress.

In the top of the sixth inning, the Mariners sent a six-foot seven-inch mammoth of a man to the plate—John Rosie, a minor league power hitting prospect from Minnesota. He'd had a good season in the minors last year, and was slated to go back to Triple A ball if he didn't stick with the big club this spring. Each at-bat was critical to his big-league career.

Denise was sitting between Casey and David, with Susan to David's left. Susan was keeping score in a program, a task which David could never understand and so had not mastered.

"Who cares about keeping score, especially in spring training? Get a life, Susan. Old people do it to pass the time, but please."

"My dad wants me to, so we can talk about the game afterwards. And he wouldn't want you to call him old, either."

"Is he back in Seattle?"

"No, he's here, but he's always busy."

"He lives here then? Retired?"

"No, lives in Seattle. He just doesn't come to every game, because of his business, but he'd like to."

"Nice daughter. Good sense of duty," David observed.

"Dad is a great guy, except he spoils Denise terribly."

"Isn't that his job, as grandfather?"

"Yes, and he takes his grandfathering very seriously." She smiled. She liked David. David liked Susan.

CRACK!

David heard what sounded like a rifle shot, but was in fact a line drive coming right at Denise's head. Denise was laughing, looking at her new best friend, Casey, her little girl hands full of popcorn and Coke, totally unaware of the approaching danger.

David had been listening to people who had been in accidents for 20 years, repeatedly telling him how everything slows down during the seconds just before impact, shifting into slow motion. Seeing the white blur out of the corner of his eye, he instinctively reached across Denise, knocking the popcorn box out of her hand, his knuckles nestling against her nose, and turned to see the ball resting in the palm of his hand.

The crowd drew a collective breath in disbelief and then, as if on cue, erupted into applause and shouts, many coming to their feet in appreciation of what they had just witnessed—a remarkable catch under pressure.

David sat stunned, in his seat, attempting to make sense of the last two seconds. Then his hand came back to life. He screamed.

"Son of a bi ..." he yelled, getting to his feet and shaking his hand in the air, to the continuing applause of the observing fans.

"What happened?" Denise asked. Her eyes were big, her popcorn missing.

"Are you all right?" Susan questioned her

little girl, with a voice beginning to shake from the delayed knowledge of what might have occurred.

"I'm okay, Mom, but what happened?"

"David saved your life, Honey, that's what happened."

"He knocked my popcorn over."

David's hand began to throb, then swell. It hurt like hell.

"Just like Kevin Mitchell's barehand catch, Honey. My big, strong hero. Are you okay?" Casey examined his hand.

"I think my palm is nothing but pulverized bones. It's all bone dust. Son of a gun."

"Are you okay, Mister?" a quavery voice from behind inquired.

"Yes, I'm okay," David stated, looking at his hand and working his fingers, hoping they would respond. The voice belonged to the ancient ticket taker who waved Casey's purse through at the gate. He had walked down the cement stairs from the top row, no small feat for someone 107 years old.

"Can I get you anything?"

"A bucket of ice with a bottle of scotch

in it, and two aspirins," David joked.

"Okay, Sir. Nice catch. You're sittin' good to get a contract." The old man grinned and ambled back up the stairs.

Things settled down, with some discussion of moving to safer seating. This proposal was rejected, especially by Denise, who now had her glove on, looking for fielding chances.

Fifteen minutes later, the ancient mariner returned to their group. He had a plastic pail of ice, a towel, a tin of aspirin, and a pint of scotch nestled into the shiny cubes of ice.

"I like this," Casey said to no one in particular, as the gentleman placed his equipment at David's feet.

"Anything else I might do, Sir?"

"Not a thing," David said, plunging his hand into the ice pail, "not a thing."

6

"Room Service," said the Spanish-accented voice through the closed door of the Pasteurs' third-floor room, number 330.

Casey rose from the king-sized bed and opened the door, allowing entry.

"I love Room Service," she said to David, who was sipping a glass of wine, poured from the same bottle he had brought to the game.

"It is truly a great invention, a civilizing influence on all mankind. I am very happy," said David, "very contented."

"So you had a nice day, Honey?"

"I had a great day. Susan and Denise are great. I'm looking forward to dinner with them tomorrow."

"How's your hand, you big, strong man you?"

"The ice helped a ton. Not as much as the scotch though." He showed her his hand, swollen, a bad bruise having formed on the palm.

"I must have caught the ball flush in the palm, otherwise I would have broken some fingers and not been able to stop the flight of the ball."

"Denise is very lucky, you're very lucky, but I'm the luckiest, cuz," she broke into song, "I've got you, Babe ...."

The phone rang. David picked it up on the first ring.

"Daddy, was that you? Huh, was it?" Lauren asked from Seattle.

"Hi, Lauren. What are you talking about, Sweetie?"

"The TV, was it ...."

"Lauren, I don't understand you. Calm down. Where's Grandma?"

"She thinks it's you! She does! Is it?"

"Put her on please. Put Grandma on,

Sweetie."

"Hi, David. Having a nice time?" Saint Esther asked.

"Yeah, great. What's Lauren talking about? What's this about the TV?"

"Did you go to the Mariners game today?"

"Yeah, and I have a bum hand to prove it, but ...."

"So it *was* you, I knew it! I told Lauren it was."

"What, tell me what you're talking about please?"

"ESPN has you making the Play of the Day. It did look rather remarkable, David. Quite an attractive catch. You look sunburned."

"Thanks, Mom. Want to talk to the star's wife? She's about to dive into room service. ESPN, huh? I'm a star!"

"She loves room service, doesn't she, David?"

"Yes, Mom. How are the girls?"

"Very proud of their Daddy."

"As well they should be."

That night, David's dream returned, as he hoped it would. This time, he was treated to more details of his newly acquired, untested talents, performing at the highest level of professional sports—at least in his head. The dream was in color, the premise the same. Thirty consecutive hits in a row. It still was vague thereafter, ending with something dramatic, but he was unable to corral the complete and total picture.

The day following his second dream, David became, not introverted, but certainly much quieter. He spent the hours after waking attempting to remember all the details of the dream, as well as putting the "facts" into some manageable perspective.

"How did you sleep, Honey?" Casey asked a little apprehensively.

"It's back, in living color. I think Chris Berman was in this one."

"Darn. I thought it might pass, like your dried salsa crystals in a packet. You were pretty sure of that idea, too."

"Hey! That could have worked. Anyway, I'm pretty good in clutch situations. Maybe I can get you tickets to some of the home games."

"Maybe you can make an appointment with a shrink."

"I don't need a doctor, Casey. I need an opportunity."

"Well, I need a shower. Remember dinner tonight with Susan and Denise."

"Where are we going?"

"Some place in the middle of the desert, sort of out of the way. Susan said it was a great place, but we should leave early and enjoy the evening weather."

Casey went to take a shower. David flipped on ESPN to hear the baseball news—trades, scores, injuries. Perhaps a team would be interested in David's talent if presented properly. He got out a yellow pad from his battered briefcase and began to figure the value of a 30 hit season.

If used properly, by an astute manager, 30 hits could well translate into 20 to 24 wins. A pinch hitter used in the late innings of a close game could dramatically improve a club's standing. David knew that over the last 20 years, in both the American and National leagues, the difference between the first and last place teams was rarely more then 25 games.

With luck and a moderately good manager, I could help a team go from last to first, he thought. David contemplated the endless possibilities. Pondering the realities was not nearly as much fun.

The tanned couple, one with a sore hand, was lost in the middle of the desert. David was riding in the passenger seat, with the seat tilted all the way back, letting the sun bake his face while Casey searched for signs of food.

"Where the hell is this restaurant?"

"I don't know," answered David, his eyes closed against the sunlight, "I can't see."

"Can't you help me, please?"

"Nope."

"Why not?"

"I'm thinking about the meaning of the dream."

"I told you what it means. It means you got a good night's sleep and dreamed wonderfully. It means you caught a ball and now your subconscious thinks you're Willie Mays. So just open your eyes and help me find food."

"You mean my subconscious thinks I'm black and greet people at Las Vegas casinos?"

"Mays couldn't keep that job. Anyway, why don't you just enjoy the dream instead of, well, whatever it is you're doing with it. Perseverating, they call it."

"I *think* it's real, Honey," David pleaded.

"I *know* we're lost," Casey said with assurance.

"Here it is. Here's the dirt road Susan said to take, 27 miles from the Texaco station after the four-way stop, in the middle of nowhere, past the big rock."

They drove onto a narrow, winding dirt road, crossing two wooden bridges that carried them over dry gullies, around a horseshoe curve, through saguaro cactuses—David refused to call them cacti—and past several dilapidated deserted shacks until their convertible rounded a sharp curve which ended in a parking lot—paved, lined and valeted.

"It's a mirage," David said to Casey. "Don't get out, just turn around and we'll go back across the desert. If we can find Phoenix, we'll stop at a McDonald's."

The valet opened the driver's door. He was a youth dressed in a cowboy hat, boots and tight jeans, which Casey appreciated.

"Please don't say 'howdy,'" David commanded with a smile.

"I sure won't, 'Pardner,'" the young man teased. "Have a nice dinner." He pointed the way inside.

"You ever lose anyone on the trip up here? This place is out in the middle of nowhere, and no signs whatever."

"We send out a posse if our guests are too late."

"Sorry I asked."

They walked into a ranch style structure, with a bricked-in patio, rough-hewn wood tables, and an incredible view of the valley below. The lighting came from the setting sun and the hurricane lamps on each table.

Susan and Denise were already seated, nibbling on what looked like ten pounds of nachos in a mountain of cheese.

"Hi, David, Casey," Denise said around a chip full of goo. "You found it, huh?"

"Just barely. What is this place?"

"A great restaurant for those in the know who have a good car and can follow directions. Like it?" asked Susan.

Casey stood with her hands buried in her pockets, gazing at the valley below. A slight breeze moved the hair at the end of her long, black braid. "Susan, this is great. I hope the food is good. I'm starving. We left yesterday," she joked

"You bet it is. Sit down. I've already ordered the whole dinner. David, here's your scotch and water, and Casey's ginger ale."

"You're a single mom. We'll pay half," protested David.

Susan said, "I ordered. I didn't say I'd pay for it."

"Oh."

"No, I'm kidding. My treat."

"No one has been this nice to me in a long time, but okay, if I can get a kiss from Denise." He got it on the forehead, a big smacking wet one.

Dinner was as expected–lively conversation, laughing, baseball talk, and some personal facts revealed for the first time.

"I've noticed you looking at my face with a certain medical interest."

"I'm sorry, I ...."

"Good surgeon, don't you think?"

"Well ...."

"It was a car accident, a bad one. My husband had been drinking and lost control. He died. Denise was a baby. I moved in with Dad. I recovered fully, but only after far too many surgeries. So what you did the other day, preventing Denise from ... well ... thanks again. It's a much bigger deal for us than you could ever know."

"Glad I was there. If I was younger, who knows? I could try out with a team down here, make some real dough."

"David," Casey warned, "don't start with that. Eat your salad and say thank you."

"Who's this?" a big, booming voice from across the patio questioned, moving toward their table. "How are my darling girls? And this must be Casey. She *is* great looking, just like you said, Denny. And is this Mr. Pee Wee Pasteur?"

"Excuse me?" David responded.

"Daddy, this is David," Susan said. "I didn't think you'd be here until later, if at all." Daddy reached to kiss Susan on the cheek, and grabbed Denise by the neck, pretending to choke her with both big rough hands. Denise stuck her tongue out, made big eyes and giggled.

"I got done sooner than I thought, besides, I wanted to meet this guy ASAP."

"Who?" David looked at Casey, puzzled.

"You. The catch. ESPN. Denise. You not so smart, buddy-boy? Hey, Sandolo, bring me my usual—a double—I'm celebrating with my new friends. Okay with everyone?" He sat down between Casey and David, reaching for some gooey chips.

Dad looked like Kris Kringle without the beard, but with the big belly. He also had a personality that instantly filled a room, regardless of its size. He possessed the wiliest eyes David had ever seen. They looked at you, through you, around you, and missed nothing while doing it. David shivered. I wouldn't want to negotiate with this guy, he thought.

Dad was dressed in a Hawaiian top, khaki pants cinched tight, and black tennis shoes. His cocktail came—a tall, very dark one, with lots of ice. He had a commanding presence, even while gulping his drink and spilling a portion of it onto a now amber palm tree on his shirt.

"So Susan tells me you like baseball, David." And they were off.

Denise started to fall asleep around 11 o'clock. Casey lasted until 11:07. Susan had nodded off long before. David and Cyrus ("I don't use a last name, just call me Cyrus") kept going with no letup. Susan finally left with her daughter and Casey, while David and Cyrus stayed to see the moon rise, then begin to descend, before the head waiter pleaded to let him go home to his wife and twelve children.

David asked astutely, "So you want us to go so you can leave?"

"Yes sir."

"Okay with you, Cyrus?" Cyrus started to snore in his seat, so David made the executive decision. They would now leave.

"We're leaving now, thank you. Bring me the bill, please."

"It's all taken care of, Sir."

"Oh!"

7

"What time did you get in last night? You smell like a brewery and look like, well, just take a peek in the mirror," Casey said, while brushing her hair.

"No. I won't do that."

"Well I guess you two like each other. You acted like he was your long-lost uncle."

"I'm not so sure now. I got a little carried away, I'm afraid," David responded, looking at Casey sideways, like Cardozo would after tipping over the garbage.

"You didn't, did you?" Casey asked apprehensively.

"Maybe."

"You didn't! I can't believe it. You must have sounded demented."

"I did, but it gets worse."

"How could it?"

"I don't have to tell you."

"Yes, you do."

"No, I don't."

"I'll call Susan and find out if you won't tell me. She'll tell me everything."

"Okay."

"Okay what?"

"Okay, I'll tell you, if you speak in a whisper, get me 13 aspirin and promise not to yell at me if I tell you most of what happened."

"All of it, and nine aspirin."

"He *owns* the Mariners. Cyrus. *The* Cyrus Sven Andvik, the bazillionaire who just bought the team. He's the new owner. He's Susan's dad."

"No. You're kidding. And?"

"And Denise is his granddaughter."

"And? What else?"

"I was overserved–it wasn't my fault–I told him about the dream after you guys left."

"You didn't, you wouldn't. No, you ... you didn't *grind* him did you?"

"Maybe."

"David!!"

"What?"

"You're an idiot."

"Aspirin, please?" David begged.

"Not on a bet."

"You promised," he whined.

"I lied," she said. "How could you? What exactly did you tell him?"

"The truth–as I know it."

"And what, pray tell, did you say? Oh, I'm so embarrassed, and I wasn't even there," she said, shaking her head in real disgust.

"I said I have 30 Major League hits. Thirty consecutive hits, when thrown by a professional baseball player. I don't know why I've been given this gift, but it's real."

"And he said?"

"That I have a rich fantasy life, I need

therapy, and I was drunk."

"He is a very smart man," Casey responded from the bathroom, while getting the aspirin for her dehydrated and demented husband.

"So we won't be seeing our new friends again," she said wistfully, "I liked them, too." Casey sighed

"Au contraire, mon amie. Cyrus is picking us up in two hours and taking us to the Mariners game in Tucson."

"Yeah?"

"Yeah. Give me a kiss."

"One condition, okay? Please, no more dream talk–promise? It makes you sound like a fruitcake. Maybe Cyrus won't remember."

"Can't do it."

"Why not?"

"Because last night the vision came back. I got more details about my abilities. Look, we're in room 330, and our rental car license plate has a 30 in it. The new uniforms for the Mariners came out on January 30th. These are messages, clues! They can't be ignored."

"And don't forget that you can be involuntarily committed for 30 days without a hearing."

"Good point" he conceded.

The drive to Tucson was uneventful, as was the game with the Colorado Rockies. The M's couldn't score against the new expansion team, their hitting being horrid. The team left 12 runners stranded in scoring position.

"We need a power hitter," said David.

"We need another starting pitcher," countered Cyrus.

"Cyrus, we need a lot of help, but hitting first."

"I'm repeating what Sammy Ellis, the pitching coach says, but I'm not so sure. I know Piniella wants another starter. He's wearing me down, so I told 'em to look around for someone, and they have."

"Who, Cyrus?"

"Bly Levin has just become available. He isn't going to stick with the Twins because of his salary, and of course he needs seven wins to reach 300 career victories, so he might be interested."

"So?"

"So, I'm talking to his agent. In fact, I'm leaving tonight to do just that."

"You! Since when does the majority owner get his hands dirty with operations and negotiations?"

"Since it's my money. Want to come to the Twin Cities with me and meet Levin's agent?"

Casey's eyes got big. She looked at David, shaking her head firmly and dared David to accept the invitation.

"No thanks, Cyrus. I'm on vacation, and I want to keep my marriage."

Casey interjected, "A very good answer, Honey. You're a smart little lawyer, just like I thought so many years ago."

"You know, I could always use another lawyer on staff. I've got other businesses around the Northwest. Smart people are still the most important asset to any company. Always were, always will be. If you want to quit hanging around emergency rooms, let me know. I've got plenty of work."

David took a calculated risk. He gazed around at the newly renovated Rockies' ballpark, near the Tucson Zoo, taking in the tanned people in the stands, the vendors screaming for business, and said very forcefully yet slowly, and he hoped clearly, "Cyrus, I don't want to be your bloody lawyer. I want to be your designated hitter."

"David!" Casey shouted with exasperation, "You promised!"

Spring training continued to be glorious. The case of *Rodriquez v. Mountain Beer* rested on David's desk back in Seattle, just as the sheepdog Cardozo rested on his back, also in Seattle, both awaiting David's return home and back to reality.

David's dream recurred four nights in a row, then ceased completely. Apparently enough detail and information had been imparted to David, if indeed any information had been imparted at all. Casey was not concerned about the dream, but she was worried that David absolutely, totally believed in it, and had begun to act upon that belief. Doctors tended to call this behavior delusional.

Casey asked Susan if her father was getting annoyed by David's continual and incessant begging.

"No, Dad likes David. He likes eccentric people, and David is definitely eccentric. So no, he isn't, but he did make a joke at dinner the other day that if the team doesn't improve soon, he just might try David out."

"Oh, no," Casey said. "He didn't!"

"Relax. Dad was just joking with Denise. She'd just asked him why older people can't play baseball."

"And he said?"

"Ask God."

"Good answer," Casey said.

"Except," Susan continued, "then Denise asked about Carlton Fisk and Nolan Ryan."

"Oh. What did he say then?"

"He told her to go to bed."

"Good grandfather."

8

Bly Levin did sign a one year, non-guaranteed contract as a potential fifth starter for the Mariners, or as a reliever out of the bullpen. Levin packed his bags in Minneapolis and was in Arizona within 72 hours, now perspiring for a perennial last-place club. Levin wanted to win 300 career games. The M's would give him the opportunity. He was seven victories short.

Levin, being 44, was the newest, and by far the oldest Mariner on the spring training roster. The age of their new acquisition was not lost on Denise, and the irony was not lost on Cyrus.

David attended several more games with Cyrus, both hoping Piniella could coax a winning attitude out of the 40-odd players left in camp competing for the 25 roster positions available to start the season, now only weeks away.

At yet another game, they were sitting, sipping beer when Cyrus turned to David. "It's been over eight hours since you last talked about your stupid dream, so let me ask you this one question. Do you play golf when you're not hanging around emergency rooms?"

"No, it's too hard," he allowed.

"Uh-huh." Cyrus sat observing an inept 4-0 loss, the fifth loss in a row. After several minutes of silence, Cyrus said, "A little white ball, a stationary little white ball on a tee. Hitting that, that's too hard. But an 86-mile-an-hour split-fingered fastball, which falls off the table, that you think you can hit, even though you've never done it. Is that correct?"

"Precisely."

"Uh-huh. So why do I even listen to this craziness?"

"Cyrus, you brought it up this time."

"Scary, huh?"

The game wore on to its logical conclusion, 5-2 Oakland. Bly Levin got the loss, giving up four runs, on eight hits and three walks. Not too bad, but not what the Mariners needed or hoped for when they picked him up from the Twins. The Mariners needed serious help, but even more they needed serious luck, both of which were difficult to come by.

Some days later, near the end of the Pasteurs' stay in the City of Cactus, the room phone light was blinking when they came back from dinner.

"It must be Mom," said Casey.

She dialed the message center. "It's not Mom. Cyrus called. He said call ASAP, no matter what time."

"That's peculiar," David said. He was looking for his swim trunks for a nighttime swim, which he always tried to take no matter what the hour, at least in Phoenix.

David called Cyrus at his hotel which overlooked Diablo Stadium, where the California Angels had just beaten up the M's.

"I got your message. What's the ASAP

about?" inquired David.

"What are you doing tomorrow morning, young man?"

"Young man is good. Let me see. I'm booked through breakfast, which I don't eat anyway .... Wait, I've got a potential meeting with the Mets. They need some help up the middle. Why?"

"Want to hit?"

David paused. "What?" he asked warily.

"Want to hit a sphere, white in color, with red seams, thrown by a highly paid 20-year-old?"

"If the question is do I want to hit baseballs tomorrow, the answer is sure, but it may not be that simple."

"David, it never is, but what in the name of God is so complicated about hitting with the boys tomorrow? I mean, excuse me David, but aren't you the crazy guy who's been pestering me about your, what, drug flashback? Nightmare? Dream? Vision? Whatever?"

"Yes, that's me."

"So show me tomorrow. Put your dream where your mouth is."

"It's not like that, Cyrus."

"Dammit, Pasteur, what's so wrong with showing me and Piniella if you can do what you say you can do? So now you *don't* want to prove it? Okay, fine with me, just don't ever ...."

"No, Cyrus. I can do it. I can hit Major League pitching."

"Okay, then what?" Cyrus screamed through the phone, interrupting David.

"But I can't hit with a real person pitching."

"Excuse me!" said Cyrus, now really getting angry, continuing to shout at David loudly enough that Casey winced from across the room.

"I only have 30 hits. That means 30 at bats against a human being."

"What exactly are you telling me? You want for me to hire a chimpanzee to throw to you?"

"I *can* hit against a machine, but I won't hit against a pitcher except in a for real game."

"Now you're dictating conditions? Now you have an agent? What is this crap? You're pissing me off bad."

"Cyrus, I'm telling you what the vision is. I know it doesn't make sense, but the Red Sea parting doesn't make sense either."

"What, now you're Moses?"

"Cyrus, let's go hit tomorrow. I'll meet you wherever you tell me to. We can use a machine. I don't expect to look like anything but what you'd expect some fat Jewish lawyer to look like, but hell, let's do it, for whatever reason. It won't prove anything though. I can only hit against people, and I won't waste my limited talent doing it in practice. It won't count and it won't prove anything."

"Just humor me. Humor an old man who is willing to suffer the ridicule of his employees. Eight A.M. I'll pick you up. Wear workout clothes, and please tell me why in the name of God I'm allowing this to go forward one more minute."

"Because I have 30 hits, and the Mariners need 30 hits. It's that simple. See you in the morning."

"He called your bluff?" Casey asked, totally amazed.

"Put up or shut up."

"Good. Tomorrow it will end," she predicted, "and none too soon. Our health insurance doesn't cover Lithium."

David dragged his sorry middle-aged butt through the hotel room door around 2 p.m. the following day. He was limping slightly, had a blister on each hand, and a mouse under his left eye that looked like Mickey on steroids.

"Tough day at the office, Honey?" Casey asked, shaking her head from the balcony overlooking the pool, her favorite location at the hotel. She was reading a thick volume entitled *Mid-life Crisis: Is There a Pill?*

"Holy smoke," David said, gently easing himself into a soft chair beside her.

"So how did my little dreamer do?" she asked, examining his hands, and clucking her tongue in mock concern.

"Rough. Very rough."

"These look like little Jewish attorney hands, not working baseball hands. Did these soft baby hands work very hard this morning?"

"Hard, but not very well, actually."

"Well, David, what did you expect? So

now is this idiot quest of yours over? Can you go back to your other dream of being President of the United States? Something more realistic, I might add."

"The dream is real. This was no test, and I told Cyrus and Lou that they couldn't judge my future performance by using a pitching machine today. Apples and oranges, I told them."

"You took batting practice with the team and Piniella?"

"Yeah, I had trouble with the curve."

"No kidding. How did you do against the fastball?"

"Couldn't see it very well, to tell the truth."

"How'd you get the shiner? Poor baby."

"Bad hop. Could've happened to anyone. Two days ago Amaral broke his nose while taking infield. It's part of the game." David opined like a veteran of many seasons, while Casey put a bandage on his left hand and examined his eye with her finger, eliciting a Jewish whine of pain.

"What, pray tell, did Cyrus tell Piniella about your paunchy presence on the diamond?"

"I'm not sure. I think Piniella thought I won an auction bid to hit with the big boys. I hit against a batting machine, took infield, shook hands, met the folks and signed an autograph."

"You didn't. For who?"

"A little boy around seven saw me hitting and asked."

"No."

"Yes."

"I bet he's disappointed."

"On the contrary. Hank Aaron is worth substantial dollars to collectors. His parents will be proud."

"That was awfully nice of Cyrus to indulge you. All of your pals back home would love to do what he let you do, given the chance, especially Freeman, your accountant. He'd die."

"I think this was more than just indulging me."

"David," she warned, purposefully squeezing a blister to hurt him.

"Ouch. No, I mean it. Cyrus wanted to know *all* the details of the dream—the specifics, the parameters, what was very clear, kinda clear, vague, and guessing—and then I hit."

"And?"

"Ugly."

"So now it's over," she declared. "I'm sorry. No, I'm not. Good."

"I don't know. I still have 30 hits. *I'm* still convinced of that. I didn't *say* I could hit against a machine, only against Major League pitching. I made that clear from the very beginning."

"Why don't you hit against Randy Johnson and show Cyrus you can do it? If you can, everyone can see. If you can't ...."

"Don't want to waste 'em. Too precious."

"You're having a breakdown. Now where did you put your Prozac, David?"

9

Spring training was winding down, opening day was a week away, and the Mariners didn't look any better than they did in late February, the young pitcher Suzuki the only high spot.

Bly Levin was struggling, and the team hitting continued to be atrocious. Ticket sales back in Seattle leveled off, then plummeted to the depths of the marketing director's feet.

Cyrus was in a worried and pensive mood.

Casey was ready to go home.

David was reading about the current baseball trades. He was looking for a team, trying to talk to other clubs who might be in the market. Nobody returned his calls.

The last game that David and Casey attended before traveling home was played at Chandler, Milwaukee's spring training homefield. The couple was headed back to Seattle the next day. It had been a memorable vacation. Casey was rested, David was driven.

In the third inning, Mardi Sheridan, a spring training bright spot, sat in the Mariner dugout, thinking about a home he was going to purchase back in Puerto Rico, now that he had made the big club. Hitting .307 for the spring, and .407 as a pinch hitter, the Mariner management had tagged him to play behind Ken Griffey, Jr. in center field, and pinch hit in those situations that called for a contact hitter with good base running speed and acumen. While sitting in the dugout minding his own business, Sheridan took a foul line drive to his jaw off the bat of Milwaukee's lead off hitter, Marques Chinn.

The ball broke his mandible in three places, causing a concussion and dislodging four teeth. Though beautifully appointed and exquisitely groomed, the stadium had not been designed with any safety protection in front of either dugout. This very dangerous condition resulted in a serious injury to an important player on a talent-shallow team.

Sheridan was rushed to the hospital, unconscious. David had seen it all, and was horrified by the injury to this promising rookie player.

"Even I could win *this* case," David said, concerned and mortified that the injury had occurred—had been allowed to occur—when it could have been so easily avoided.

Later that evening, David and Casey dined in a small, intimate Italian restaurant (are there any big, noisy Italian restaurants?) thinking about Seattle, their waiting girls, and their shaggy dog. The dream was temporarily forgotten in the anticipation of returning home.

"This injury hurts Cyrus a ton, doesn't it David?" asked Casey.

"I'm afraid it does. The M's were already pretty thin, but now ...."

"Well, I have had enough sun and sleep. I'm ready to go home. You?"

"I guess," David answered. "It's been awfully nice, getting away from the office and the whining clients. I miss the girls, and I can't sleep as well without Cardozo's 90 pounds on my chest at night, but ..." he trailed off.

"But what?" Casey prompted.

"I had the dream again. First time in over a week."

"Oh, Honey," Casey said sincerely. She leaned over and gave her husband a big hug, took his face between her hands and kissed him deeply. "Even if you can't hit, you can talk like a preacher at a tent meeting. Let's go home. I'll be a mom, you be a lawyer, and I'll make you forget this whole Arizona vision. It's probably just the change in the water. Besides, I don't want you to hurt your face anymore. Old men like you don't heal as fast as the young do."

David flew home with a tan and a mission. The tan would fade, but the mission would not.

Back from Arizona, David changed his routine.

Now, every morning he rose at the ungodly hour of 8:30, woke the dog, and jogged until his knees and lungs screamed for mercy, which usually occurred at about a quarter of a mile from his front door.

Cardozo only wanted to walk, just as his Dog Union prescribed, but David held the leash and bought the groceries. So Cardozo ran, stopping only to water the neighbors' lawns.

David's neighbors were stunned. Even though he had lived in the neighborhood for 14 years, most of the neighbors rarely saw the attorney. Waving and smiling was usually the most interaction he would ever have with them, with one exception. If *anyone* under the age of 16 came to the Pasteurs' door selling *anything*, David and Casey would buy it. And when a neighbor knocked on the door soliciting for charity, any charity, the Pasteur household would determine how much the biggest gift so far had been and double it. It was never more than $100, and it was great PR. One can't have enough PR, David thought.

David wasn't disliked—he was just a relatively unknown personality in the neighborhood, which was fine with him.

However, there was one worm in the apple. Colonel Robert Powell, U.S. Army Retired, knew David, hated him, and hated everything David owned, liked or produced.

The Colonel was over 60, a widower—his wife had probably committed suicide—a meticulous housekeeper and gardener with a close-cropped lawn and gray hair to match. His politics were slightly to the right of Genghis

Khan's. Several of the neighbors speculated openly about his mental health or his lack thereof. He drank like a soldier and constantly patrolled the neighborhood on the lookout for personal slights. He was paranoid about other people's successes, certain that they had come at his expense. If someone else's lawn was greener, they must be stealing his water. If someone else was noticeably happy, the Colonel's self-appointed mission was to change that immediately.

The Colonel lived four houses down from David, in a smallish bungalow. He had an expansive view of the mountains, but kept the blinds and curtains drawn at all times, just in case the sun came out and tried to lighten his mood. The Colonel didn't like lawyers and hated Jews, children, Hispanics, blacks and dogs. So when David began to get into shape by jogging with Cardozo, the Colonel took notice and set out on yet another mission to do what he could to stop it.

When the Rodriquez case began to receive media attention in Seattle, the Colonel made it clear that "the spic chick and her Jew lawyer" should lose, die, and be dismembered. He told this to all who would listen, including Lindsey and Lauren Pasteur, when they played near the Colonel's house.

One day the girls came home crying because of what the Colonel had said to them. David then explained the word "asshole" to his daughters.

David returned to his office after his Arizona adventure to find messages stacked to the ceiling, clients wanting his attention, and the Maria Rodriquez appeal languishing. He had new clients to interview, including a couple who was sitting in their living room watching COPS on the television when their front door flew open. Actually, it had been kicked in by a ten-man SWAT team with loaded rifles, shotguns, pistols and an attitude. The elderly couple was rounded up, held at gunpoint and interrogated for 45 minutes before the police determined that they were not, in fact, crack dealers hoarding Uzis, but retired special-education school teachers.

Another matter awaiting David's legal attention was a severe dog-bite case involving a little boy.

"Maybe Cardozo could be an expert witness," David mused to his secretary, Catherine. "What else?"

"George Freeman, your softball coach and accountant called, said he needs your $350 sponsorship money by Wednesday or *you* won't start this season. Aren't you a little old for softball? Last year you limped until October," she observed.

"Have you spoken with Casey since we came back from Arizona?"

"No, why?" she said, pawing through a stack of papers that she'd been saving for David to review.

"Good. Don't."

Casey and Catherine were good friends. Catherine had been David's secretary before he'd ever met Casey.

"Marry her," she'd advised when she first met Casey. "You won't find anyone better." And, as with most of what she recommended, he did what she told him to do.

"Why not talk to Casey? What's going on with you two?"

"Because I'm the boss, and I said not to. I hate the way you two share information. I have no privacy."

"You don't deserve any privacy. You can't be trusted with secrets. Oh, I forgot. Who's Cyrus?"

"Why?"

"He called. He sounds nice. Left a concise, straightforward message. He knows how to utilize staff. He's probably successful."

"Yeah, I'd say so. We met in Arizona."

"He wants you to go to the Mariners opening night. Wants you to call him back."

"Okay, later," David instructed. "What else do you have?" he asked.

"Nothing more for you right now, but I've got to call Casey immediately," Catherine said.

Opening night at the Kingdome. Fireworks. Spotlights panned the stands and the field. A new season, a new beginning. A terrible start. The pre-season projections forecast the M's as dead last, for the second season in a row. It was a disappointing crowd. The brass bands and opening-night festivities seemed forced and dismal. The M's looked like they would fulfill their predicted role as bottom-feeders.

Bly Levin, the veteran pitcher signed to stabilize the pitching staff, had been hit like a punching bag all spring. Still, his experience and years of knowledge helped the younger players in the clubhouse to master the pressure of the Big Leagues. Despite Levin's lack of success on the mound, Piniella was glad to have him on the staff to begin the season.

David and Cyrus sat in the owner's box, with Denise, Susan, Lindsey, and Casey. By the seventh inning of the first game of the season, the M's were down 6-2. Bly Levin came out of the bullpen to give up three runs and two walks. The Mariners had committed two errors and Lindsey and Denise were falling asleep. More people in the stands would have done likewise, but they had already left the cement Chia Pet, a name many Seattleites had come to call the ugly, squat, unpainted stadium at the south end of downtown.

One of the marketing people for the M's had come by to commiserate with Cyrus and confirm yet another marketing meeting for the next day.

"If we don't have a competitive team, we can still provide a good evening of entertainment," stated Cyrus to David after the marketing staffer left the box. "If we can just figure out how.

"Good baseball is the product we're selling. Good doesn't just mean Major League play, unfortunately. The Northwest has five Minor League franchises that will all draw people to their real grass fields, rather than watch us inside a building, and they have a cheaper price tag for their product. People need to see a competitive team or they won't come. If we can't be competitive, then we need to market better and smarter. If you're not good, be smart.

"Do you have any visions about marketing?" Cyrus inquired with a chuckle.

"Nope. I'm still looking for a team—to market myself. I'm thinking of contacting the Everett Giants to see if I can hook on with them. Single A ball is better than wasting these hits I've been given. Besides, the traveling won't be so hard on my family," David said through a mustard smeared grin.

The Mariners rallied in the eighth inning, scoring three runs. In the ninth, the Orioles led 9-5. The M's were able to get a runner on second base with two outs, but stranded the runner when the pinch hitter, a 23-year-old rookie, struck out on three pitches without swinging the bat.

Cyrus turned to David. "Don't say a word."

"I wasn't going to. However I did find 30 cents on the street last night when I was jogging with Cardozo. Just thought you should know, the signs continue to appear everywhere. You're passing up your date with destiny."

"Just pass the beer."

10

The season continued to be rocky. The fans dwindled to a trickle.

Piniella juggled the lineup daily, trying for a winning combination. The marketing team was pulling its hair out. Some didn't have any more to give and left the organization for, if not greener pastures, at least more hirsute ones.

The head of public relations was a 28-year-old MBA from Harvard, who had been on the job six months. It was he who suggested that something "big," "different," "bold," "innovative," and other lovely adjectives be implemented.

"Stop thinking like a regular baseball franchise. Let's face it, we're not. Do something dramatic, something different—hell, hire a stripper. Who cares? Just get people talking about this club."

If Cyrus and his staff didn't come up with something soon, well, the cash flow and the income picture would look like the team batting average—ugly.

At the end of the first three weeks of the season, the Mariners had won 4 games, lost 12 and had an average attendance of less than 8,000 for their home games. There was no cable television deal, despite pre-season promises that an offer would be forthcoming. The reason no deal had been offered to the Mariners was simple, the cable company said. They couldn't sell adequate sponsorship because the team had not, and probably would not draw flies, unless things changed, dramatically.

After another series of bleak income forecasts and bleaker concessions projections, in combination with no viable gimmicks to sell bad baseball to the Northwest public, Cyrus wearily met with David Pasteur—lawyer, father of two, softball player, owner of a shaggy dog, and would-be pinch-hitter for the Seattle Mariners.

Cyrus' 110-foot yacht bobbed in the middle of Puget Sound, while the snow-capped Olympics shone brightly in the noonday sun. Cyrus and David sat on the large fly bridge in leather deck chairs, a bottle of Jack Daniels half full between them on a teak-checked table. The fly bridge instruments twinkled in the sunlight as David sipped his icy drink. Cyrus drank the whiskey straight, like the talk they'd engaged in over the last two hours.

"One more time, Pasteur, *all* the details you can piece together. How many hits?"

"Thirty."

"Singles, doubles, home runs?"

"Hits. I don't know what kind."

"Can you *control* anything about this talent, if that's the phrase?"

"To a point."

"*What* point?"

"I don't know."

"Can you walk? And if you do, is it counted as a hit?"

"I'm not sure. It's not clear. I think not,"

David answered, pouring himself his fourth drink, trying to answer as honestly as his ego would allow.

"Can you be hit by a pitch?"

"Yeah, I think so. I mean, I'm not Casper."

"These are consecutive at-bats?"

"Yeah, I'm pretty sure of that. Thirty hits if the pitcher is a professional."

"Your defensive skills, which I've seen, are they affected by this vision thing?"

"Evidently not, but I'll work out, improve my game, speed, and hand-eye coordination in case I'm needed to play. But the dream's about hits. I got 'em and you should use 'em." He was feeling a wee bit cocky. Alcohol will do that.

"Do you know how preposterous this sounds?"

"Yeah. What about Piniella?"

"Piniella will go crazy, ballistic, nuts. But I'm still the owner."

"What does he know?"

"Not much, a little. He thinks that a marketing gimmick is coming up and it might somehow affect his team. He's nervous and apprehensive. How the hell am I going to tell him about you, make him understand?"

"You can't. You just have to tell him *you* believe."

"But I *don't* believe. It's preposterous on its face. My gut says you're an idiot, but as a marketing gimmick I just might be able to package and sell an idiot with a dream. You're Everyman, the middle-aged could-have-been-should-have-been person with a dream to play baseball, who finally gets a shot at the fantasy. It needs work, but ...."

"Am I getting a shot, Cyrus?" David interrupted.

Cyrus didn't answer. He sat staring at the mountain tops, like Buddha, with a drink. "Maybe."

"Who do we tell about this dream?"

"Just Piniella," Cyrus suggested.

"I agree," said David. "What about the sports writers? There could be a feeding frenzy."

"We'll cross that bridge ... later."

"When do I sign? How about the Director of Personnel? He needs to know."

"It's my call. I just tell him to sign you."

"Salary?" David asked.

"Don't push. Major League minimum only because I have to."

"How about incentives?"

"I'll let you live. What about your law practice, David? Are you sure about this? It's not much but it's all you have."

"I won't meet clients at night on game day."

"Thanks," said Cyrus. "How about batting practice?"

"I don't take it."

"Fielding practice?"

"I take that."

Cyrus, deep in thought, finally said, "What in the name of God are we talking about? I need medical help."

David smiled. "We're taking us to the Pennant, that's what we're talking about."

They looked at each other and picked up their respective drinks. They did not toast, but drank heartily, continuing to gaze at each other over the rims of their glasses, two reasonable men about to engage in an unreasonable act.

The girls were in bed. Cardozo was finding interesting places on his body to lick. Casey was drinking a cup of tea in the den. ESPN was on the TV, and David's brain was spinning like a dreidel.

"Casey, we need to talk," David said, turning down the big screen TV, which showed a couple of ex-jocks trying to talk cute on *Sports Center*.

"Okay, I'll talk to you if you want. I'm your wife–it's one of my jobs."

"I talked to Cyrus today on his boat. Nice day. Interesting conversation."

"So that's where you were. I called your office and Catherine wasn't sure. She said you were acting all mysterious."

"Yep."

"And?"

"I'm going to sign with the Mariners."

She put down her cup of tea and looked at her husband. "I think that's fine, Honey. Want some ice cream?"

"Casey, it's a done deal. He's going to sign me. I'm on the roster. Cyrus talks to

Piniella tomorrow."

"No! C'mon!"

"Yes!"

"No!"

"Yes!"

"Why? Why would he do it? He's not a stupid person. He's a bright man, a businessman, and a successful one at that. Or at least he was until now."

"Honey, I've got 30 hits. I really do. Cyrus thinks that, if nothing else, I'm a great marketing gimmick."

"No! You can't be serious!"

"Okay, maybe not a great gimmick, but a gimmick nonetheless."

"What will everyone think? I have friends in the community. The girls will be pilloried."

"Depends."

"On what?" she asked.

"My RBIs."

Casey groaned.

Cardozo licked.

David smiled.

The next day, Piniella went ballistic.

"I saw the fat guy swing, Cyrus. What in God's name are you talking here, signing a fat attorney to put people in the stands? You crazy, or what? Bill Veeck you're not."

"No Lou. I'm the owner. Maybe eccentric, but still the owner."

"Whoa, just a minute. I've got my reputation! I've got integrity! I've got ...."

"A contract," Cyrus interrupted, "a four-year, one-point-three million dollar contract, with my name on it and your name on it. You work for me."

"Not any more. I quit."

"Goodbye."

"You're kidding, right? I'm fired?"

"No, but if you quit .... Listen Lou, he's got 30 hits. He'll be a pinch hitter. You utilize him like he's a member of the team, cuz he *is* a member of the team. He signs today in a private ceremony. You're invited."

"Cyrus. tell me what you're doing. I thought you wanted a winner for Seattle. You told me I had the power to run the team. Now ... now ...." Piniella was beside himself, searching for a way to stop this madness.

So Cyrus told him the entire story. The dream, the vision—30 hits in a row, no more no less, against a Major League pitcher. Minimum salary. With the falling attendance, what was there to lose?

"I wouldn't be doing this *just* for a gimmick, Lou, but of course that's a big part of it. Actually, it's most of it, but still ...."

"Still what?" Lou screamed. "You think he can hit a 90-mile-an-hour fastball? The son of a bitch can't even see his shoelaces. You crazy?"

"So he'll drop ten or fifteen pounds. I've decided, Lou. It's my team"

"Yeah, but it's my ass." Piniella paused, running his hand through his hair. "Okay, Cyrus, okay. Have him show me. Have him hit one lousy ball. Show me it's even possible."

"Lou," Cyrus reasoned, "if David did hit four dingers off the wall, off Randy Johnson or Chris Bosio, would you say 'okay? Sign him?'"

Piniella sat in his leather chair in his cozy office, rubbing his stubbly chin. "No. That doesn't prove anything," he responded. "Four lucky pops. But remember, I've seen the son of a bitch swing. Is he disabled?"

"Exactly. That's my point, Lou. David can't prove it to me or to you, or to anyone. He just does it, or he doesn't do it. Simple as that."

Lou sat there, staring, pondering, trying to find a face-saving compromise. He wanted to keep this job. He liked the nucleus of the team, he just needed time—time Cyrus couldn't afford.

"Do you believe in God, Lou?"

"Of course I do," Lou answered.

"Can you prove it?"

"Of course I can!"

"Okay, how?" asked Cyrus, "How do you prove the existence of God?"

"Ya just know. You *feel* God. You know He's with you. You believe."

"It's called faith, Lou, and you have it or you don't. Unlike God, David's faith is in his dream, but our faith in David *can* be proven without us having to die and see our Maker by the Pearly Gates."

"Okay, Cyrus. Who the hell would we send down to make room for Pasteur? Whose heart are you gonna break because of this stupidity?"

"You're the manager. I don't want to interfere," Cyrus said as he left Piniella's office, "but you've gotta make room by midnight tonight. Okay, Lou?"

"Shit!"

The scene reminded Casey of a presidential ceremony. The wife, the two children standing around watching the dad be sworn into some governmental position. Similar, but different.

David, in a three-piece suit, signed a one-year Major League contract with the Seattle Mariners for $109,000, not guaranteed. The team photographer was there for the signing. He was very confused because, quite frankly, David didn't look like, act like, or in any way resemble a Major League prospect, let alone a signed one.

The PR man, David Remer, flitted around the room, his mind racing, trying to make sense of this marketing opportunity.

"Who is this guy?" he whispered to the photographer.

"New guy."

"I know that, but from where?"

"I don't know. Did he play in Japan with Suzuki? He looks American."

"How the hell do I know? Cyrus said he was going to do something innovative. So this is it? This is innovative?"

"Who got cut to make room for pudgy?"

"Bly Levin."

"No kidding. How old is this guy? The team age is going to go up on this exchange, by the looks of him. What does the press release say about this transaction?"

Remer rustled in one of his folders and, finding the right piece of paper, said softly, "The press release says Bly Levin is leaving, free to 'find a home with another club. He leaves the Mariners 1-3 with an ERA of 6.74, six walks, two strikeouts.' This'll be no big surprise to the beat writers, I guess. Levin has just run out of arm strength. But this is the guy who is going to replace him? Is this the marketing gimmick?" Remer shook his head sadly.

The morning after the press release, sports writers descended on Levin in the clubhouse as he cleaned out his locker.

"Will you look for another team, Bly?"

"I don't think so. I'm done with professional baseball."

"Why not? You're now only five games from 300 career wins. You could find another team. The season is still young."

"I know, but I've told my agent it's over. I don't want to take some kid's chance to fulfill his dreams of being in the Show. I've had 23 great years. I'm very grateful for those years. Most people never get the chance. I've had 23 years of chance, and I'm not going to take away some kid's spot on another team, especially since the season's already started, and this hypothetical kid has made that team already. Then I come in and bump him. No, that wouldn't be right, so guys, I'm done playing. This is my last locker. I've thrown my last pitch. Sounds like a movie," he said sadly. The writers were touched. He was a class guy, and this was a sport that was more and more being dominated by jerks. The writers would miss Bly Levin. So would the sport.

"Who are they calling up to fill your spot? Any ideas?"

"I heard some flame-thrower from Calgary, but they didn't consult me—they just fired me. Can't blame them. Age will take its toll no matter who you are, and management has to respond with youth."

"What now, Bly?"

"Now, I get on with the rest of my life. Grow up and get to know my kids better."

ESPN ran a retrospective of Levin's career, noting the changing of the guard, how time and old age speak to us all, sometimes in whispers, sometimes in shouts, but everyone has to listen eventually.

David, apparently, was deaf.

The reporters all wished Levin well and wrote glowingly of the career and the man. Buried among the numerous articles that resembled obituaries was a blurb on page six reporting the signing of David Pasteur, recently promoted to the big club from a place that was somewhat unclear to the author of the article.

The day after the formal signing, the Pasteurs went to dinner at Ivar's Salmon House, a landmark seafood restaurant on Lake Union, near the ship canal. The restaurant had outside tables, where one could assist the dietary intake of seagulls as they swooped from above, doing aerobatics for french fries.

"Daddy, are you going to be a baseball

player now?"

"Yes, Lindsey, I am."

"Are you going to be famous?"

"No, probably not, infamous maybe, but one can never tell."

"I told my friend Roger, and he said I was a fibber, and his brother John, who's older, said I was, too."

"Well, you're not, so don't worry about it. Eat your food."

Lindsey threw a french fry for a white sea bird, who caught it in midair and flew off for some quiet.

"I hope I can do that if the time ever comes," David said pensively.

"Have you thought about what you're going to tell your clients?" Casey asked. "I mean, one day you're behind your desk asking if their neck hurts and boomski—you're a, uh, anyway, you're unavailable. I think they need a word from you about this career change." Casey wiped the ketchup from Lauren's mouth. She was very messy. She'll make a good surgeon, David thought.

"I'm sending out a letter explaining this six-month sabbatical, or whatever you want to call it, telling people I'm still an attorney. I'll still represent them. Nothing will change except that it might be a little more difficult to whine at me. I'll probably lose some clients, and that can't be helped, but hey, I'll probably get some, too. Think of it—'*I* have a power-hitting litigator.' 'I can see *my* attorney on TV.' '*My* attorney is that jerk in the ill-fitting uniform.'"

"Can you really do this?" Casey asked for the hundredth time.

"I haven't got the slightest idea. Doesn't make much sense on its face, does it? But nothing ventured, nothing gained."

"What are you now, a fortune cookie?"

11

The day before David was scheduled to report to the clubhouse, Piniella called a team meeting. He gave some background about the release of Bly Levin, told the team about management's continuing search for a middle reliever who could replace the projected innings Levin was scheduled to pitch, and further, Piniella announced that David Pasteur, a new prospect, had been signed and was to report the next day.

"Where's he from, Skip?" asked Buhner, a 220-pound, strong-armed right fielder from Texas. Jay Buhner was a big, rangy right-handed hitter who hit with power when he didn't strike out, which had been occurring too often lately. He was a free spirit with a rifle for an arm, but he'd never quite achieved the promise which was anticipated by the scouts and prognosticators. He was currently hitting .235, with two home runs, but was striking out on a ratio of 1/10.

"I don't know much about him. I guess he's had a peculiar career, a little older than a normal rookie," remarked Piniella, avoiding eye contact with the group and shuffling his feet like a dancer with a bum leg.

"Hey, so what?" laughed Rich Amaral, an infielder from upstate New York. Amaral had been in the minor leagues for ten years, quitting three times, always coming back in the spring. Years earlier in his first season with the pros, he, at 31, had been the leagues oldest rookie, a player with a great attitude and foot speed. Now, as a seasoned veteran, he was a well-liked, gritty player.

"Older rookies," Amaral opined, "are a special breed. Hungry, yet not pushy, warm and sensitive, yet standup kinda' people," he kidded.

"Take a walk, Pops," said Griffey. He was the star of the team, one of the youngest members despite his super-star status.

"Quiet," commanded Piniella. "Listen up, will ya? He reports tomorrow. It's um ... uh

... a corporate decision, so we run with it. He might look, ah ... a little rusty. Some of you might have seen him before, hanging around in Arizona. But we all work for the management. They give me the ballplayers, I give them the wins. This is a team game, and he's, uh, he's gonna be, he's signed, so ..." he trailed off.

The team couldn't understand Piniella's discomfort. He was shifting his weight from foot to foot, running his hands through his hair, and in all respects acting like he had just been caught sleeping with the boss's wife.

"Now let's talk about yesterday's game, when you guys missed two signs, couldn't bunt and missed the cutoff man. I'm serious about this year. If you guys can't perform, I don't give a shit about your contract—you're gone, hear me? Gone. I'll play Double A players before you guys. Think. You gotta think, not just react. It ain't that tough, guys. Think, relax, and we'll start to win. We got more talent here than ya think, but if you're making mental errors, you're not gonna be here to make 'em, capice?"

Silence.

"Okay?"

More silence.

"We got a game tonight. Let's go over the lineup ...."

David awoke at 6:00 A.M., butterflies the size of condors banging away in his stomach, his first game just hours away. The sun was barely up. Casey slept beside him, without the birds circling in her belly.

He rose, retrieved the paper and brought it back to bed. He turned to the sports page, wrinkling the paper in the morning stillness. The M's had lost again, by one run. Yet another editorial on Bly Levin appeared. David scanned an article on the possibility of congressional hearings on the viability of the antitrust laws that governed baseball, and a report on a high-school phenom from Portland, Oregon, who had pitched his fourth no-hitter in six games. The M's could use him, David thought. Have the governor waive algebra, and the youngster could head north to Seattle in a heartbeat. Could happen.

David sat up, watching Cardozo sleep peacefully at the bottom of the bed, snoring slightly, sleeping the sleep of the dumb and fed.

"Go for a walk? A walk?" David questioned the black and gray fuzzball in a whispered voice, just to screw with his puppy's head.

Cardozo lifted his head, looked at David with disdain out of one half-opened eye, sighed, and replaced his head on the quilt until the folds covered his black gumdrop nose.

"No, huh? Okay, I don't want to either. It's raining."

The phone rang. It was too early for good news.

"Hello?"

"Pasteur, it's me," said Parker, "Seattle Times."

"Yeah," David said warmly.

"I'm sitting here at my desk drinking bad coffee, smoking my third coffin nail, when I come across the weirdest damn thing."

"What's that, besides the fact you're up?"

"The M's just signed a rookie with the same name as you."

"No kidding," David said suspiciously, the birds beginning to fly faster in his abdomen. "So?"

"So how many David Pasteurs are there?"

"A bunch?"

"No, not a bunch. So I made some calls and this smells like Alice in Wonderland on acid. No bio, no stats, no nothing. A rookie from outa nowhere, Counselor. I gotta wonder."

Beat. Beat. Beat.

"So what are you wondering?"

"About you. What I'm wondering is about you."

"Excuse me?"

"Are you this rookie?" Silence. Followed by more silence.

"Maybe," David finally said in a whisper.

"Bullshit," replied Parker.

"No, I'm afraid it's true," David replied. "It's me. It's a long and peculiar story."

"Double bullshit. *You* replaced Levin? You talk to me, Pasteur. What's going on? Is Cyrus nuts? I know *you're* nuts. You blackmailing someone?"

"Just listen. I've been signed by the Mariners to fill an open roster spot. I signed a couple of days ago and will suit up for tonight's game against Cleveland. That's really all there is to it. It's a league minimum contract, $109,000, and it's not guaranteed beyond that ...."

"That's all there is to it?" Parker screamed. "Are you crazy? This story is huge. This is bigger than the Bill Veeck midget gimmick. The midget was only three foot nine, but at least *he* could play ball."

"How did he do?" asked David.

"Walked."

"Good for him."

"Who okayed this deal, the Tooth Fairy?" Parker barked, returning to the subject of a lawyer in a baseball uniform.

"The owner. That's why they call him an owner. He owns the team, and makes the big decisions."

"I gotta get an exclusive on this deal. Listen, Dave ol' pal, I'm coming over now with a photog. We gotta talk."

"The team wanted this kept low-key, uh, until I could perform, so I'm not sure I feel very comfortable ...."

"It's clear to me that *you* are not well, *Cyrus* is not well, the *team* is definitely not well, and I'm coming over right now. Tell Casey no coffee, thanks. I'll only be staying a couple of days."

Click.

"Who was that?" Casey asked, awakening against her will.

"Parker, reporter from the *Times* who covered the Rodriquez case, who now thinks he's gonna get a Pulitzer."

"So, it's started."

"Yeah, it's started."

That afternoon, after settling down with a Valium, David reported to the equipment manager, Jim Lopez, for his gear. The fitting went well enough, but they had to search to find cleats for the indoor carpet that was the Kingdome field.

"Where's your bat?" David was asked by Lopez, who had held the same position for 16 years. He'd probably been wearing the same shirt as well. He was in his 50s, and firmly believed he would have no more really great stories to tell his kids, until now. "We don't supply bats. Who the hell are you anyway? You don't look like no rookie I've ever seen, and I've seen a lot. You look like a damn accountant."

"Lawyer."

"What?"

"Forget it. I'll get a bat later."

The clubhouse was filled with ballplayers. David thought that made sense. He walked into the locker room and spotted Piniella talking to a young black man who was barely a man. He looked about 15, but had to have been at least 20. They weren't fighting, but the conversation didn't look friendly or deferential.

"Pasteur," Piniella said, looking toward the double doors, where David stood forlornly. "In my office." He pointed toward the back of the locker room. David hefted his newly acquired equipment bag, sans bats, and headed in the direction indicated by Piniella's pointed finger. He walked by the open dressing cubicles of players he had cheered for a few weeks earlier while eating dogs and gulping beer. The stares were cool. Most of the players didn't associate the newest rookie with the guy who was ambling back to the office, but Buhner, Griffey and Bosio did. David read their expressions. Contempt was a good word to describe it, utter contempt.

No one nodded his head in greeting. No

one smiled. To David it felt like a prison yard, and he was a stoolie. It was a long walk to Piniella's inner sanctum, one which David made in silence.

David waited for Piniella to open his door, then he followed him into the office.

Piniella went behind his desk, cluttered with papers, cups of coffee, letters. David was nervous. Piniella was pissed. They stared at each other without saying a word. It was a very loud silence. It was so quiet that David could hear the wall clock tick, and it was an electric clock.

David decided to break the ice. "So," David said, "nice to see you again, Mr. Piniella."

Piniella said nothing for a few more moments, and instead just stared. Finally he barked, "You blackmailing Cyrus?"

"No, but it's a reasonable question. It's the second time I've been asked that today, come to think of it." He attempted a laugh. It came out a snort. He sounded like a pig. He thought he was going to pee in his pants. A pig that peed its pants was not a good start.

"A dream, huh? A bloody dream?"

"Yeah, hard to believe, huh?" David began getting even more nervous.

"Okay goofball, here's the drill. Thirty hits in a row, right? So I figure you go 0-1, your vision thing is crap, we cut you like a piece of meat, and we're all done. If Cyrus insists on keeping you around anyway, I quit. Just so you and I are clear about this bullshit, okay, Pasteur? 'Cuz this PR crap ain't me."

"Okay, you're the manager. What's that mean to me in real terms?"

"In real terms? God, you even talk like a lawyer. It means you start as the DH tonight."

"No, really. I thought ...."

"Yeah, really. So don't unpack. You're gone by 7:30 tonight, asshole, and I want you out of here by 7:31. Got it?"

"Can I ask you one question?"

"What?" Piniella could barely restrain himself.

"Where do I get a bat, you know, so I can hit the ball tonight?"

"Shit!" Piniella said. "Out!"

David, head spinning, left Piniella's office and looked at his watch. It was 4 p.m. Game time was 7:05. He asked the clubhouse boy to watch his stuff.

"Who's gonna take it?" the kid asked. Everybody's a comedian.

On the way out of the clubhouse, David literally ran into the well-muscled, right-handed flame thrower from Kobe, Japan. Suzuki was backing away from his locker and into Davids distracted path. They collided. David fell. Suzuki looked around startled, then bowed deeply.

"I'm sorry—my fault, wasn't looking. Hey, you okay? I'm, uh, your new teammate. Pasteur, no relation to the great scientist from France."

Suzuki continued to bow, saying nothing. David did not know the proper etiquette to gracefully allow the other party to stop bowing so he rose from his knee, looked around the clubhouse, saw people staring at him as if he was fungus growing in a shower corner and slid out the door.

On the team six minutes and already I've been involved in a collision, David thought. Who knew?

David left the Kingdome, hailed a taxi and went looking for a sporting goods shop in downtown Seattle. Quickly.

"Wait here, I'll only be a minute," David said to the cabbie as he exited the cab and quickly walked to the store.

He entered and accosted a young clerk. "I need a bat, please. I'm in a hurry, where might they be?"

"Right this way," said the 20-year-old clerk. She had a chirpy personality, straight white teeth, long blonde hair, a name tag that read Traci, and a body sculptured by aerobics and sweat. "Here they are." She pointed to a wall full of bats almost proudly, as if they were her children.

"Good, but where are the wood ones? These are all metal."

"Oh, golly. Wood. Who uses wood? Are they legal?"

"Yes. Please, I'm in a big hurry. Do you have any?" he asked impatiently. She pondered the question with agonizing slowness.

"Let me check. I'll call Doug."

Doug appeared. He was the manager, much older, but no wiser.

"Well, we may have some in back, but I can't tell you where." He smiled the smile of the inane.

"I'll look myself, okay? I'm in a hurry."

Together, the three located a cardboard box full of wooden bats. The box had dust over the logo—Louisville Slugger, the kind the big boys still use, but only in the pros.

The last time David had used a wooden bat, he was in high school, in the mid-60s. He'd been a contact hitter back then, using a thick-handled bat, which also had a thick barrel, more surface to get on the ball. David went through the case of 30 bats. The very last one he examined, the thirtieth bat from the box, was a thick-handled, big barreled, Nellie Fox-like bat, exactly like he used in high school. He smiled. Traci smiled. This was indeed an omen.

He paid for the bat using his credit card.

"Is this for your son?" inquired Traci, as she ran the card through her computer, checking his credit in some far off city.

"No, it's for me. I'm going to use it up the street tonight. Can I use the phone?"

"You a bouncer?" she asked as he strolled to the store phone.

He dialed Casey, told her that he was starting tonight, to find a sitter and come down to the ballpark with her mom. Then he called Cyrus.

"I heard about your meeting with Piniella. He just called. He's hot. I told him hit or not, you're on the team until I can market this idea, so, uh, good luck. By the way, I don't intend to lose Piniella over you, so hit one tonight, Mr. Psychic.

"I'm sending a car for Casey. She sits with me tonight, so in case you fall on your face, we can hustle her out of the park before the mob forms. You're on your own.

"By the way, the reporters are beginning to circle and flock. Who's Parker? He woke me up at 6:30 this morning, wanting a quote and an explanation. Pushy s.o.b. I like him," Cyrus chuckled over the phone.

"Well, Cyrus, you wanted to publicize this deal win or lose, so here we go."

"Dave, one last thing."

"What's that?"

"Don't screw this up for me, your town, or your career. Just relax and have fun." Cyrus hung up.

David signed his credit card slip for Traci. She gazed at the signature. "Pasteur. Any relation to the guy who invented rabies?"

"Cured rabies, and no," he said.

"But are you a somebody?"

"We're all a somebody, Traci. We all have gifts, and can help others with those gifts, so yes, Traci, I am a somebody. And after tonight, I'll be an even bigger somebody."

"Gee," she said. "Who are you?"

Ah, celebrity, he thought. "Just listen to the M's game tonight and call me in the morning. You might be part of something big."

David climbed back into the waiting cab, its motor still running. He arranged himself on the back seat with his bat in his lap. He had told Traci not to wrap it. How do you wrap a bat, anyway?

The cabby said nothing until David got out at the Kingdome entrance. "Hey, buddy, I thought people brought gloves to the game. Ya got it all wrong!" He laughed heartily as he counted his tip, shaking his head at the dumb guy who was trying to get into the Kingdome with a bat.

It was one hour till game time. The team was on the field taking batting practice and running sprints, all except the young man who had been jawing with Piniella when David first walked into the clubhouse.

"Hi. I'm David Pasteur," said David, extending his hand.

The kid shrugged, looked at David's hand but didn't take it. "I heard about you. You're the new guy?"

"Starting in an hour."

"I gotta go do some sprints." He left. "Jerk," David muttered.

David got dressed sitting on a three-legged stool in front of his open locker. He was alone, very alone. He wanted to joke around with Casey. He couldn't. She was more uptight than Piniella. Besides, she was sitting in the stands drinking, and she didn't drink.

David's eyes fell on the afternoon headline of the *Times* sports page, which read ROOKIE LAWYER TO "TRY" and below in smaller type, New Owner Attempts Gimmick to Raise Attendance. The byline read Pete Parker. David read the article:

> Today marks an historic day in baseball, as well as for the Mariner franchise. The Mariners, inept for years, today attempt to go down in baseball history as not only bad, but now embarrassing. The owner of the team, Cyrus Sven Andvik, fired Bly Levin, a 23-year veteran,

and replaced him with one David Pasteur, a personal injury lawyer with no, that's none, zero, zip prior baseball experience. "Due to sagging attendance, and poor play on the field, something needed to be done," said PR director David Remer. "We felt Pasteur could contribute to this team, despite his lack of experience. Don't judge this personnel move until later, much later."

Pasteur, when interviewed in his North Seattle home, told this reporter that he had hit over .350 consistently in the slow pitch E league in Mountlake Terrace, where he captained the Ambulance Chasers to a second-place finish in last year's league play. Team Manager Lou Piniella said that Pasteur would start tonight as the designated hitter and made it clear that he was not consulted on this personnel move. "I manage whoever they give me to manage," Piniella stated, "and they gave me this guy. That's all I'm gonna say."

A larger than normal crowd is expected for tonight's game, at 7:05.

> The Baseball Commissioner's office is reportedly looking into this situation, but was not available for comment.

David put down the paper. He had to throw up. So he did.

The PA announcer spoke David's name as the designated hitter, to boos, heckles and a few cheers from the 35,000 beyond-curious fans.

David took off his cap during the National Anthem, just like the other players, but the similarity to the other players ended there. David sat at the end of the bench, alone, excluded. He had seen Casey and Esther in Cyrus' box. They looked worried, like patients before surgery. He felt awful. If hitting was 80 percent confidence, as Ted Williams had said, then David was ... a lawyer.

David came to bat in the third inning of a scoreless tie. Amaral stood at third base, smiling and dirty. He had just taken Marty Reid deep to left, his line drive bounding away from the Cleveland left fielder. Amaral had slid into third just ahead of the tag. The crowd stirred. So did David's bowels.

"Now batting, number 30, the designated hitter, David Pasteur," the PA announcer boomed. The crowd buzzed. It didn't do much other than buzz. No applause. Not many boos, just a general confused expectation.

David got up from where he was kneeling in the on-deck circle, wiped his new bat handle with old black pitch, and walked toward the batter's box. Showtime.

The pitcher David faced was a six-foot-two, 29-year-old curve baller with 35 career wins and great control. He hadn't shaved that day, and he didn't appreciate being placed in this no-win situation, especially with a runner on third. On the other hand, it was better to face someone named Pasteur than, say, anyone else in organized baseball.

David dug in. He'd seen it done on TV just the other day in the sports bar he frequented. He wished he was there now. He looked at Reid. Sixty feet six inches didn't look like a great distance. It looked more like six feet six inches. Reid got his signal from the catcher, nodded his agreement, and went into his windup.

The ball went right for David's head. It was a blur, a blur that was going to kill him. He was going to be killed in his first at bat by a blur. He had to dive out of the way. Now.

He dove from the batter's box like a veteran soldier in a firefight. It was a strike, down the heart of the plate. The umpire screamed his decision at David, still sprawled in the dirt.

The crowd laughed, booed, jeered. The Cleveland dugout went crazy, yelling taunts. Casey cringed. Cyrus shook his head. David almost soiled his pants in front of the home crowd.

David brushed himself off, trying to appear nonchalant, and climbed back into the box, attempting to still his shaking hands. He looked at the umpire. "Good curve."

Reid's next pitch was a fastball. David didn't swing. One swings *at* something. He had never even seen the ball, only heard the pop of it hitting the catcher's mitt.

"Two!" yelled the umpire. David thought he saw the umpire sneer as he said it. Piniella smiled in the dugout, Casey began to cry in the stands. He thought he saw Esther consoling her daughter.

David stepped out of the box to check his shoe bottoms for mud. They were clean. Big surprise, as they were playing inside a dome.

He took two practice swings and returned to the right side of the batter's box, looked at the pitcher and took a deep breath. Reid smirked. David didn't blame him.

The windup. The pitch. A curve, he was told later. A curve that broke too late, so that the ball hit David's bat as he bailed out of the way trying to avoid getting plunked yet again. The ball struck the bat, caromed off its fat barrel and looped ten feet over the third base bag, then rolled six more feet, stopping on the edge of the carpet. The Cleveland third baseman never had a chance. The left fielder had even less of one. David had a hit. The Mariners had a run.

Casey sat next to Cyrus, dumbstruck. The crowd went wild. Cyrus almost wept. Esther did.

Piniella pulled David after his second at bat, a swinging bunt single. The ball rolled down the first base line 46 feet from home plate, where it ran out of gas and sat on the chalky white line quivering like a living thing.

David went two for two. Piniella could make no sense of the events that he had just witnessed, but he reasoned that if David *did* have 28 hits left, he had better use them judiciously. Piniella was beyond skeptical, but he wasn't stupid. The Mariners won 1-0. David was in the Show.

David was inundated by reporters after his first game in the Major Leagues. He sat in front of his locker, his bat gleaming in the ambient light as it leaned against the side of his wire cubicle. Reporters and cameramen formed a half circle around the rookie attorney ballplayer perched on a wooden stool. He dripped with sweat, not from exertion, but from the bright camera lights.

After the last out of the ninth inning, David had jumped from the Mariners' bench and added himself to the conga line which had formed to congratulate the winning pitcher. When David went to shake hands with his team-mates, several of the players refused to extend their hands. This social slight was not lost on the host of observant sports reporters, who generated questions for David in the post-game interview and feeding frenzy.

"Pasteur," yelled the hairless reporter for the Seattle CBS affiliate KIRO TV, "where'd you play your ball before tonight, if you can call that playing?"

"Mountlake Terrace Slow Pitch."

"C'mon, where? We got a right to know."

"Well, I did play in the Lynnwood Rec

League three years ago, but that was C competition, so I changed leagues."

"David, tell me about your first hit. What did he throw you?"

"A fastball, hard. It hit my bat. I ran. You guys probably saw it better than me."

"Pasteur, you really a lawyer here in town?"

"Yeah. *Rodriquez v. Mountain Beer* mean anything to you?"

"No," the reporter answered, "but I drink the stuff."

"What are you doing in a Mariner uniform, anyway?" prodded another.

"Hitting."

"Who signed you?"

"Cyrus, but I presume he represents the entire franchise."

"How did this happen?" shouted someone else over the growing mayhem.

"With a pen."

"He means how did it happen that you were scouted in the first place? I mean, just look at you," said a bespectacled, potbellied reporter for an all-sports radio station, KJR.

"Good organization, I guess. It's been no secret in North Seattle that I wanted to play professional ball, and I guess I was just a lucky local prospect who got found. And what the hell do you mean just look at me? What's wrong with me?"

"This is crazy, Pasteur. Is this a media gimmick you guys cooked up? If it is, it isn't going to work. Bill Veeck is long dead, and Seattle and the league won't stand for it. You're being used, we're being used, and ...."

"I'm two for two, pal," David interrupted hotly. "Good gimmick, don't you think?"

"What do your teammates think of this bullshit, Pasteur? They paid their dues to get here and you ain't no Michael Jordan."

"They haven't shared their views with me yet. I'm a rookie. I'm going to have to earn their respect, and other people's also, if I can. If I can't, I can't."

"Have you been timed from home?"

"Yeah. It takes me about fifteen minutes to the clubhouse."

Some of the reporters even laughed. At least Pasteur would give them some good copy.

"Your second hit, David, was that a hit and run play?"

"No, it was a swing and pray play. Listen guys, all I know about what happened tonight was what you saw. There are good ballplayers and great ballplayers, and then there are lucky ballplayers. Tonight I was a lucky ballplayer. I'd rather be lucky than good. It wasn't pretty, but hell, I'm not pretty. Anyway, it worked, at least tonight. So chalk it up to beginner's luck. I think I can contribute and help this team. If I'm wrong, I'm gone."

"Are you starting tomorrow?"

"Ask Lou. I'm a rookie–what do I know?"

"How does it feel to replace a future Hall of Famer like Bly Levin, a guy with *your* credentials and skills?"

David answered, "I was offered a contract. I signed. I played. I've never met Mr. Levin. If I did, I'd ask him for his autograph. I was in law school in Minnesota when he was a rookie with the Twins. I have nothing to do with management and its decisions, but Levin has proved himself a great player. I've had two at-bats in one game, so there ain't no comparison."

"Do you think ...."

"I'm not paid to think. I'm paid to compete." He had been waiting a lifetime to give that answer to someone.

David thought that last answer sounded pretty good, just like all the stupid interviews he had heard over all these many years. This was easy. Give them trite answers to their stupid questions and everyone will get along. Just be careful not to speak about the dream or alienate anyone too soon. Don't sound foolish or combative and, just like in court, quit while you're ahead.

"Oh brother!" some reporter exclaimed, rolling his eyes with disdain.

"Did you know the Baseball Commissioner's office is looking into the circumstances surrounding your signing with the Mariners?"

"No, the Commissioner hasn't called me, but I'm listed and he can ...."

"Do you think signing a guy like you is in the best interest of baseball? Doesn't it tend to degrade the entire institution?" asked a stringer for *Time Magazine*. He was a 24-year-old crew-cut, pompous, officious ass.

David turned to the circle of reporters. "That question is leading, compound, and therefore objectionable, but then so are you. So I'm not going to answer." Ricky Henderson would have been proud, David thought as he slipped into his snug jeans.

The reporters laughed, congratulated David on his peculiar first game performance and moved on to talk to other players for their evaluation of the last three hours.

David left the clubhouse alone, walking out into the cool night air and into Casey's waiting arms in the Kingdome parking lot. She shook her head as he approached.

Casey said, "May you live in interesting times."

"Now you're the fortune cookie. Let's go home." David remarked, sliding into the passenger seat of his car. He was asleep before she released the parking brake.

12

The next day's press release from the Mariners office read:

> Mariner scouting personnel has once again uncovered a diamond in the rough. Manager Lou Piniella is in the process of doing some polishing of that diamond, David Pasteur (no relation to the scientist).
>
> The Mariners, constantly on the lookout for talent wherever it may be, recently signed a highly talented local softball player and attorney as an adjunct to the Mariners hitting lineup. Playing in his first Major

League game, Pasteur, age 43, drove in the only Mariner run in a sterling three-hit performance twirled by starter Greg Hibbard.

Cyrus Sven Andvik, the new owner of the Mariners, was the first of several executives to contemplate extending a contract to Pasteur, after viewing what has been described as his picture-perfect command of hitting mechanics.

Further, the Mariners have no knowledge of any investigation or any intent to investigate the circumstances surrounding this recent signing of their potential new star by league officials.

The Mariners will resist any probe at any level of baseball regarding this signing.

ESPN led with the story the next day. The local media carried it that evening. The national media were buzzing, not over the fact that some unknown middle-aged lawyer went two for two at some relatively meaningless game in some state near Alaska, but rather over Cyrus' obvious attempt to milk the press like a cow's udder. The PR gamble was working. Within 48 hours season ticket inquiries were up dramatically, and the local press was clamoring for as much information as it could find, uncover or invent relative to this unknown hitter, the litigator Pasteur.

The next day was an off day before traveling to Los Angeles for three games at Anaheim Stadium. David went to the office to take care of business.

The phone never stopped ringing. He got calls from AP, Reuters, *Sporting News*, three judges, and every client he had ever represented, along with several he hadn't. Not all the calls were friendly.

"I want my file back, Mr. Pasteur. I want to go to an attorney who cares about being an adult, not running around in short pants. Act your age! You're fired." It was always something.

"Maria Rodriquez on one," the intercom squawked.

"Hi, Sweetie. I was going to call you."

"I thought we were pals. You never told me ...."

"Maria, it happened so quickly, it just evolved ...."

"You never said you played ball. Why not tell me? I'm hurt and I'm angry."

"It's not like that, Maria. It just happened, it's all very peculiar."

"You sound real dumb, David, real stupid. What do you mean it just happened? You sound like a teenager caught out too late."

"I can't talk about that, but I can talk about your appeal, and we should."

"Okay, but I want you to know I can help you with your swing. You're pathetic. I saw the tape. I was embarrassed to call you my attorney." She laughed.

"Just cause I couldn't see the seams on a split finger fastball."

"I'm not sure you could see the mound!"

They talked about her appeal, the due date on the brief, and how to recognize a change-up.

Casey took David to the airport where a

chartered jet would whisk the team to Southern California for a game against the red-hot Angels. The Angels were tearing up the American League, getting off to their fastest start in years. This would be David's first road trip.

"David, remember you don't travel well, but you travel worse without me. So what you need to do is ... *not* be yourself. These people don't like, understand, or know you. Please no Jew jokes, no black jokes, no ... oh, you know what you do. Have they assigned you a roommate or will they let "Pops" sleep alone due to your age and condition?"

"Yeah, I'm getting a roommate, just like in college. Maybe we can become pals, chase chicks, copy each other's notes during finals, cram together, and pull all-nighters."

"You scare me to death, but listen to me David, you got two hits totaling 73 feet. If you think for a minute that you are going to strut around Los Angeles with visions of ...."

"Honey, I know where you're going. Relax. I have not brought the Wade Boggs memorial straight razor on any road trip since the softball team went to Wenatchee on the 4th of July. I will be a good boy. You be a good mom and pray that I increase my feet per swing. I love you. Watch the TV. You'll be able to recognize me. I'm the pudgy guy with a new tan. Anaheim here I come. I wonder if the Whiskey-A-Go-Go is still open?"

Anaheim, California. A road trip, a roommate, a member of a team. Well, maybe not a member, David thought. He sat by himself on the flight down the coast. Generally, a row to oneself was a sought after prize, but David wanted to sit and chat with anyone willing to chat back. Maybe next time, he thought, I'll bring Cardozo. He'll talk to me and there's obviously going to be room for the dog if things continue like this.

David knew team acceptance would be slow in coming. He knew he was the ultimate outsider of all outsiders, and he knew he was a freak in a world of physical perfection, but all that was intellectual mumbo-jumbo. A social slight is a personal wound when inflicted by an individual. When inflicted by a group of people in concert, this personal wound deepens, and when tacitly approved by a formal organization, the concept changes to social outcast. David, always a social creature, naturally wanted to mix with this new group of people, but it takes two to talk, and no one wanted to talk to David, or even acknowledge his presence. The lonely flight led to a lonelier bus ride to the team's hotel.

David unpacked his bag in his hotel room.

He looked approvingly at the mini-bar, the good-sized room with two double beds and that most important piece of equipment, the TV remote. David smiled, thinking of other hotel rooms and other memories.

David had often discussed with his male friends the ultimate male socio-sexual sports fantasy. It involved a deeply comfortable lounge chair, a large alcoholic beverage, and several big-screen TVs tuned to different exciting sporting events, while a beautiful, young, accomplished female attended to the occupant's every need. The chair and TVs were located outside, under the blazing sunshine, and overlooking a picturesque vista, while a responsive and easy-to-use remote control rested comfortably in the hand that rocked not the cradle, but the lounger. At the conclusion of all the sporting events, the female and the debris would be whisked away, the sunshine remaining, one's tan growing darker. The only debate that remained was the size and responsiveness of both the remote control and the female.

The door to the room opened abruptly as David came out of the bathroom after he finished unpacking. A young black man with earphones and a huge blue nylon bag banged into the room. He threw the bag onto the furthest of the beds like a shot-putter. The youth did not look at David, but lay down on the other bed, on which he had not deposited his bag, and closed his eyes. David could hear the rap music leaking out from beneath the padded earphones, the bass beat making the pillow jump, but not the young man's head, which was still as death.

David recognized his putative roommate as the young man involved in the heated discussion with Piniella days earlier. David now observed him more carefully—closely cropped hair, powerful upper body with large shoulders and smallish waist. Not very tall for a pitcher. Only 5 feet 10 inches, he possessed muscular thighs, but smallish hands. He wore gold on his fingers and around his thick neck, and new Reebok high tops on his feet.

David walked across the room to the small round table in one corner, sat down and took out some legal papers to review, waiting for the closed eyes to find him.

An hour later the muscled youth moved. He rose from the bed in one motion, earphones still in place, and walked out the door refusing to look at David. He let the door click shut with finality. David concluded it must have been something he had said, and further concluded this guy was a jerk.

His name was Xavier Allison Washington. He had been on the team just four weeks longer than David. Xavier had left high school 18 months earlier and had played semi-pro ball in some inner city area in the Southeast. He was found by a Mariner scout and immediately signed. This season, Xavier had pitched eight innings in relief over five games in the majors, most of which were already out of reach. He had done a mediocre job. A fastball pitcher who had impressed in spring training, the team decided to keep him, as they were very thin in the bullpen and Piniella was inclined to take some chances with younger, untried throwers. David was vaguely aware of Xavier's gang-related activities while growing up, and of his marvelous potential to play at this level. Sports reporters wrote about his brushes with the law and hoped he would grow up and settle down. But David was damned if some punk kid with an attitude was going to treat him with disrespect. They were both new to this life and league. David was entitled to be treated with common courtesy. When David worked in the public defender's office years earlier, many criminal defendants he represented thought the world owed them a living and that David owed them his all. Rarely was a thank you or common courtesy extended. He didn't put up with that attitude then, and wouldn't put up with it now, unless of course he had to.

An hour later, Xavier came back in the room, sipping a can of Coke with his head tipped back, the damn earphones still cemented to his temples. Xavier began to assume the lay-down position when David blocked his path to the bed and mouthed the words, "Screw you" over the drum beat sounds of some rap group. Xaviers eyes got big. Disbelieving, he whipped off the earphones, squared his shoulders and growled, "Say what?"

"Hi." David brightened, extending his hand. "We must be roommates, if not, I gotta charge you rent for your bag and resting space."

Xavier was perplexed, wary, and not too swift. A bad combination for an ice breaker conversation. He allowed as how it might be his room.

"Oh, good. We *are* roommates. Forget the rent then. You can call me Mr. Pasteur, Pasteur, Your Honor, Dave or Hey You, but you cannot pretend I don't exist, since I do. You will treat me, and I you, as a civilized person on the same team attempting to achieve the same goal. Any questions, Mr. Washington?"

Washington just looked at this person who was literally in his face, took a step backward and said, "Name's Xavier, man."

"What does your best friend call you?"

He didn't answer.

"I'll call you X, okay, and you call me Your Holiness because of our massive age difference and the respect you will grow to have for me in the days to come. That's Holiness with an i."

X shook his head and expressed the opinion that David was crazy. He took another step backward and, for the first time, let a small smile enter into his eyes, if not onto his lips. He quickly pushed the smile out of his thinking and off his face.

"No? Okay, then call me Roomie, or Pasteur."

"How old are you anyway?" inquired Xavier as he headed for the bed nearest the window. "I got grandparents your age."

"I'm 43, but I look older naked. How old are you, X?"

"Nineteen."

"Well, then that makes me older, doesn't it? Now I have a question for you, X, and that question is simply put. How can you listen to that screaming, unintelligible so-called music all the time without your brain leaking out your head and without going deaf?"

Xavier glared, insulted David's parentage and said, "You ain't no ballplayer. What you doin' here?"

"Good question, X," David replied, trying to keep this conversation light. "Here's the easy answer. I got lucky so accept that fact. Let's just get along. I can learn a lot from you, and you might just learn something from me."

"I got nothin' to learn from you." Xavier examined his earphones minutely.

"I didn't mean about baseball but other stuff. Life isn't all baseball."

"Says who?" He chugged the rest of the can of Coke, looked at the waste basket 20 feet away, and lofted the empty can in an end-over-end toss that landed dead center at the bottom, all net. He smiled, more of a smirk, then spun on his new high tops and slammed out of the room again.

David thought, as he returned to his round table covered with yellow pads, that it had gone pretty well. At least there hadn't been any knives involved.

David took fielding practice during the pre-game warm-up. A routine flyball as observed while sitting in the stands with a beer, looked totally different than when one circled under it in the vast expanse of a twilight sky. The ball fungoed so high, so far, so wiggily that David's neck became kinked just waiting for the ball to come down.

David's warm-up with the team had a distance to it. No bantering, no ribbing and no help was offered by anyone on the team, including the coaches, whose job was to instruct. David did not ask for anything and nothing was offered.

The game started at 7:05. It was clear from the first pitch that both starters had left their good stuff in the bullpen. Both struggled and both teams' bullpens were utilized early and often, but with little effect. By 10:30 that evening, the score was tied at 5.

It was the eighth inning. The Mariners' new shortstop, the sure-handed Felix Fermin, led off with a double over third base. Buhner failed to get the runner over to third on two foul balls, and eventually popped up to second base. One out. Next up was Tino Martinez, the first baseman who was in the last year of his three-year contract with the Mariners. He had enjoyed a good spring, but when the season began in earnest, his swing stayed in Arizona. A slick fielding first baseman, Martinez needed a hit in a critical situation to regain his confidence. He worked the count full, fouled off the next two pitches, then drove a hanging slider 338 feet to right center field for a long out. It allowed Fermin to scamper to third base. Two outs and a runner in scoring position. The crowd looked toward the on-deck circle.

The next batter for the Mariners was to be the number nine hitter, Rich Amaral. He had gone 0-4 this evening, striking out twice. Piniella looked down the bench, seeing Pasteur sitting alone at the end of the dugout near the water cooler, a new batting glove twirling on his fingers. Pasteur gazed at his shiny shoe tops, knowing he was being scrutinized by the skipper. He liked thinking of that word, skipper, especially since it had nothing to do with large bodies of water, because David got seasick in the tub.

"C'mere Pasteur," Piniella called down the bench in David's general direction in a voice full of hesitancy and uncertainty. David got up, and headed to where Piniella stood, slipping on his batting glove in expectation of his number being called. Or was that just in football, he wondered?

"Pasteur, this guy throws a lot of sneaky stuff that breaks down and away. He has a curve which breaks late. Also watch out for ...." Piniella hesitated. "What the hell am I talking for?" he interrupted himself. "Just grab a bat and get a hit."

David turned from Piniella grabbed his fat bat and went to the on-deck circle. As he took a few practice swings, Amaral stopped in front of him on his way back to the dugout. Amaral looked into David's apprehensive eyes.

"Take his ass deep, Pasteur. You can do it—just don't get fooled by his change-up. Concentrate. Watch his hand release the ball."

It was said quietly, honestly, with no sarcasm. Those simple words made David feel unbelievably good, like he was a ballplayer, a real ballplayer and part of this team. At least for now. David stepped up to the plate, aware Casey was watching at home, as were thousands in the stands. He was keenly aware of Amaral on the bench.

The first pitch from Bill Clarke, a veteran of nine years and three Major League teams, was a slow curve thrown behind David's head. Intentionally. A deliberate intimidation that was totally uncalled for under the circumstances. David stood there furious. There was no need to do that, he thought. Who the hell was this smug smirking jerk out there, picking on a rookie? Something snapped. Who knew why, but little David Pasteur in his second game in the Major Leagues, charged the mound with his bat. Or at least charging the mound was what David thought he was doing. What he actually did was to take three steps toward the mound, then stop dead. The pitcher was six-foot-four, 240 pounds and had been an excellent wrestler in junior college.

Clarke, who was smirking after his first pitch (which landed in his catcher's glove behind David's right ear), now began to look with amazement at this smallish, thick-waisted, middle-aged, probably stupid person coming at him with a bat in his hand. His face changed from smirk to smile as he tossed his glove to the side of the dirt mound and stepped toward the approaching figure.

Three steps toward the mound, David's rational self took hold. He froze in midstride, looked at his right hand, which gripped a deadly weapon pursuant to the criminal code of the State of Washington, for it could be argued that he was threatening a human being with a weapon, to wit, a Louisville Slugger. Even the name of the weapon was damning.

David concluded he was in the process of committing a Class B felony in front of 43,735 witnesses here present and a multitude of witnesses back in the Northwest via television. As an officer of the court, a potential defendant, and *not* a stupid person, David lowered the immense and dangerous weapon and began to turn back toward the batter's box from whence he had come.

Too late. Clarke hastened off the mound, grabbed David by the scruff of the neck, lifted him off the ground like a mother cat grabbing her kitten, and shook him like a mixed drink. He then flung David through the air in the general direction of first base, many feet away. It was quite an impressive toss. David thought he had been transformed into a slider, thrown low and away.

David lay in the grass, stunned. He tried to get to his knees, but before he could pick himself up, he observed from the corner of his eye the entire Mariner bench beginning to empty like a swarm of angry gray-clad bees leaving late for lunch. The swarm from the bench was led by Amaral, who was closest to the field. The next few minutes were a slow-motion blur. The flashes that David remembered came to him as if he were watching an all-male dance troupe perform under strobe lights—freeze frames of intense activity as 60-odd athletes went at it under the lights. David later remembered being on the bottom of a pile, listening to swear words issued by sweating men in uniform, and grunts of effort mixed with some laughter. He remembered a fist whizzing by his ear and missing, then being picked up and moved from spot A to spot B and gently deposited. Later still, David remembered grabbing hold of Buhner's back while Buhner restrained an Angel from further involvement or interference. The videotape later viewed made it appear as if David, Buhner and the Angel player were all dancing in a conga line but not to the same music.

The altercation lasted two or three minutes, or maybe it was an hour. David wasn't sure.

When order was finally restored, Clarke was tossed from the game, along with Amaral. David was spared for the time being. A new pitcher for the Angels was allowed to warm up until he was ready, instead of the seven pitches usually allotted to a bullpen relief pitcher.

The Angels manager, upon determining that David was not going to be removed from the game by the umpire, did not argue the issue. It was clear the manager wanted his stopper, Lou Rago, to face Pasteur and not anyone else on the team. Pasteur would do nicely.

After both teams returned to the dugout,

David came to bat again. The count remained at one ball, no strikes. Rago's first pitch was a fastball, high and away. David was still looking at Rago's release point when the pitch was called, a ball. David backed out of the box and looked at the third base coach for a sign. Sam Perlozzo gave David a sign of disgust, followed by one of exasperation. What kind of a sign could he possibly send? David stepped back in, settled his batting helmet on his balding pin head, and pondered the situation like a lawyer with no baseball talent might do.

One, the count was 2 and 0, runner on third, two outs. Rago knew David couldn't hit a Major League fast ball, especially since the batter had trouble picking up the flight of the ball until it was being thrown back to the pitcher.

Two, the infield was playing back.

Three, David figured Rago would throw a fastball down the middle and maybe low. Ergo, David would attempt to bunt for a hit, bringing in the runner from third.

Rago reared and threw a fastball up, not down. David squared into the pitch, heard a "thunk" as the bat was knocked from his stubby fingers. He took off toward first base. Fermin, on third, streaked toward home. The ball had been poorly bunted directly down onto the plate but then careened 30 feet straight up into the air. Fermin crossed home plate before the ball finally settled into the pitchers glove. Rago, being a left-handed pitcher, needed to make a full turn toward first base and fire a throw to his first baseman to get Pasteur for the out—quickly. He made the turn, caught his cleats on the pivot, dropped to the ground from a jabbing pain in his knee, and failed to throw the ball at all. Single. Run scores. 6-5, Mariners.

The Mariners' next batter, Ken Griffey, Jr., laced the first pitch over the head of the Angels' center fielder. David took off from first base, looking to make the turn around second. He was setting up his feet to hit the inside corner of second base, while looking to pick up where the ball was bouncing in center field and identify what his third-base coach had in mind. He saw Perlozzo pinwheeling his arms, urging him to hurry to third-base. David was so excited as he pumped his short legs around the dirt infield, intent on beating the ball to the bag, that he forgot to put one foot down before picking the other foot up, resulting in a spectacular spill between second and third. For the second time in twenty minutes, David lay prone in the dirt while thousands looked on.

David scrambled to his feet just in time

to feel the leather glove of the shortstop, ball tightly cuddled within, slap against his shoulder.

"Out!" screamed the umpire, struggling to contain a laugh. David looked back to find Griffey shaking his head in a sad half-smile of disappointment.

"Nice hustle," he said, trotting out to center field, the inning over.

The Mariners hung on for a 6-5 victory. David hung around to get his knees mercurochromed. Back in Seattle, Casey needed CPR.

David had 27 hits left. Two days later, he was suspended.

13

The road trip went by in a haze of close wins, swinging bunts, and bus rides. The Mariners returned from their extended road trip playing .500 ball, having won 8 and lost 4.

David was suspended for one game by the Commissioner's office, for his participation in the altercation. He considered appealing the Commissioner's ruling but decided he couldn't afford competent counsel, what with the cost of attorneys' fees these days. Besides, he rather liked being suspended. Like a horse bloodied in battle, he now belonged.

The altercation, which David persisted in characterizing as a misunderstanding or a misinterpretation of body language, solidified the team in a way no other event could have done. The rush onto the field was, if not a rush to judgment, at least a rush to protect one of their own. Without analysis and based on pure instinct, the team bench had emptied.

After that, the group became as one. The players concluded that this small, balding, affable lawyer who couldn't hit his own face, apparently was able to produce crucial runs in critical situations. This was just plain good luck for the organization. The players, with the annoying exception of X, began to seek David out as a friend, and in some cases, as an advisor. After all, free legal advice was still free legal advice. The tone of the clubhouse was loose and the attitude of the team one of optimism. This was a new feeling for an organization with a history of losing seasons dating back to 1977. For this team, optimism was unheard of.

When David stepped off the M's charter plane at the end of the road trip, Casey and the girls were there to greet him. Casey was wearing David's favorite outfit, and the girls were washed, combed, starched and smiling. Cardozo waited impatiently in the car, examining his shaggy paw for the wristwatch that wasn't there.

David disembarked from the plane between Mike Blowers and Greg Pirkl, two of the larger players. Of course, compared to David, everyone on the team was a giant.

"Where's Daddy?" asked Lauren. "Did they leave Daddy in Oakland? You said they wouldn't leave him there, didn't you? Where ...."

"There he is!" Lindsey shouted, pointing. "I can see his bald spot! Daddy! Daddy!" Lauren broke from Casey's hands and ran through the crowd of players like a tailback through the line, searching not for a hole, but for her father.

Dan Wilson, the Golden Gopher Mariner catcher, watched the blonde four-year-old begin her search with a look of determination on her face rarely seen on a pitcher. He picked her up and handed her down the line, player to player, until Fermin deposited little Lauren in the skinny arms of her somewhat pudgy but smiling father.

"Here she is, Amigo. She has missed you grande," said Fermin, in the South-of-the-border accent that fluctuated with his batting average.

"Hi, Snug-face. How's my little person? A new dress, any new teeth, hmm?" He kissed her until she squealed in little girl pleasure. "I'll give you a nickel if you tell me where Mommy is."

"I want cash. You bring any cash, Daddy?"

"Yes, I did, Honey. Just for you, cash on the barrelhead."

She giggled, smiled and hugged David tighter.

Lauren had developed the cash gene somewhere in utero. Her first spoken word of English was not Mama, or Dada, or dog. It was "cash card." It was months before Lauren connected her perceived need for a cash card as being related to her parents' unwillingness to explore this possibility, thus Lauren began to call her parents Momma and Dada. Four years later, Lauren still had no cash card, but her need for American dollars continued unabated.

Casey and Lindsey spotted David and Lauren stumbling in the departing line. Reporters and camera crews circled the disembarking players, while a small group of supporters who had also met the plane stood noisily to one side.

Casey looked radiant. She came forward to hug her husband, but before she could, a reporter stuck a mike in David's face and began to bark questions.

"David, you're six for six, with six game-winning hits. Can you keep up this torrid pace?"

"No, listen. I'm not used to all this. I want to see my family, have dinner, forget about baseball and get some peace and quiet. Be a pal, okay? Talk to me later."

"Good luck with that, Dave. You're hot. Better get used to this because we've got a job to do, and this is it. So can't you give me just five minutes?"

"No, later, please." David moved past the reporter on his way to Casey when six little kids surrounded him, asking for autographs. David put Lauren down and began signing autographs. Finally, twenty minutes after landing, David met Casey and steered her into the cool night of the parking lot.

They climbed into their red van, where Cardozo sat tapping his foot impatiently. Cardozo spotted David and started spinning like a top, a gray and white whirling dervish, hair flying, in a tight circle, yipping with delight at the return of the Alpha dog.

"How come you don't greet me like the puppy does? That's the welcome I deserve, Casey. C'mon, spin in circles for me," said David, grabbing her by the shoulders.

"Go soak your head. Uh, girls, let's tell Daddy to go soak his little pin head. And speaking of proper behavior. Let's talk about your behavior in L.A. The suspension, the entire embarrassing debacle. What on Earth were you thinking? When I saw you heaved around like a sack of potatoes, I didn't know if I should laugh, cry or scream. I'm sitting at Mom's with the girls, my brothers are all there, and you step up to the plate. What happens? Wrestle Mania! You do that again, David, I'm serious—I'm taking your bats and balls away, and that's final. Do you understand me? I am not allowing you to act like ...."

"A boy?" David helped, buckling Lindsey into her seat.

"Exactly. A boy. A five-year-old boy."

"I am shamed, truly shamed, but it worked. It was the catalyst for closeness."

"Sounds like an engineering text," opined Casey. "Like you had any intention or idea of bringing the team together like that. Why don't you and Rodney King hold a joint news conference? 'Can't we all just get along?'"

"I love you, Casey. Be nice. I'm back ten minutes and you're all over me."

"Welcome home, Mr. Big Shot. This is

the real world so start deflating that head of yours and drive us home."

The next home stand developed a pattern, a pattern of craziness, too little time, too many late nights. During the days, David even did some lawyering.

He sat in his office with Catherine one morning around 6:00 A.M., before the office phones went berserk. He and Catherine could do nothing with the phones continually ringing, so 6:00 A.M. was the only quiet time they had to talk to one another.

"Hi. Nice to finally see you again."

"Catherine, miss me?" David asked, while examining a stack of papers taller than Lauren.

"We have to talk," spoke Catherine. A dark serious tone in her voice.

"I hate that phrase. It's never, 'We have to talk, someone wants to give you a million dollars.' People always use that phrase when you have a disease or something. Is the lump cancer? Okay, go ahead."

"Are you going to be a lawyer anymore or what? Your calendar is still the living thing it always was. Clients call, new clients want to see you, client interviews, scheduling. I need ten more people or I quit. I'm dead serious. I'm going to have a breakdown."

"You can't quit. I still have pictures of you with those farm animals."

"You have no idea where they are," she joked back, only slightly amused. "You don't know where *you* are most of the time, let alone six pictures. For instance today at 11 o'clock you're in court with Judge D'Amato. Did you even know that?"

"No!"

"Yes. His bailiff confirmed and he wants *you* there."

"What case?" he asked.

"Powers v. Brevik," she answered.

"Oh, are we Powers?"

"Jeez, David! Yes! Rear-end, bad arm, nice lady."

"This is all new to me, Catherine. The dream didn't talk about this kind of problem. Who knew?"

"You said you did. If you can dream about hits, why couldn't you dream about the other consequences, and fix this like you did the team's morale? By the way, you were crazy going after that monster in L.A. You acted like a teenager with testosterone poisoning."

"Enough already! Okay, let's get you some help. I'll interview some college girls to come in and ...."

"Oh sure, perfect. Some Trixie for David's ego. I think not. I'll take care of it. By the way, that $109,000 salary that you're expecting to earn isn't going to go far, and I can't run this office for long without some cases settling and a little cash flow. You're the lawyer, remember. I can't make the money–I can only keep it for you."

"Yeah, okay. So what else is on the agenda?"

"Cyrus has a real problem that's developing with endorsements about you and the team and Major League Baseball. He needs a meeting. Wants to know if you have an attorney. He's serious. He's stunned by the size of this thing, and it just keeps growing."

"Try to book him in ... whenever. What's next? I'm swamped," David said while fingering the long-neglected stack of somewhat important papers.

"Next is Maria's appeal."

"I'll get to it soon. I need some quiet time. It's under control. It's not a priority yet."

"The time is running, David. We have deadlines to meet," she cautioned.

"I know, don't worry. It's my problem. I've got it handled. What else?" David asked, looking at his calendar. It was a war zone of different colored inks.

"The Seattle Symphony, the zoo, Greenpeace, the Boys and Girls Clubs and about 650 other organizations all want either donations, sponsorship or some of your time. What am I supposed to do with these requests? You're a big deal now."

"Talk to Casey. Let her handle it. She can figure out what to do with these requests."

"Uh, David, listen to me carefully. Casey's not having that good of a time with this thing. You may not be aware of that, and nobody's blaming you, but really, she wants to keep Lindsey and Lauren away from all this publicity. Her phone starts ringing at 5:30 in the morning and doesn't stop until late at night. She may not complain, but she doesn't want a job."

"Yeah, I've noticed. We just changed the phone number, but ...."

"Keep Casey away from all this craziness. She jokes about this stuff, but it's your dream, not yours *and* hers. And another thing ...."

"I'm listening," David responded, feeling like a little boy who doesn't understand how the world really works.

"I am very proud of you, and I think you deserve all this adulation. But please, let's not get too full of ourselves and our luck and let's use it correctly. Try not to hurt anyone, even unintentionally, especially the folks we love, okay? Keep your feet on the ground and your head away from your backside."

"You worry too much, and you don't need to. I'm okay."

"Worrying has been my job for the past 20 years, and it will be for another 20. I worry so you don't have to."

"Gotcha."

"One more thing?"

"Okay, what?" he asked, exasperated.

"I need 25 autographs for the Childrens' Hospital. Here, start signing, and be there Saturday at 8:30 A.M. I set this one up myself, okay?"

"At five bucks a pop, sure. Give me a pen"

14

David stood in the wood-paneled courtroom, waiting for his case to be called by Judge D'Amato's bailiff. Eight other lawyers were milling around, most without clients in tow. The hearing was to argue why an insurance company should be allowed to send his client, Rose Powers, to an "independent medical examination." This term was actually shorthand for the defendant's hand-picked doctor, who would have already written his report stating that David's client had never sustained any injury. The defense wanted an IME, as they were called. It needed to be scheduled before May 18th, which was exactly two days ago. David's argument would be that it was too late to schedule one now. The defense would just have to try this case without their prostitute, i.e. doctor, testifying for them and criticizing Rose's treatment, while telling the jury that she should have discontinued her care a month after the 40 miles-per-hour rear-end collision had occurred. It was an important motion for both the plaintiff and the defense.

"Pasteur, is that you?" asked Tom Schwanz, the attorney for Allstate, and David's adversary for the morning.

"Hi, Tom. Looking for more widows to cheat?"

"What are you doin' here, David, slumming?"

"I'm an attorney, remember? And a good one, too, as more than one person who wanted free tickets has told me."

"Well, you're certainly not a hitter, I can tell you that. How the hell did you work that deal with the Mariners, anyway? I was at the first game, and I had no idea. They announce your name, and I about fell off my seat into my frozen malt."

The two chatted amicably for a few minutes, pausing each time the bailiff spoke up.

"How come you're fighting this issue, Tom? You blew the date. You don't get an

IME. It's over. Let's just settle this case, or you're going to have to stand in court with no bullets in your gun while my doctor tells the jury she'll never walk again."

"I thought she injured her arm and shoulder, not her back," Tom said, thumbing through his file with a look of alarm on his face.

"Great plaintiff's doctor, don't you think?"

Tom rolled his eyes and shook his head. "Well, Judge D'Amato is a big defense guy. I've had great luck with him. He'll extend the time limit, allow me the IME, and then you're cooked. How did your client run up $8,200 in medical bills for a bump on the arm in a collision of 15 miles-per-hour?"

"It broke in two places, and the impact occurred at 60.

"So what? She had a good recovery. And anyway, D'Amato doesn't like the plaintiff's bar, and there has been no prejudice to your client if she now has to submit her arm to my panel of highly respected physicians and surgeons. The time limit's only a guideline to justice, not an impediment to the truth."

"Hey, that's good. What matchbook did you copy that from?"

"Powers v. Brevik," intoned D'Amato's

bailiff. She was a 26-year-old stunner, with great legs and a silky voice, who could make "pass the water" sound like an invitation to the heights of carnal pleasure.

"Ready, Your Honor," Tom responded, striding forward from the back of the courtroom and placing his file on the bench before the gray-haired, rheumy-eyed judge.

"Well, gentlemen, what are we here for today? I've read your motion, Mr. Schwanz, and it appears to me that you want me to order an IME and allow you to examine Mr. Pasteur's ... is it *the* David Pasteur?" The judge squinted closely at David.

"Yes, Your Honor, I'm here representing Ms. Powers, who ...."

"Are you *that* Pasteur? My grandkids are wild about you. They're always pestering me—do I know you, can we meet him please, can you get us his autograph .... Boy. And what happens? You walk into my courtroom. Ya know, Counselor, I played ball at USC about a hundred years ago, but you, you're something else. Since it's my courtroom, I guess I can do anything I want, right? So can I have your autograph for the grandchildren? It would make them very happy."

David, somewhat taken aback, gladly and

promptly acquiesced. After more discussion about the team chances and the next tough road trip, the litigants returned to the subject at hand, but only after David told D'Amato that he had to attend a team meeting and was running late.

"By all means, Mr. Pasteur, let's not keep you." He turned to Schwanz. "Now, why in the world, Mr. Schwanz, should I grant your motion when the time has clearly passed for your doctors to examine Mr. Pasteur's client?"

"Your Honor, it appears that ...."

"Mr. Schwanz, you heard about Mr. Pasteur's time problems. I'm prepared to rule unless you want to add to your written materials by way of a new case you have overlooked?"

"No, Your Honor, but the law allows you to use your discretion in cases where ...."

"I will deny your motion, Mr. Schwanz. Mr. Pasteur, have you prepared an order?"

"I have. I'm handing it up to you now, Your Honor."

The judge signed it with a smile. "Good luck, David. I really appreciate the autographs. I'm going to be a big hero this weekend. Knock 'em dead!"

David packed the Powers file into his beaten briefcase and began to leave the courtroom.

"David," Tom said.

"Yes, Tom? I've really got to go. I'm in a hurry."

"Two quick things. One, get me a settlement demand on this case. We'll be settling this pretty quick now, and second, my boy is nine and ..." he hesitated.

"No problem, Tom. What's his name?" He took out a piece of paper and started scribbling.

"Timothy. One other thing, Pasteur. Are you having as much fun as it looks like you're having?"

David snapped his briefcase shut. He gazed up at the ceiling, thought a moment, and said, "More. Much more."

David had not gotten a hit in six games. This was because he hadn't played in six games. He was warming the bench for a very good reason. The last six games were all major blowouts, with the M's winning five and losing one. The team had become downright competitive. All the experts agreed that if the bullpen could hold up through the middle innings and keep the game close, the M's could surprise everyone. Close was good. Keep the games close, get lucky, and who knew?

The team was also getting some breaks. Errors were made by opposing players with gold glove pedigrees, opposing balls were bouncing over outfield fences for ground-rule doubles instead of triples, and of course, there was the David phenomenon.

Piniella, David and Cyrus met several times to talk about the future. The M's were in second place, actually tied with Texas, both teams one game above .500. David's role was being defined on a daily basis as *the* pinch-hitter, no matter who was pitching. Veteran, rookie, left or right handed pitcher—it mattered not. Piniella would use David only once a game, and only in the late innings. David had 22 hits left, and there was a lot of baseball still to be played. The date was June first, and 116 games remained on the schedule. Thirty hits were not many, and each one had to be utilized with precision, care and effect.

David told Piniella that he wanted to work with the hitting coach, to really learn the art of hitting. It could do no harm, and might even do some good. Besides, it would make him feel more like a part of the team.

"I don't know, David," said Piniella, while having coffee in Cyrus' office on one of the rare sunny days in Seattle when the rain and clouds gave way to Chamber of Commerce weather. "If it ain't broke, why fix it? You can never be a hitter. I'm not sure you can even improve. I'm not sure I want you to improve. I mean, your swing is so damn unpredictable that nobody knows how to play you, how to pitch to you. You don't even know what you're doing out there, so why screw with it with this 'art of hitting' crap?"

"Because, Lou, I'm still a ballplayer. At least, that's what I am this year. And players need their skills honed—quickness, bat control, seeing the ball. I could use the work, and again, I might improve."

"What's the harm, Lou?" Cyrus asked. "The dream is real or it isn't. If it's real, well you can't do any damage to it, and if it stops, batting practice won't help get it back. So what the heck. If Sal Romero wants to teach, let David learn what he can."

"Actually, Romero can't figure out why I won't let him help. He doesn't understand why David's the only player who doesn't ask for help, yet needs it the most. I told him not to mess with Pasteur's swing, if that's what you call it."

"So I work with Romero on the batting tee and the machine, but how about taking pitches from a non-professional, live person? The dream said ...."

"No!" Cyrus shouted. "Absolutely not. I've got too much invested in this project to start fine-tuning it. This is not a contract, or a negotiation with some deity. Stop pressing. No live hitting, period. The vision has so decreed."

"Okay, no live hitting," David backed down.

"And we still keep this a secret, just the three of us."

"What happens if it gets out?" Piniella asked Cyrus.

"Now how the hell is it gonna ...."

"It just could. Then what?"

"Well, just see that it doesn't. All of us, see that it stays right here."

Texas came to town for an important

early-season series. Mike Rennie and Randy Johnson, the anchors of both pitching staffs, were to pitch in the opener. Both were veterans, both relied on the fastball as their out pitch, and both were having great early starts. Mike Rennie was 6-2 with an ERA of 2.2. Opposing hitters were batting .230 against him. A veteran of 22 seasons, Rennie was destined for the Hall of Fame on the first ballot with over 315 career wins. Randy Johnson was having his best start in seven years, a 7-1 record, opposing hitters batting .194. Both the Rangers and the Mariners figured to be in the hunt late into the season, barring injury and bad luck.

Despite the fact that Seattle baseball was played indoors on a bad green carpet, and that the day outside shone gloriously, the Kingdome was a sellout. This game, scheduled as the nationally televised game of the week, featured CBS's first team of announcers. The city was electric about even the slim possibility that this could be the year.

The game, as expected, was a pitcher's duel, with no hits allowed by either pitcher, into the fourth inning. Then, with no one out and no one on, Edgar Martinez doubled down the right field line, sliding into second head first.

Casey and Esther sat with Cyrus in the

owner's box. The place was rocking, fans screaming, the big screen monitor showing scantily clad women standing on their seats waving M's Pennants at the rest of the country. Never before in the long, depressing history of the club had anything like this ever happened.

Mike Blowers, a dead pull power hitter, was up next. A steady, young veteran, Blowers had hit ten home runs so far this season. He had medium foot speed, but had a good eye for the strike zone. He'd been with the M's after graduating from the University of Washington and had rarely been asked to bunt, testimony to his ability to hit for power.

Piniella flashed the bunt sign to the third base coach. It had to be a mistake. You don't bunt with Blowers up and no one out, not this early in the game, thought David.

Martinez, on second base, was already in scoring position. A single would most probably allow him to score. The third base coach looked for confirmation and got it. The coach passed the sign to Blowers. Blowers asked for confirmation. He also received it, but still couldn't believe it. Blowers turned to call timeout from the home plate umpire, who said, "No, let's hit. Get in the box." Blowers looked one more time at the third base coach, perplexed. He'd seen the sign but knew he must have misread it.

David saw the confusion. He knew Blowers was unsure, and an unsure hitter is an ineffective hitter. David made a decision. He left the bench, went to the top of the dugout and yelled to Blowers, "Bunt on the son of a bitch—he's too old to field it!"

It was one of those incongruous moments when, for no apparent reason, the crowd quieted as one entity. The stadium became as still as a church sanctuary. It was into this unexpected silence that David Pasteur had yelled his insult at one of the greatest pitchers of all time. More than a living baseball legend, Rennie was a bank president, and David respected bank presidents. He had yelled to alert Blowers, not to insult Rennie. Now he had done both.

Rennie looked over at the dugout to search for the voice. Stepping off the rubber, he spotted David and smiled the smile of a serial killer. David's insult was of great magnitude, a moment of monumental disrespect, not to mention poor judgment. Piniella was livid. Pasteur had just shouted the sign to Blowers for all to hear. Casey heard it, the 11-year-old-boy on the third deck heard it. But would Rennie believe it? No one *shouted* signs. Even idiot lawyers with softball experience.

Rennie settled on the mound. He toed the rubber, straightening his cap. The Texas infield was still back at regular depth. They had all heard the statement, but they also knew that Pasteur had shouted it, so why pay attention? Besides, why would Blowers be bunting? It wasn't the right tactical situation for a bunt.

Blowers bunted Rennie's first pitch back to the mound. Rennie looked at Martinez streaking his way to third base, picked up the dribbler, hesitated, whirled and fired to first. One out, runner at third. Zero-zero tie in the bottom of the fourth. The sacrifice worked, but the run was still 90 feet away.

Buhner was up next. He was waiting, kneeling in the on-deck circle. Piniella called him back to the dugout. Buhner was pissed. Not only was he not going to be allowed to hit in this crucial situation, he was being pulled from the entire game, and it was still only the fourth inning. He flung his helmet at the dugout wall in disgust, looked at Piniella and Pasteur, then sat down at the end of the dugout, his ego badly bruised.

"Pasteur, you're up," Piniella said. "You deserve to get buzzed for what you just did."

"What? It's way too early for me. It's Mike Rennie. I don't want to, Skip, I don't think I'm ready for this."

"Get up there. This ain't no democracy, Pasteur. You're hitting."

"Say goodbye to my family. They've been wonderful to me."

"Now, Pasteur! Get up there!"

"Now hitting for Jay Buhner, number 30, David Pasteur," the PA announcer blared.

Pandemonium. Whistles, shouts, craziness. It was only the fourth inning. Were the M's going to let David actually *field* a game? Casey prayed it was an ugly rumor.

Rennie looked at the paunchy, scared poser and shook his head almost sadly at what was about to be done. His first pitch was clocked at 96-miles-per-hour. Strike. Rennie took a little off the second strike and threw it by David at 94-miles-per-hour. David's bat never moved off his shoulder, as if it were cemented to his uniform.

Rennie, ever the professional, would play it straight by the book, David thought while he adjusted his crotch. He'll waste one pitch, low and away or high and inside. David would have to guess as to location, because he certainly couldn't react in time to actually hit the damn ball. He guessed that Rennie would try to scare him for the unintended insult and come in high and tight with his waste pitch. That's what he did. David positioned his bat so that the ball, if it were to come in on the rise, would make contact with some part of the bat or his jaw. David did not swing. He just placed the bat across his body on the diagonal, like Little John and Robin Hood over the river, jousting for position.

The ball caught the top two inches of the bat and skied over 130 feet straight up, directly into an overhanging PA speaker located in fair territory, rattled around for a while until it caromed off the speaker, and fell on two bounces, finally picked up by the Texas catcher. He stood watching while Martinez whizzed by him to score from third. 1-0 Mariners.

David stood on first base, once again not too sure exactly what had happened. As all batters know, when one hits the ball, one runs like hell toward first base. There is nothing tricky to it. Hit the ball, run to first. Don't stop to look where the ball goes. This hit was no different than all the others. David ran as fast as his elderly legs could carry him, head down, steaming. He did not see where the ball had been propelled after he heard the thunk of bat meeting ball.

"What happened?" David asked, Sam Mejias, the first base coach.

"You got all of it this time. Great looking hit. You drove it deep—deep into the home plate speaker." He chuckled. "They never had a chance. Clean hit. Martinez scored, and you get another RBI. I'm still not believing this."

David saw Amaral, his pinch runner, trotting out from the home dugout toward him. Apparently he was done for the day.

"Now running for Pasteur, Rich Amaral."

"I'm being pulled?" questioned David to the coach.

"This is a surprise to you, Counselor? What with your foot speed and recent track record on the bases, if you'll forgive the pun? Nice job. Go sit down."

David left first base and trotted toward the dugout. The crowd rose. His first standing ovation ever. He neared the dugout entrance, tipped his cap to the crowd in acknowledgment of their appreciation and, missing the first step, fell down, disappearing into the dugout.

David's hit so unnerved Rennie that by the end of the inning, the Mariners had scored three more runs, and never looked back. The

M's won the game 6-1. David had 21 hits left.

The Mariners were tied for first.

15

On the next off day, David held a picnic in his backyard for some of his teammates, neighbors and friends. In the midst of the barbeque, someone knocked on the front door, hard.

Casey answered the door with Tino Martinez by her side, holding a pitcher of orange juice in his big first baseman hands. Casey swung the heavy wooden door open, revealing an enraged man in what looked like a South American army uniform. It was the Colonel, with an attitude.

"You havin' a party, Pasteur? Cuz if you are, there's going to be big trouble. Some car ..." the Colonel looked past Casey toward Martinez, taking in his size and ethnicity, and continued, "some beaner car is blocking my damn driveway, and I'm moving the damn piece of beaner junk with or without your help. Also, tell your big-headed husband if he continues to run by my house with that mongrel mutt barking and shitting everywhere, I'm going to have to shoot 'em both. Got that, Missy?" He glowered at Casey.

The Colonel had been unpleasant many times before. He had been verbally abusive before. However this was an escalation of noticeable proportions. Clearly the mental illness his neighbors suspected was galloping forward.

Martinez, who had witnessed the encounter from behind Casey's back, set the pitcher of juice down on the hall table and stepped toward the spittle-flecked chin, which continued to move.

"Excuse me," said Martinez, "but please lower your voice, state your problem, and act like an adult."

"That your beaner car on my property, huh, Mister? Cuz ...."

"My car is the red two-seater Mercedes parked down the street. It's legal. You're not. Get off this property please. We're having an enjoyable gathering."

"Who do you think you ...."

Martinez stepped out on to the porch, picked up the Colonel, and walked him down the walkway onto the street. He put him down and said quietly, "I'll tear your head off, Mister, then rip your guts out of the bloody hole. Got it? Just leave. Now."

He spun on his heels and walked back to Casey, whose eyes were bigger than usual.

"You okay, Casey?"

"Thanks Tino. He's getting worse. He was never likable, but now .... Let's go eat some of your beans, and don't let David near the barbeque."

"We heard he's dangerous near open fires. He can just watch. He's good at that."

Tino and Casey returned to the yard from the house. Tino set the orange juice down on the picnic table and picked up the remainder of his beer. Casey had lost considerable color in the intervening few minutes. David noticed.

"What happened?"

"That was the Colonel knocking. He's more crazed than usual. His eyes were big, and he was ranting. He scared me this time. He's not right, really not right. Tino moved him on."

"I smell trouble, David, especially since he lives so close," said Tino, finishing his second imported beer.

"Can't do much about it now. Just keep the kids away from his house and win the Pennant."

Felix Fermin said "Isn't that a non sequitur? Or is my English just bad?"

"Shut up and eat, Fermin. Before I was a designated hitter I was a wordsmith." They all laughed as they wandered back to the party.

David surveyed his back yard, where 30 people were socializing. David had a stack of car insurance policies in front of him, along with a glass of white wine. He had been reviewing both of them with equal vigor. David believed for years that one could not have enough auto insurance, since if one were to get seriously injured it would, statistically, be on the highways of this great land. He had been known to demand that a party guest leave, go home, and bring back their insurance policy so he could review it on the spot. He had saved the economic lives of several families, who very soon after increasing their coverage at David's urging, were involved in serious car accidents.

One young family went over an embankment within hours of increasing their coverage. They insisted that money was tight, and they already had full coverage.

"Full coverage in insurance parlance means the state's required minimum, the lowest limit a company can sell to a consumer. You need more. You have a family, and it's cheap for what you get."

"I just met you," said the new father at a party, holding a beer in one hand and a sleeping baby in the other, "and you're telling me my insurance agent is wrong? He's in the insurance business. How come you know more?"

"Well, I do. He's wrong. I'm right. Get more insurance. You're underinsured."

The father reluctantly did, and within a month, his young wife was in the hospital, and their new baby had ten stitches and a cast.

The case settled easily due to the amount of funds available, and now the family was in a new home, with some savings in a bank for their child's college education.

David was almost done with the team insurance review. Because of the team's salary level, he recommended that they all carry a million-dollar umbrella policy, in case they ran over a surgeon's family in a hospital parking lot.

Amaral said, "Okay, you tell me what and how much, and I'll buy it. Uncle Sam takes enough off me already. I sure don't need some greasy ambulance chaser to .... Oh, excuse me ... anyway, you know."

"I do know. Buy more." David looked up and saw Maria Rodriquez strolling by with the hitting coach, Romero, talking, logically enough, about hitting, a passion for Romero. He had been the hitting coach for several batting champions, in both the American and National Leagues, and had been hired by Piniella to work with the Mariners' young hitters because of their age and Major League inexperience. David had begun to work with Romero as well, never allowing him, or anyone else to throw any "live" pitches. David would utilize the batting tee like five-and-six-year-olds just learning the game. He and Romero would work on the mechanics of hitting. David was a poor mechanic.

David was told when Romero first saw his swing, he concluded that David could possibly be helped to improve, but that pure talent played an important part in the science of hitting.

"When God passed out baseball skill, you musta been havin' a couple of pops, cuz David, you got no natural nothin'."

"Thanks. Good to hear it. You wanna help me or not?"

"You want to learn?" Romero asked.

"As much as I can," responded David.

"That might not be much, but what the hell. Pick up a bat and let's try."

It was explained to David that fear was the fundamental factor that stood in the way of hitting. Fear was a reasonable and instinctive reaction. If the ball hits any part of your body, it's going to hurt like hell. Sometimes it will injure you as well as just hurting you. It could also kill you.

"If you can overcome the fear, then you can begin to work on the mechanics of the exercise itself."

"How do you overcome the fear?" David asked his guru, all ears, very interested in this particular answer.

"I dunno. Most players don't. Mantle never did. Told me he would wake up screaming in the night sometimes, from a bad dream about a bad pitch. The good ones don't overcome it—just learn to live with it."

David had told Maria about this conversation. As a college pitcher, she hadn't known the real, brute terror of a badly aimed professional fastball, but it made good sense to her. She asked to be introduced to Romero. David did so soon after his first hitting lesson, and the two had gotten along famously from their first meeting.

"Do you think Sal and Maria have something going?" David asked Casey as they strolled around the back yard. Cardozo followed the couple like a chaperone.

"They both love the game. She's a fox. They have you in common. Who knows? Maybe they do, or maybe they will. Finish your insurance policies, pour me an orange juice and please stay away from the flames on the barbeque. Remember what happened last time you put something on the coals.

"By the way, Catherine said Maria is going to finish her degree then look for work in baseball in some capacity. Do you have any ideas?"

"You know, I just might have some very good ideas about her future." He smiled.

David put the girls to bed that night, after promising Lindsey he would try to be home for her Father-Daughter school day lunch, an annual social event where the girls dressed up in the clothes of what they wanted to be when they grew up. David hoped she would dress up as a heart surgeon or an arbitrage broker. She was leaning toward pinch hitting as a career.

"No, Honey, there's no future in it. There's a sexual bias in the industry. Maybe own the team, like Uncle Cyrus, but not play on it."

"You do."

"You're smarter than I am. To own is much better, trust me."

Lindsey looked very seriously at her father, pursed her lips, cocked her head like a cocker spaniel and said, "Mommy said to be very careful when you say 'trust me.' How come?"

"Because Mommy loves Daddy very much, and she loves you even more. So trust is important when you love someone, understand?"

Now she really pursed her lips. She knotted her brow and said, "Is that a no-squirterer?"

"You have to stop talking to Fermin, Lindsey. English is not his first language, y'know."

David padded down the hall, stepped over the breathing gray and white pile of fluff, and sat in the red antique barber's chair, which stood in the center of the master bedroom picture window, overlooking the Sound. Casey was in her nightgown, reading a cookbook.

"Explain to me again why reading recipes relaxes you. You're so bizarre."

"Explain to me why reading Nazi-torture-spy-sex-trash thrillers relaxes you."

"I get ideas through reading. Knowledge is sacred."

"Well, so do I." She smiled.

David left the shiny chromed chair and asked, "Want to pureé something?"

"Maybe." She smiled again.

That night the bedside phone rang at 2:00 A.M. David, after several rings, was reluctantly drawn up from his deep sleep.

"Hullo..." said David groggily into the darkness.

It was Xavier. He had been pulled over

for driving erratically and was now at the police station demanding David's attention.

"Is the officer there?" David's brain cells received the message that being awake now would be important.

"Yeah, he's listenin' to me," said Xavier. "Everything I say."

"Put him on, please."

A short pause, then, "Sergeant Randolph here."

"Sergeant, good evening. My name is David Pasteur. I'm an attorney. I appreciate your speaking with me. What is Mr. Washington in custody for?"

"Suspicion of DWI, resisting, speeding, and equipment violations. No proof of insurance."

"Have you breathalyzed him yet?"

"He won't agree until he talks to you, but I'm not waiting for you to get down here, so be clear on this, Sir."

"No, I understand. Was there an accident?"

"No."

"Anything else?"

"He's real belligerent. Says he's a Mariner. I've never heard of him. More bullshit hype, I'm sure. A real punk."

"Well, Sir, he's kind of a jerk, I'll grant that, but he is on the Mariners. Tough life, bad history at home. This could kill his way out."

"You *the* Pasteur? The old guy, pinch hitter?"

"Well, 43 ain't too old, is it?" asked David, climbing out of his warm bed and trying not to wake Casey. He cradled the phone, waiting for X to get back on.

"Is he still listening?" asked David.

"Yeah."

"Okay, just answer these questions with one word. Press the phone to your ear so he can't hear me, okay?"

"Yeah."

"How many drinks?"

"Not many."

"Give me a number, you jerk. You called me. I'm back in my warm bed in a hot minute if you don't want my help. How many?"

"Four beers."

"Speeding?"

"Yeah, probably."

"Snort anything?"

Silence, then more silence.

"Okay, say nothing and be polite to the officer. Take the BA test and put the Sergeant on the phone again."

"Okay, you comin' or what, cuz I ain't spendin' the night here."

"Yes, I'll come. Just shut up."

David picked up X at the police station soon after receiving the call from his teammate. He spoke to the arresting officer at length and whisked X out of the prison environment. They left X's car at the station and took David's car to the all-night Denny's for a recap and conversation.

They sat in an orange booth in silence. It was not a companionable one. X did not make eye contact with David, which was not new, but now doubly annoying, as it was close to 4:00 A.M. and David was exhausted. He was damned if he was going to speak first. One more silent cup of coffee and David was gone.

The Denny's was near X's apartment in Kirkland, across Lake Washington from David's house. X was subdued, worried, still angry. He asked how David had gotten him off. David's opinion was that it had more to do with luck, and his own skill as a lawyer, than with X's charming personality.

More silence.

"We've got to talk," David said.

Xavier snarled. "I don't want no talk. Ain't nothin' to talk about."

"Bullshit," David snapped back. "You're blowing the chance of a lifetime like this. You doing drugs?"

Xavier ignored the question and ordered more coffee. He stared into his cup under the harsh restaurant lights, swirling the brown liquid around with both hands as if to give warmth to the now cool cup. He maintained the strained silence as he twirled the cup on the table top.

"I'm taking that as a yes. Give me a dollar, then I'm your attorney. If I'm your attorney, I can't tell anyone anything you tell me, okay?"

"I don't want you to be my attorney. I want you outta my face." Xavier glared at David, his fingers tightening on the mug.

"X, what are you so angry about? People who are angry all the time are usually scared. It's okay to be scared of something. This is the big time, lots of pressure, lots of attention ...."

X smacked his fist on the table between them. "Pressure? What the hell you know about pressure? I ain't scared of nothin', Pasteur." He paused momentarily, a peculiar, puzzled look spreading on his face. "And how the hell did you get on the team, anyway? You ain't no athlete. You blackmailing someone?" Xavier pinned David under a suspicious stare.

David took a very deep breath, gathered himself, and looked at X across the table. "You really want to know?"

"Yeah."

David then decided that if any trust was possible between them, he would have to share a real part of himself with this angry and scared youth.

He ordered breakfast for them both and told X about the dream, how he'd met Cyrus, the promise to tell no one—all of it. It took an hour.

X never interrupted, listening intently. David thought he had done the right thing.

Build a bridge, show your own frailties, and common ground can be forged.

"That's crap, Pasteur. If you think I'm buyin' any of that bullshit, you can kiss my ass. I didn't finish high school, man, but I ain't stupid. You got pictures of somebody?"

"Forget about me then. Answer me this: Are you willing to jeopardize a promising career by being stupid, angry, and confrontive?"

Xavier exploded, shouting invectives and creative insults at David across the table. Two disheveled drunks in a booth four tables down turned to look at the scene.

"Shut up!" David hissed. "You don't want any help from me, fine. I got problems of my own, Mr. Washington. You can take care of your own police problems. I'm exhausted, I'm tired of listening to your shit, and I'm not getting paid for this. You're paying for breakfast and then I'm taking you home."

They said nothing on the ride to X's apartment. As David pulled up to the building, X turned to him.

"You gonna tell anyone about this? You better not talk me down."

"I'm not sure at this point. I wash my hands of you. Now I only think about the team and whether you can hurt it."

"I can pitch, man. I've proved that. I can play. Don't screw with me."

David said nothing.

X started to get out of the front seat of David's car, stopped, looked back at David under the dim dome light and said, "That dream shit for real?"

"I said it was," David said, annoyed. "By the way, I'm not letting you or anyone else screw with my year in the sun, got it? Goodnight, and shut the door."

X slammed the door, turned on his bootheels and swaggered into the apartment complex without looking back.

On the way home, David's mind raced a mile a minute as he drove north on I-5, the main traffic artery of Seattle. What did he owe X, he wondered. He owed him an attempt to help. Well, okay, he'd done that. Now analyze it as a baseball man, as an owner of the team, and ask what do you do about it. You get rid of him. He's trouble, now or soon. Get some value for him early in the season, before his problem surfaces and he's no longer marketable.

A young, unproven black reliever was no

white veteran Steve Howe, but then, there shouldn't be any Steve Howes in baseball. That was the worst message baseball could ever have sent to its young, up-and-coming players: Screw the rules, I'll figure a way around them, especially if drugs are involved, because the league doesn't really mean what it says. Look at Howe, David thought, a seven-time loser, and the Yankees give him a raise, for God's sake. Why wouldn't Xavier look at David as a meddling white guy who had no sense of the problems he might face? Realistically, Xavier might not face any. Howe didn't.

There was no doubt in David's mind that X was trouble. David shrugged his shoulders, shook his head and decided to talk to Cyrus. Let him talk to Piniella or not. Let them decide what they wanted to do with this time bomb. He would present the facts as he knew them, and let management evaluate their import. David was a player. These weren't player problems.

David did not meet with Cyrus right away. He decided to wait until after the upcoming road trip. The trip would take the team to Texas, Chicago, Baltimore, and Minnesota. David was looking forward to returning to the Twin Cities, the place of his legal education at the University of Minnesota, and where he learned how to freeze to death in the month of May. Minnesota was to be their first stop on the trip. The law school invited David to speak to the student body on the topic "Lawyers—Curse or Cure for Social Ills." Casey wanted to know what credentials he had to speak on that, or any other issue regarding law and society.

"I'm 12 for 12, with 14 RBI's. Them's my credentials. I can speak on just about any issue put to me knowledgeably and articulately. Go ahead, ask me about the mating habits of the Russian musk-ox, the filling pressures of the heart, anything. Go ahead, just ask. I know all," he said jokingly.

"Okay," she said seriously, "what do you know about assholes who think they are something special and can speak on any subject presented to them, even if they can't? Tell me about wives who didn't sign up for all this attention and suddenly have to cope with reporters, phone calls ...."

"I just hope that these are hypothetical questions," said David, now turning serious himself.

"I hope you come down to Earth on your own, before something or someone brings you down with a big, ugly thud, because it's coming, David. I'm tired of it, and I'm tired of you."

"So what the hell is the matter? I thought we were doing okay"

"Well, we're not. This has been an ordeal for me. I get stopped at the grocery store. The phone rings all the time. You're gone more than you have been at any time during our marriage and I ... I don't like it." Tears leaked down her cheeks. "I don't like the attention. I don't like people asking me questions, and I really don't like you beginning to think like this is really *you*, as if you have anything to do with this so-called success.

"I don't understand it, but I'm forced to live with it. The girls get treated differently. It's subtle, but it's there, and I don't like that either. Your office is crazy. Catherine is on Valium, and the worst thing, the very worst thing is that you don't even know any of this is going on. You're totally oblivious to the problems your ego is creating for others. So to answer your question, Mr. David Pasteur, no, we are not doing very well. And what are you doing tomorrow? You're leaving for two weeks. Again."

"Yes," he whimpered, "I'm leaving. What, you want me to stay and hang around emergency rooms? This is a road trip! I'm a ballplayer. Ballplayers travel, got it?"

"So just go. Enjoy your fame, have a great time. We can do okay without you," she said, clenching her fists open and closed. She usually did that before she threw something.

"What did *I* do, Casey? I dare not ask, but are you perhaps in the midst of a PMS episode? This seems to have come out of nowhere."

Casey could not believe what she just heard. David could not believe what he had just said. Three letters. Three letters that send most women, and especially Casey, through the roof into the sky and far out into the ionosphere.

PMS. Men can't ignore it. Men can't understand it. Men can't deny it, and they're ordinarily not even allowed to inquire about it.

As Casey turned quietly and left the room, David muttered to himself, "I just don't get why she acts this way. They will appreciate me there even if she doesn't here." He packed his bags, drove himself to the airport and left for Minneapolis.

David eyed the assembled law students, 50 percent of whom were female, which he was glad to see. When he had attended these hallowed halls of jurisprudence, they were dominated by men. The college of law had been 98 percent male. It was the early '70s, and law was still a male-dominated profession. The four females in his class were identifiable only because their voices were somewhat higher than those of their male classmates—but only somewhat. Otherwise, they looked like guys, including the facial hair. Things had changed. David stood behind the lectern in the speaker's hall, peering out at all the long, straight blonde hair of the young Nordic would-be lawyers.

David wore a three-piece, blue pinstripe suit with a red-striped tie. For the first time in a long while, David dressed like an attorney. Of course, at this time, he really wasn't an attorney, which is probably why he'd begun to dress like one.

His talk went well. David spoke about the role of a PI attorney in keeping the playing field level for the consumer, given that the insurance companies had all the money and most of the power, and totally controlled the pace of settlement, assuming they even wanted such an event to occur. His talk was well-received, as David knew more lawyer jokes than the ordinary lawyer baiting insurance adjuster.

"So in closing, if you're smart enough to get in and stay in law school, you probably should have applied to business school and earned an MBA. It's not too late. Keep that in mind when you can't find a job, or don't like your job if you do find one.

"Thanks for your attention. Any questions?"

There was strong applause, followed by many raised hands.

"Yes?" David said, pointing to a female second-year law student, who possessed a body that would stop traffic in rush hour, even if she were to wear a gunny sack that was many sizes too large for her five-foot two-inch frame.

"Mr. Pasteur," she began, uncrossing her tanned, bare legs and smiling.

"Call me David. My father is Mr. Pasteur."

"Okay, David. Here's my question, actually three questions. Are you starting tonight, are you free tonight, and could I have your autograph?"

Laughter erupted in the hall. I love baseball, David thought to himself.

"What does that have to do with my

chosen subject, a subject that I spoke so eloquently on just moments ago?" he said in mock anger.

She retorted, "What does that subject have to do with baseball?"

"Nothing, however, this venue is dedicated to academics, not sport. I can speak to both. I should only speak to one."

Another voice interrupted, "Do you like baseball better than the courtroom?"

"Yes, of course," he answered.

"Hey, David, did you attend school here at the same time as Winfield? You're both Golden Gophers, aren't you?"

"Well, Winfield is a future Hall of Famer. I'm a fluke. A cute fluke with a lawyer's physique and a mind like a razor, but a fluke nonetheless."

The blonde lady law student began to suck on a number-two pencil while observing David as he spoke to the room. She caught his eye so as to demonstrate her ability to envelop most of the length of the writing instrument, while smiling through her eyes and squirming in her seat. David began to blush. Then he began to perspire. He considered himself an excellent flirter, but this lady, she was an all-star practitioner.

"Excuse me, I didn't get the last part of your question," he said to a student in the front row.

"Can you keep up this remarkable pinch-hitting pace?"

"It's a long season. I'm not sure I have the endurance, but using as my guide the young David Winfield, who continues to outperform much younger men, I may be able to keep hitting the ball with some consistency. Golden Gophers seem to have staying power." Much laughter ensued.

David looked at his watch and noticed it was time to get to the Metro Dome, the downtown "baggie" dome built after David left the Twin Cities in 1972. "One more question and then I have to go—and I love saying this—to the baseball park to work."

More giggles. More applause.

The blonde raised her hand again. David looked at her, debated, and called on a law professor he had seen around campus, 20 years earlier. He apparently liked the job security. He also wore the same jacket and stained shirt of years gone by.

"Mr. Pasteur, my question is this. Leaving a law practice, and the clients who depend on you, to do this rather peculiar endeavor, strikes me as both childish and irresponsible. Can you justify your acts within the context of the Code of Professional Responsibility?"

"No," David said, "but thanks for asking." A jerk then, a jerk now, he thought as he left the podium, eyeing the blonde with the pencil.

That evening, David pinch hit in the eighth with a man on second base. This particular hit was a comebacker to the right side of the mound. The pitcher went to glove the lightly struck ball, but failed to set his feet properly while trying to deduce what base to throw the ball to, first or third. He decided to go to first base, for the sure out. His feet slipped, changing his throwing motion to the Twins' first baseman, the toss pulling him slightly off the bag. David had gotten a good jump out of the batter's box, for a lawyer, and beat the softly thrown ball to the base. The official scorer, who had attended David's law school talk, awarded David a hit.

Despite David's successful at-bat, the Twins got out of the inning without giving up a run, and went on to win the game an inning later.

After the game, David left the visitor's clubhouse to catch the bus back to the hotel for the night. The crowd outside the locker room door was filled with autograph seekers, mostly interested in Ken Griffey, Jr.'s signature, and that of Edgar Martinez. David signed autographs, when asked, of course, but a pinch hitter's autograph, even a hot pinch hitter outside one's home field, was not an important or valuable commodity. In public, and without his uniform, David was not very recognizable as a Major League player. He was somewhat disappointed with his national recognition quotient, but believed that it would change as the season progressed and the Mariners continued to win.

"Hi, David." A throaty female voice pierced the din of youngsters' shouts and prayers for the players to stop and sign.

"Hi," David said, searching for the face with the voice. He spotted the blonde law student with ease. She was taller than the other autograph seekers, who were mostly children. She was also prettier than most women in the world, even after their makeovers were completed.

"Loved your performance, David, both at school and on the field." She said this while taking his arm as one would that of a long-time friend, and led him gently away from the door of the waiting bus.

"And you are?"

"Who do you want me to be?" she asked impishly.

Oh brother, he thought, be careful. This was what he had hoped for and dreamed about for close to 43 years, but what male didn't dream of such a meeting? Yet, a fantasy is one thing. This could be something else—like heaven.

"To answer your question, I'm Leigh Stanton of Chicago, Illinois. I'm 23. My father is a rocket scientist. He does shuttle propulsion systems for NASA. I love baseball, older men, and adventure. I believe you represent several of the things I'm fond of. In case you are wondering if I'm chasing you, the simple answer is yes. I'm aggressive, smart, and I'm a legal and emotional adult with adult needs, or maybe, just wants."

They continued to stroll away from the stadium. David began to have difficulty swallowing, breathing, and walking. He said nothing. He wanted to clarify the situation, but not stop it. He pondered the right thing to do, then discarded the ponder.

"Do you have a response, or questions to my opening remarks?"

"How are your grades?" Now that, David

thought, is the lamest question ever asked in the entire history of this sort of thing.

"That's cute, but you don't care. You're just nervous. That's okay. Some people say I can be a bit overwhelming at first, but I'm not, really. I'm glad you didn't say something about briefs. Anyway, my car is over there. I'll drive you to your hotel if and when you want to go back. I assume you're married, so we need not speak to that irrelevant issue."

"What makes you think it's irrelevant to me, Ms. Stanton?"

"One indication that I cite, Counselor, is that you continue to walk with me away from the stadium, away from your bus, and toward my clutches, if that is not too strong a word."

David thought that was a good answer and an accurate observation. He followed her like a little lost puppy.

They strolled to an outside café in the downtown core and sat under a tabled umbrella, having left the team bus behind in the stadium parking lot.

She was a great conversationalist, smiled a lot, and asked appropriate questions, i.e. all about him. If she was a typical groupie, all the stories he had heard about that particular class of female were woefully incorrect. This was a neat lady. Aggressive, to be sure, but a self-possessed, self-confident, gorgeous female.

They continued to sit at the outside bar in the early summer night, talking about the law school experience, today's dating mores, and how much money she was going to inherit should her widowed father, the famous rocket scientist, predecease her.

It was a very large inheritance indeed. David liked pretty women with lots of money.

"I said he was a rocket scientist, didn't I? He's very smart, and invested wisely. I'm not going to have to worry about food and shelter for a long time. I'm a lucky girl. You can be lucky too."

He sipped his tall scotch and water and, hesitating, asked, "Why me, of all the people in the world?"

"Why not you? You act like you have never been hustled before."

"I've never been hustled before just for the uniform, for the baseball garb I wear, and when, in the distant past, I was approached, it was for my personality, wisdom and inner light. I have a nice inner light, I'm told."

"You're scared to go to bed with me, aren't you?"

"No," he protested. Why would he be scared? "You're a little girl, I'm a big, worldly man. I have wisdom and that inner light. You are very attractive, and I want to sleep with you for the rest of my life. Scared? Pshaw!"

She said nothing, sitting demurely in the bar chair with one leg tucked underneath her small bottom.

They sat for a while longer, staring at the flickering candle in the middle of the polished black table. It was a silence filled with the price of celebrity being calculated.

"Want to see my etchings?" she interrupted. "I live only blocks from here. We can walk there, and you can continue this silent internal debate you are obviously having. I promise I won't make the decision for you, but I am very persistent, and you won't be sorry."

"I like etchings," David replied.

Leigh lived on the top floor of an older, brick apartment building in a studio—not a studio apartment, but a sprawling, open-walled artist's studio with large floor-to-ceiling windows which looked out over a grassy park, and of course one of the 10,000 lakes that dotted the state. There were several easels set about the room, with long wooden worktables full of artist's accouterment, brushes, pallets, and a throwing wheel tucked into a corner. On one end of the large room, a tall masonry fireplace was set into the wall with an unlit fire built within. In front of the fireplace, positioned on and around a red and blue Oriental rug that covered much of the parquet floor, were floral patterned couches, pillows, and an ornate coffee table. Indirect lighting, from some hidden place, cast a warm glow over the seating area.

David stood in the middle of this large, comfortable space, turning slowly, like a ballroom light. Several impressive oils hung in simple frames on what walls did exist in the tastefully decorated studio.

"This is my place. Welcome to it," said Leigh, as she kneeled in front of the fireplace, struck a long match and lit a blazing fire in just seconds. She turned to David. "Well, what do you think of my law school digs? Better than a dorm?"

"You do have etchings. You're a most remarkable person. You are an artist, a law student, a rich girl, and further, you're not bad looking. What in the hell am I doing here at 2:00 A.M. with someone like you, in a place like this? But, more to the point, what do you want with me aside from the obvious?"

She stood up. "Want a drink?" she asked, avoiding the question by asking one of her own. "I'm going to slip out of these too-tight jeans. I'll be right back. Look around if you like."

She turned her back on David, who now sat on the comfortable couch, staring into the flames, contemplating his immediate future. She walked toward a corner of the room and opened a recessed door. As she walked away, Leigh crossed her arms in front of her and pulled off her yellow short-sleeved blouse, exposing her perfectly tanned back to David's gaze. She stopped and slowly turned toward David so that he could see her high, pink-tipped breasts as she dangled the blouse from one hand.

"Could you pour me a glass of wine, please? It's in the icebox. I'll be right back, and we can continue this discussion."

"Sure," he croaked, eyes transfixed on her radiance.

"Thanks," she smiled. Leigh turned back toward the door, and as she did, David heard a zipper being pulled forcefully down. It sounded like a sheet being torn in two in a quiet church. The sound also tore to pieces any resolve he might have had. He had never cheated on Casey, never thought he wanted to. On the other hand, he never really had the opportunity to test himself. It takes work to cheat, hard work, and David didn't have the energy to work that hard. However, this situation was easy labor.

What the hell am I going to do? he thought. I mean, this isn't like deciding to have open-heart surgery. This is just sex, isn't it? A private memory to take with me through the years to come, after an hour or two of private pleasure. No one will be hurt. It could, in fact, allow me to gain additional insight into who I am, knowledge which can be useful, as all self-awareness is useful.

In fact, not to do what is so obviously in *her* best interest would be impolite, insensitive, and therefore not in *my* best interest. There, the decision was clear, his duty plain. If she invited him to be intimate with her on this particular night, he would, of course, accommodate her needs.

He did not know how long he had engaged himself in this internal debate, but when he looked up from his reverie, Leigh was standing in front of him wearing a D. Pasteur Mariners jersey, #30, which hung down to just below her well-muscled upper thighs. Two buttons closed the garment, the other four buttons stood open, revealing glimpses of something that God had built perfectly. David smiled at this beautiful young woman, who had made it so clear that the night was still young, even if he no longer was.

Don't analyze—act, he told himself.

"Where's my wine?" she inquired, with a small pout that accentuated her high, Nordic cheekbones.

"I forgot. Forgive me?" he whimpered.

"You're forgiven, Dave," she said.

"How can I make it up to you?" he asked.

"I think I know a way, but let me do this first." She walked over to the fireplace wall, and bent over to flick a hidden switch, casting the room into darkness, but for the fire's flames. As she bent over to flick the switch, it was revealed to him that Leigh wore nothing beneath the jersey, and she wore a thong bathing suit when sun tanning. David's heart began to palpitate as Leigh walked back to kneel in front of his stockinged feet.

"Just sit there and be still, while I enjoy myself entertaining you."

She unbuttoned the two remaining buttons and shrugged out of her shirt. She reached for David's belt, which she began to unbuckle with the expertise of a practiced nurse.

David's hand slowly covered hers, gently lifting it to his mouth, kissed her open palm and said "We're not going to make love Leigh, because ... actually, I don't have the slightest idea why we're not. I will not regret this decision, because I'll probably commit suicide when I get back to my hotel for my stupidity in not spending the night with you. Thanks for the offer, the conversation, and this unbelievably nice memory, which I promise you I shall never forget."

He slowly rose from the couch, helped her up from where she knelt, put his arms around her naked shoulders, and embraced her forcefully, feeling her damp heat. He broke his hug, kissed her deeply and long, then broke away from the kiss as well. He spun away from her and strode out the door without looking back. He almost started to cry.

He didn't feel very well on his walk back to the hotel. The temptation had almost overwhelmed him. There was more to this dream stuff than this dream stuff let on. Who knew?

16

The team zoomed through June playing .500 ball, then in July won seven straight games against the American League West. Going into the All-Star break, the M's were tied for first place with the California Angeles, three games above .500.

David had collected a total of 14 straight hits. The city of Seattle was truly crazed. The Mariners had finally become contenders, a team that could win in the crunch, as well as overcome the mistakes that all teams make in a long season of pressure.

Cyrus was having the time of his long life, and Piniella was being toasted as the genius manager who could recognize new talent and develop older talent, melding the two to achieve consistency, the hallmark of a winning team.

Xavier and David never again mentioned the night of police and breakfast. They continued to room together on the road, deciding not to call attention to their strained relationship. An icy truce prevailed until David accidentally found in X's night stand a waxed paper packet of the sort that often contained cocaine. David neither opened the packet to confirm his suspicion, nor confronted X with his discovery. X had pitched infrequently in the Mariners surge in June. He continued to make no friends in the clubhouse, choosing not to socialize in baseball circles.

David called Cyrus to discuss this still troubling issue, and to review the first half of the season. David requested Piniella attend the mid-point summit as well.

Once again, they met on Cyrus' boat, in the afternoon of an 80-degree day. The boat was headed to a dinner location across the Sound. The warm sun beat down on the middle-aged men, while visions of October danced in their heads.

"I gotta tell ya, Pasteur, this is the damnedest thing I've ever been or probably ever will be involved in. I've had to learn not to question, just accept. That ain't in my nature, and it ain't so easy ...."

"I know, Lou. No one can explain it, but I'm glad we kept this dream thing between us. Any other way would just be too risky, too disturbing."

All agreed. Despite the probing questions posed by the stream of reporters over the past months, the dream was still secret.

"I'm afraid I need you guys to consider a request. I can't tell you the reason, but trust me, you should trade Washington fast. He's not good for this team. Hell, he's not even good for himself."

"Why, David? Washington is a legitimate Major League pitcher. He's raw, overthrows the ball and needs work, but we need all the innings we can get."

"I know all that," David said. "Still, trade him now. ASAP."

"David, you have to tell us more," said Cyrus.

"Is this another part of your vision, or a new one?" asked Piniella. "Maybe you think you can pick personnel as well? Do you want to manage the team, pick the lineups, make the roster moves? How about running the league?" Piniella snapped, with mounting hostility.

"I didn't mean to step on your toes, Lou. But this isn't dream-related—it's fact-related."

Cyrus didn't laugh. "Just tell me, David. Why do you feel so strongly about this kid? I know he's a pain in the ass, but ...."

"I'm putting my lawyer hat on now. I don't want to tell you. If I tell you, when asked by another GM or manager, you would have to tell them. If you don't know, then you don't know, and you won't have to lie about it."

"Still a lawyer, aren't you, Dave?"

"Yes, I'm still a lawyer, and I *know* Xavier is in trouble. His problem will surface sooner or later, but there's no question that big trouble is coming. I'm selfish. This is my season my half a season. I don't want Xavier or any other person to screw with what's left of my career, so please, get rid of him now, while he still has value. Probably more value now than he'll have in the near future. He needs help, doesn't want it, won't take it. Trade him."

An Orca whale broke the surface of the water, sailed into the air, and crashed back into the dark, cool Sound. "Good slide," remarked David, breaking the uncomfortable silence that followed his opening argument to his bosses.

"What do you think, Lou?" Cyrus inquired.

"I hate to give up a promising young pitcher on a non-professional's intuition ...." David opened his mouth to protest and Piniella raised his hand to stop him.

"Now wait till I'm done," he said. "David here feels strongly, and I understand that, but this is not related to the vision thing. We have no facts to evaluate Pasteur's opinion about letting Washington go. David is still no baseball man. Intuition is no substitute for fact and judgment."

"That's a fair statement," said David. "But I have some facts to back this up. I just ... well, I can't talk about it."

Cyrus peered closely at David, evaluating the situation. "Okay, maybe we'll try to move him, attempt to get another middle reliever. I'll make some calls, ask around," he said.

"If you're set on this, I guess we could showcase him in the upcoming White Sox series, get him some innings. If he does well, his value could go up," Piniella offered reluctantly.

"Okay, we try to move him. Maybe to the National League, get another middle reliever, and worry about the second half of the season later," Cyrus concluded.

"I don't like this at all," said Piniella.

"No one does," David replied. "Pass the scotch."

Shortly thereafter, Xavier Washington was traded to the Texas Rangers for a player to be named later, plus a left-handed, power hitting, AA prospect. Not a great deal for the Mariners. In fact, it sucked.

Piniella was very disappointed in the swap, believing that the Mariners lost major talent in the deal. Cyrus did what David asked, because David had requested it. Cyrus had decided to do, at least for this year, whatever David asked him. The proof of the pudding was in the eating, and this meal was being eaten in first place in the American League West. Cyrus would continue to use David's recipe for the rest of the year.

On the third Monday of July, Xavier Washington held a press conference in Arlington. The sum and substance of his statement was rather simple. The Seattle Mariners were owned and run by a crazy old New Age cultist who believed in the occult, crystal balls, fortune tellers, astrology, and visions. Satan was lurking in the Mariners' background, if not in the dugout itself. As proof of these outrageous accusations, Xavier described his ex-roommate, David Pasteur, as a spirit-worshipping Hebrew, who had made a pact with spirits (evil spirits, perhaps the devil himself). Because Xavier was a true born-again Christian, he could not and would not tolerate this kind of conduct in his presence or on his team. He had therefore demanded a trade, despite having been a productive member of a first-place team. That this trade may have jeopardized his position in professional baseball could not be helped, and he had to speak up and tell the truth. Evil was present in Seattle. The world needed to know.

The media, coast to coast, erupted. National and world press began literally pounding on the Mariners' corporate doors, begging for answers and copy. A slow news summer had just changed. *Hard Copy* was planning to expand their show to 12 hours just to cover this one event.

The questions continued around-the-clock from across the country, from ESPN, sports call-in shows, Larry King's producer, and of course the local media. The White House hadn't yet called, but was expected to ask for clarification. The headline in *The Wall Street Journal* read: A PACT WITH THE DEVIL: DAMN MARINERS FOR REAL?

David sat observing the gray, ashen faces wearing expensive business suits and silk ties. The emergency meeting had started at 5:00 A.M.

"What?" David exclaimed as they looked at him accusingly. "It's the craziest thing I ever heard. It's so absurd, so bizarre, of course no one believes it, do they? It's just going to be a media circus for a while. It will blow over. I'm right about this. Trust me." Damn, he thought, there's that phrase again.

"No, you're wrong, David," offered Remer, the PR executive. "The bigger the lie, the more believable it is, and this is colossal."

"So Cyrus, what do you suggest? Should I retire? No—I have an idea. I'll build a dunking stool in the back yard, strap Casey into it, and invite the press to see if she drowns. If she does, I'm innocent. If she lives after being submerged for ten minutes, I'll move to Salem. Massachusetts, not Oregon." David thought that was pretty funny. Apparently, he was alone in that thought.

"Lighten up, guys," David continued. "I'll hold a press conference, answer the questions, explain about the dream, and defuse the issue."

"Whoa, David. They'll crucify you for not speaking about it from the beginning. Everybody, even this crowd here, is pretty pissed. The dream won't play well."

"Screw 'em. It wasn't then, nor is it now any of their business. The dream was mine to have, and to share with whom I chose. I chose Cyrus. Unfortunately, I also chose to confide in Xavier."

Cyrus looked up from examining his too short fingernails. "You what?"

"Yeah. I told Xavier. It doesn't matter now, but I'm sorry. It felt okay at the time. I misjudged him."

"We had an agreement, dammit!"

"I blew it. Really, Cyrus, this is totally my fault. Who could ever have thought that that slimeball could weave this .... Oh, who cares. What's done is done. Let's just try and fix it, or at least contain it. Gee, I sound like the Nixon White House," he said.

"So David, how and when? How do you handle the press, and when do you hold the conference?" Remer asked.

"The sooner the better, I think. Why not today? Book a room. My inclination is to not take this thing very seriously, to treat these absurd accusations for what they are—an attempt to disrupt this team and to punish me personally for some imagined insult, while diverting attention from *his* ERA. But you're the pros—you went to PR college. You tell me. I'll take any suggestions. What do the textbooks say about denying charges of devil worship while trying to improve one's on-base percentage?"

There was some strained laughter in the room, gallows laughter, but laughter nonetheless.

"About tonight's game, want to play, or should you stay home?" asked Remer while finishing his twenty-fourth cup of coffee in 16 hours. "I'll write a release about the press conference, but what about tonight?"

"Which is less distracting to the team?" asked Cyrus.

"You mean which is worse, getting a sharp hot stick in your eye or a sharp cold stick in your eye?" asked David.

"I guess it doesn't matter, but I'm deathly afraid of the religious crazies coming out in force, and God only knows what they ... pardon the pun ...." said Remer.

"It can't be helped. If they pay for a ticket, they get to scream for us, or at us.

They get to wave signs reading JOHN 3:16, or THE DEVIL MADE ME DO IT. So let's deal with what we can control," Cyrus explained to the room full of note takers, who all shook their heads in unison as the boss man spoke. "The goal for all of us in this room, and out on the field, is to keep our cool, keep playing solid baseball, and ride this nightmare out. Lest we not forget, David is a big part of why we are here, both in this room and in the standings. So now the world knows. David was told he could hit in the majors, and I guess he can. The devil be damned. Xavier be damned ...."

David interrupted, "And God bless us, every one."

The hotel ballroom where the press conference was to take place was strewn with wires, cameras, and reporters from all over the country and beyond. They waited patiently for a story some observers had dubbed the best candidate for the Tabloid Hall of Fame. The Kerrigan-Harding story was nothing compared to this. A little bump on the knee versus baseball, the occult and a lawyer. *The New York Times* was at the conference. So was *First Edition* and the esteemed Long Island newsletter, *Occult On Parade*.

David peered from behind the curtain, observing the noisy, jostling throng. Cyrus decided the best way to meet the press was with Casey standing by David's side. Dressing up the two girls in devil outfits was nixed. David was not particularly nervous because he was having trouble taking the accusations seriously. He believed that by showing the world he was taking all of this with a less than worried attitude, the situation would be defused more quickly. Of course that's what Clinton thought when he first mentioned that river front property in Arkansas.

At exactly 10:30, David appeared from beyond the curtain to take his place behind the wooden podium. He wore a three-piece lawyer suit, while Casey appeared in black pants and a bright yellow blazer. She sat in a chair to David's right, crossed her legs and looked at her husband as he adjusted the neck of the microphone and peered into the intense camera lights. He cleared his throat.

"The United States government today announces that negotiations between the nation of Tasmania ...."

David looked up in mock confusion, then down at his notes, perplexed, and said, "This isn't the State Department briefing? Oh my, am I embarrassed!" He smiled. No reaction. He took a sip of water, coughed and continued.

"The real reason I am forced to stand before you this morning, instead of sleeping in my warm bed, or representing the injured innocents of the Northwest, or God forbid, working on my craft—baseball—is because of events that began a while ago.

"Four months ago, I had a dream. A dream like millions of little boys, young men and some women have every spring—to play the game of baseball. The difference between their dream and mine is simple: I know Cyrus, who happens to own a baseball team in the city where I live. I badgered him, I begged him, I cajoled him, until he finally allowed me to tell him about my dream.

"It was a simple dream, a clear vision. I knew I could hit Major League pitching. Not necessarily like a Major Leaguer, but like a ... uh ... a me."

The room was totally silent. One could hear the whirring of the cameras as David sipped a glass of water, looked at Casey and continued. Thirsty work, this dream talk.

"Cyrus took a chance that my vision was real, and not the fevered imagination of a schizophrenic attorney with a blood sugar problem causing hallucinations. The Mariners decided, and I think wisely, that the details of this dream would be kept private. It no longer is, so rather than have it distorted, manipulated, and misstated, I will share it with the world through you.

"I've been given one year. One single year to get 30 consecutive hits. I don't take hitting practice, as you know, and that's part of the dream as well. I had a dream. A dream not as noble as Martin Luther King's, a dream not as grand as peace on Earth for all time, but my dream—a little dream for a little man from a small city in the Northwest corner of America.

"I confided this vision to Xavier Washington in a private moment, as an example of what some talent and perseverance could achieve, if you have a ton of luck to go with it. I asked him to keep my dream confidential and private. He said he would.

"Xavier betrayed that trust, and in addition, manufactured lies, attaching bizarre motives to Cyrus' and my activities. Activities as simple as wanting to play baseball, if I could, in Seattle, Washington, and help this franchise achieve a goal—a winning season.

"I am not a follower of the occult. I am

not a devil worshipper. I am not a crook—oh, wrong line again. I feel sorry that Xavier needed to spread lies in this most unproductive way. I have a half of one season left to play in my short baseball career. On the other hand, Xavier could pitch for years, but may not, with the juvenile performance that we all witnessed at his press conference 24 hours ago.

"So, in closing, let me say this. Xavier Washington, get a life. I've got one, with or without baseball. It's just more fun with baseball. You owe Cyrus and this entire community an apology. You owe baseball an apology. Baseball is too important, too much fun to be associated with the likes of you, or the devil. Besides, it would be a "sin" to let this season get lost in the "evil" of Xavier's lies. I only hope that Seattle will not become the pun capital of the country. Instead, I hope it will become the baseball capital. Thank you for listening, thank you for caring, thank you for sharing. It should also be noted that my new policy is that autographs are free, questions are a buck apiece. Any questions?"

The room exploded into chaos, with grown men and women waving their hands, shouting, vying for attention—the noise level similar to that of a jet engine being tested in the middle of a Whitesnake concert in a concrete bunker. David spotted a female reporter wearing a tight black leather jumpsuit with a large brass zipper with attached pull-ring, waving her blood-red fingernailed hands in a motion sure to attract his attention. It did. Then David remembered Leigh Stanton's high white breasts, begging for his touch, and called on a fat white guy with three chins and a tie recently used as a table-cloth at a pizza-eating competition, which he had obviously won.

"Please explain to me why a businessman with Cyrus' acumen would do what he did—hire you—without the devil being involved. The devil, who is the mortal enemy of thy Savior, the Lord our God, who died for our sins and cast out the black angel from Heaven above?"

David thought to himself, I should have called on the zipper chick. Who knew?

"Excuse me, I got lost right after you said 'please explain.'" David pointed to another reporter in the back of the packed room, who looked to be very young, with a bad complexion. He wore a loud blue and lime green sport coat, probably from Brooks Brothers.

"Sir," he inquired, "these peculiar charges seem to be based on no provable facts, but only Mr. Xavier's alleged observations of *your* conduct. What might he have observed to make him say what he did? Are you saying he made it *all* up?"

"I'm not sure, but it's an excellent question." The young reporter beamed brighter than his sport jacket, no easy task. David looked toward the heavens, or the ceiling, depending on who might be interpreting the gesture, and responded, "I don't know what Mr. Washington *thinks* he saw. Perhaps he spied on me while I was sacrificing a baby lamb on the portable altar in my hotel room while in New York, accompanied by the hooded, candle-holding Satanist. But that's only a guess. It could have been anything."

David next called on his friend and local reporter, Pete Parker, who had broken the story what now seemed to be years ago.

"Yes, Parker, what's on your mind?"

"David, are you apprehensive that all this will negatively affect your performance on the field, and thus affect the team and the season?"

David stood still, looking intently at the questioner, who asked the one question David knew could not and should not be joked away. "Yes, I am," he said seriously.

"How detailed was the dream? Did it tell you anything else, like who will win the Pennant?" asked the zipper chick, a smirk on her round, powdered face.

"No."

"Have you told us everything about the vision? Any home runs? Can you walk, or just hit?" This said with derision by a reporter from *Sports Illustrated.*

"I guess we will both see, but I can tell you, I've been working on seeing the ball better in the strike zone. However, I rather doubt after today that any self-respecting Major League pitcher is going to throw me too many balls, but if they do it four times, I'll gladly run to first."

The conference lasted an hour. Some reporters wanted to speak to Casey about how all of this had affected her. Did she believe in astrology? What was her sign? She handled all the questions with quiet aplomb, speaking clearly and directly to the questioning party. She couldn't wait for the ordeal to be over. Cyrus had begged Casey to attend the conference, for although looking solely at David, one could imagine he might be engaged in any number of nefarious acts, viewing Casey, one could only conclude that she was the epitome of middle-American womanhood and thus clearly a proper representative of baseball. No devil worshipper, she.

The press conference made the lead story on all the sports shows and most of the tabloid news programs. The evening news even ran the story, from the perspective of the business of baseball. They posed the question of what a one-season superstar would do to the autograph, baseball card and memorabilia markets, especially if Pasteur continued to 'live the dream,' which, most conceded, was still very unlikely. If scarcity equaled value, Pasteur's ability to play only one season could easily disrupt the baseball markets and the stable price of autographs.

The evening of the press conference, the Kingdome was sold out for the home game with the Kansas City Royals. Signs festooned the domed stadium, most in support of Pasteur. An instant poll, taken hours after the press conference, showed overwhelming support for Pasteur, some support for Xavier, and almost no support for the devil, except in those areas known for their covens. The networks asked what might have happened if David had signed with the California Angels.

The KC Royals were having a mediocre season, with the league's worst combined team batting average. However, they boosted a good group of starting pitchers and an excellent closer, in the person of the 36-year-old forkball pitcher, Nick Cominos.

Over the years the Mariners had developed an unfortunate team habit: They would not, or at least did not, win when performing in front of a large home crowd. They could win in front of large away crowds, but the sad fact was that, over the last 15 years, excluding opening-night crowds, the Mariners were about 10-60 when playing before crowds in excess of 40,000 fans. This particular night, 42,000 were in attendance.

The Mariners jumped out to a 4-0 lead. It appeared that past history and Xavier's accusations were having no negative effect between the white lines. But then, in the sixth inning, as the Mariners starting pitcher Greg Hibbard was cruising through the Royals' batting order, a line drive off the bat of Duff Tussing hit Hibbard in the foot, causing his emergent removal from the game. The partisan crowd came alive as Hibbard left the field, limping to a standing ovation, and hand-held signs were displayed to the TV audience across the country. The Mariners replaced him with "Goose" Gossage a middle relief pitcher having moderate success this season. The Goose promptly gave up three runs and was quickly pulled from the mound, leaving two Royals in scoring position. The third M's pitcher, Roger Salkeld, warmed up in an attempt to save the win for Hibbard.

The Mariners dugout yelled encouragement to their new pitcher, Salkeld, who had a terrific first half of the season, having won eight and lost two, with an ERA of 3.2. He was one of the surprises of the pitching staff, being rock solid with opposing runners on base. A stocky, wiry young man, Salkeld had a good screwball, a sneaky change-up, and always threw around the plate. Unfortunately, he also gave up a lot of home runs, a bad trait for a relief pitcher, whose stock in trade and longevity in the Major Leagues depended on not giving up runs in the late innings.

On this note, in front of a packed house, Salkeld only had to throw two pitches before the Kansas City right fielder took him deep to left center for a three-run home run, giving the Royals a two-run lead, and silencing the crowd. Piniella left Salkeld in, as he struggled to end the inning, which finally happened on a line drive double play to the M's shortstop, Fermin. A sign appeared in the center field stands: WITCH TEAM WILL SHOW UP? And so it had started, pun city. The spectre of the last 24 hours had crept into the delicate psyche of the pitchers, disrupting the peculiar chemistry that exists between pitching mechanics, concentration, and confidence which was the fear of all in the Mariners bullpen. The season had progressed so well that it was rare for the M's to lose a lead in the late innings. Now, in front of the home town crowd, within hours of "the vision thing," the M's had given up a huge gopher ball and the lead. The dugout was silent as a morgue as the team trooped in, to fight their way back into the game, if they could.

The mark of a good team is to not lose games in the late innings. The mark of a Pennant contender is to win games when behind in the late innings. The crowd sensed that this was an important game, not just in relation to the standings, but for the negative psychological effect a defeat now could have. The team felt a common icy fear. It was time to overcome.

The Mariners' first batter was Rich Amaral. He had become a good friend of David's and had even requested David become his sports agent after this season.

"With your special relationship with Cyrus, you can really grind the old goat for me, make up for all those years in the minors. What do you say? Be my agent, and I'll give you an autographed bat."

"Whose?" David asked, grinning. "Yours ain't worth squat."

Amaral worked the count full, then poked

a pitch over second base for a hit. He stole second on the first pitch to Edgar Martinez and scampered home on Martinez' double. Next up, Tino Martinez worked the Royals pitcher to another full count, then fouled off ten straight pitches before striking out. Dan Wilson, the catcher who had a career high of two home runs so far this season, sat on a fastball and drilled it to left field, off the wall for a standing double, scoring Martinez. The rally fizzled thereafter, as the Mariners stranded two runners in scoring position due to a missed sign.

No runs scored for either team as the Mariners came up to bat in the bottom of the ninth, still behind 6-5.

The Mariner bullpen turned their baseball caps upside down and around with the bills turned up, in a "rally cap" position. Cominos, the Royals' ace closer, stood on the mound twirling the ball in his sweaty palm, awaiting Ken Griffey, Jr.'s approach as the lead-off batter in the bottom of the ninth—a crucial half inning. The tension crackled through the stadium.

Griffey took two quick strikes. An unbelievable hitter with the count against him, he looped a single to right. Piniella flashed a hit-and-run sign to Eric Anthony, the swift outfielder up next who always made contact.

Cominos threw a slider low and away. Anthony connected and sent the ball through the hole vacated by the Kansas City second baseman. Griffey, who took off from first base just as the pitch was thrown, now headed to third, beating the throw from the Royals' right fielder. The throw allowed Anthony to advance to second base. Still no one out.

Buhner, the big Texan leading the team in RBIs, popped out to the catcher. Mike Blowers, a backup infielder tonight, came in to hit for Fermin. He tapped a come-backer to the mound, and was thrown out by 70 feet. Two out, runners on third and second, bottom of the ninth. The crowd chanted "Milk Man," a nickname for David coined in one of Parker's early columns. Signs appeared over the Mariners' dugout: THIS HOUSE IS BLESSED. Another read ASTROLOGY THIS!

Piniella looked at David, sitting next to Amaral.

"Okay, David, look for a pitch to make contact. Don't try to drive it. Stay loose. He'll come inside."

"I hate inside," David joked, as he grabbed his bat and blue plastic batting helmet, and self-consciously readjusted his blue and white batting glove. David had been studying Cominos intently. He thought the pitcher would start him off low and inside or high and tight. Come to think of it, he had no clue where Cominos would pitch him. This was the first at-bat after the dream disclosure, and David wondered just what kind of reaction he would get. He didn't have to wait long to find out.

As David walked toward home plate, the Royals dugout began screaming at him, accusing David of carnally knowing Satan, and taking drugs to induce visions. One veteran player wrapped a towel around his head and pretended to peer into his "crystal" baseball.

"Here's your *future*, Pasteur," taunted a younger ballplayer from the middle of the Royals' dugout. He produced a noose and was "hanging" himself, with his tongue lolling out of his mouth. Funny stuff, David thought, giving them credit. He dug in, settled in, and waited for his future to unfold.

Cominos' first pitch caught the inside corner for a strike. The crowd cheered encouragement to Pasteur. The next pitch was a slow curve, which hung out over the middle of the plate. David timed it late and barely tipped the ball causing it to dribble weakly to the first base coach, bouncing foul. Strike two. Griffey at third clapped his hands in encouragement. The team rose to their feet as did the crowd. Cominos wound-up and delivered a slider that spun, then broke on the outside corner, late. The umpire hesitated, uncertain, then punched him out—strike three. Game over. Dream shattered. Total silence in the stands. The Royals erupted onto the field, sprinting toward the mound as if they had just won the World Series. Players danced around Cominos as if he were a May Pole, and they, the colored streamers.

17

David sat in his den, sipping a diet orange, stroking Cardozo's fluffy ears, and staring blankly at the test pattern on the TV. It was 3:00 A.M. the night of his first out, his first K, his first Major League failure. He could not fathom how the dream had been so wrong. The dream clearly revealed, he remembered distinctly, consecutive hits. David perused and reviewed the dictionary on his arrival home, examining the word and the concept of "consecutive" in a desperate search for answers. The pages of small print offered definitions that were clear, unambiguous, and not subject to lawyerly interpretation or shadings. "Consecutive: One after the other. No breaks. An event immediately following another event." David's 'vision' was flawed by reality, the worst kind of flaw. He was despondent. He was embarrassed. He was a failure.

When he arrived home from the Kingdome, hours earlier, he had gotten a call from Catherine, who that day had received a notice of opinion from the Court of Appeals. The appellate court had ruled that the trial court judge had indeed decided correctly in the Rodriquez trial. The jury had acted with passion and prejudice in awarding plaintiff the amount of damages specified. The trial judge had acted properly when he attempted to reduce the jury award. The court further ruled that the case should be returned to the trial court to determine a proper amount to be awarded to the young female pitcher, or, barring that, a new trial should be held. It was so ordered. David had lost the appeal, lost the game, and lost the meaning of the vision, all within the last 12 hours. Life was uncertain. Life was shit. Gooey, yellow, runny shit.

David came home to find his family asleep. He walked upstairs to kiss his sleeping daughters in their stuffed animal-filled room, decorated in yellow and white. They were too young to snore, he observed, and that was good. Snoring females were a "Bad Thing." Snorers were never accepted as full citizens as they grew up, being the victims of discrimination in housing (thin walls), employment access (business trips) and of course, marriage proposals (who wants to sleep with a Toro chainsaw?). Much would be denied the snorer. David vowed his daughters would never snore. Snore school would be attended if necessary. David, of course, snored. Double standard be damned—he was a realist.

As he left the girls' room he stepped in something warm, mushy, and darkly tan, barely seen in the dim nightlight. Cardozo had apparently ingested too many table scraps too fast, only partly digested them, and heaved up the remains on the carpeted floor at the foot of Lauren's bed. David let out a sound of disgust as he shook his bare foot free, attempting to dislodge Cardozo's meal from between his toes.

After leaving the goop for Casey to clean up in the morning, he strolled to his den in an attempt to make sense of his recent debacles.

All in all, this had been less than a mediocre day.

David heard the brass doorknob turn, and the den door squeak open. Casey peered into the bluish, flickering light, and saw David keeping company with the test pattern. She wore a short, blood-red nightgown that hid very little. She rubbed sleep from her eyes as she sat on the floor next to David's chair, putting her chin on his jean-covered knees.

Cardozo slept peacefully nearby. Casey picked up the remote and killed the TV picture of the Indian chief's head.

"Want to talk?" she asked.

"Not really. I'm trying to sort it out. Do you know about the court of appeals?"

"Yes. I'm sorry. Catherine called. She spoke to you, huh?"

"Yes. When I got home."

"What's on your foot, Honey? It looks like a crusty disease. It can't be athlete's foot, you're not an ..." she teased, with a loving smile.

"Just an exclamation point to the last 24 hours. By the way, you were quite perfect at the press conference this morning. You looked great, acted better, and defused all the crazies. Thanks for coming. I know you hated to do it."

"You're welcome. So?" she persisted, while wiggling closer to her husband, letting one of her gown's spaghetti straps fall off her shoulder.

"So, what?" he asked.

"What the heck *is* on your foot?"

"The contents of *your* dog's stomach, which was deposited at the foot of *your* daughter's bed, which I stepped in after finding out that *you* had lost the appeal then *you* struck out, ending *your* dream. You're killing me, Casey!"

Casey smiled. "I'm sorry I let you down," she said. "I was looking for the change-up. He froze me with the fastball," she joked.

They sat quietly, listening to Cardozo snoring contentedly in between his whimpering dreams of chasing bunnies.

David finally asked the question: "How could I have misunderstood the dream so completely? I know what 'hit' means, and I'm sure the vision said 'consecutive.'"

"So the dream was not perfect. So what? Who is. It could still be mostly right, couldn't it?" Casey reasoned hopefully.

"No, it's all or nothing. I'm pretty sure of that. I think I have to quit now. Damn, but it was fun while it lasted."

"Don't be so dramatic. Let's just analyze the word 'hit' before you do anything rash."

"What do you mean, dammit? Can you give me a glimmer of hope?" he asked.

She pulled back from her lap dog position and sat cross-legged in front of the chair, reached for a yellow pad and pencil, and began to make notes. Some minutes later, she looked up, placing the pencil in her thick black hair like an old-time stenographer.

"Just listen," she began.

"I'm all ears, Honey."

"A hit can mean several things. It's a very useful word used in a multitude of contexts. For instance, one can be a 'hit' at a party. If one gets a punch in the nose, that's a 'hit,' Bill Clinton smoking a controlled substance is a 'hit.' A blackjack term for one more card or chance is a 'hit.' There's a 'hit and run accident,' and, of course, a baseball 'hit.' We'll take that one later. One could be a 'hitter' on campus. A bomb 'hits' its target. One can find or 'hit' upon an idea. Then there's Mafia killer with a contract ...."

"Did you major in English? This is very clever. I'm very impressed but, Honey, what the hell does this have to do with my shattered career?"

"Who said *your* interpretation of your dream is the correct one? You *are* now a hitter in Seattle, you are taking a huge *chance* as in gambling, although tonight you busted.

You often look like a Mafia killer when you wear your old suits, and if I'm not mistaken Mr. Pasteur, a.k.a. 'The Milk Man,' you are 14 for 15 against Major League pitching. Your dream is probably fine. Maria Rodriquez' appeal is probably not. Her brief was not your best work, and it should have been. You didn't pay attention to her case. She trusted you. I trust you.

"Maybe today was your wakeup call. Maybe Xavier's garbage was just that—a call to evaluate priorities. He also did it to distract you and the team. Your no-hit performance was long overdue and quite coincidental. Maria's appeal was not. I think trust is a big part of this. You broke your promise to Cyrus, and now to Maria. I guess I don't want to know if you've broken any other promises."

"Like what?" he whined.

"Please, I know about temptations. I'm not naive, and I know you are a spineless male who cannot say no when offered gifts of the fleshy variety ...."

"What?" David protested. "I've never ...."

"No, don't tell me. I'm just really tired of all this. I loved our life before. I don't like or want this pressure. I don't want to be famous. I don't want to be a player's wife."

Casey looked so sad, so unhappy that David could only look at his lovely wife, saying nothing.

"Know what else?" she said, picking at the den carpeting, avoiding eye contact with her husband.

"What?" David asked apprehensively.

"I'm sick and tired of always having to clean up the lamb's blood from the altar. I'm also tired of that damn bleating ...."

David slid down from his leather lounger and took Casey into his medium-muscular arms.

"Casey, you don't have to worry about us. I'm a good boy almost all the time."

"Now that's real comforting," she said.

"And," he continued, "casual sex is just *too* expensive, and remember, I'm Jewish. Just give me these next few months, after which I will never play professional sports again," he grinned.

"On one condition," she bargained.

"Okay, what?"

"Take this stupid silk thing off me this instant."

He did.

Within weeks of David's press conference, the value of his autograph had zoomed into the rarefied air of a Pete Rose, Joe DiMaggio, Mickey Mantle, or Yogi Berra. The economics of baseball autographs was simple: The more a particular autograph existed in the marketplace, the less valuable each autographed baseball, picture or slip of paper became. A ballplayer who played for six years would, on the average, sign ten thousand items. Combine the number of items signed with the popularity of a particular player and one has a general equation of value. Of course how good a player is helps a ton also.

Dave "The Milk Man" Pasteur, also known as "The Counselor," was literally able to create wealth with his pen, not unlike a king named Midas. Before his press conference, his signature was being traded for ten cents and a bucket of warm spit. David now had a $30 signature. Ah, David thought, the vagaries of American culture. Who would have thought that bizarre accusations combined with TV coverage would equal a trading frenzy for ten-year-olds? David was inundated with kids wanting his autograph, pushed, encouraged and beaten by their parents to acquire as many prized signatures as possible.

"I want Griffey's autograph, Dad, he's my favorite. I don't want Pasteur's, I want Junior's."

"Listen to me, you little brat. Griffey will be here for the next 50 years. You'll have a lifetime to get his autograph. Don't you know anything about appreciation? Now, push yourself up to the front of that line, hold your position, and get the fat guy to sign till his fingers bleed. Got it, Timmy?"

David was not called upon to re-test his dream or his baseball skills for 12 days following his strikeout. During that string, the M's lost seven games and won five. None of the games were close. What David did when he wasn't hitting in the late innings was worry in the early, middle, and late innings about his skills. Had his peculiar skills headed south, disappeared, vamoosed, scrammed, vanished? Or were they still lurking somewhere in the recesses of his agonized soul? Sitting on the bench, game after game after his strikeout, was just plain torture. If David had misread his vision, so be it. But he needed to find out sooner than later. He prayed for a close game, where he could be tested once again.

During one game, David even asked Piniella to let him hit, despite the score being 9-2, just to end the suspense that was giving him diarrhea and other ailments.

Piniella barked at David as if he had asked to swap wives. "Go sit down, Pasteur. I'm managing here," he yelled. "If you want to do something to help, dream me some bloody runs, okay pal?"

David concluded that his request was ill-advised.

The other activity that David engaged in besides worrying was retaining a law firm to form a nonprofit foundation. Career or no career, David could trade on his celebrity for years to come. Consequently, he and Catherine decided to channel revenues into a foundation which could do, as Catherine observed, "I guess whatever you want it to, David. Not only can you be the senior partner in a one-man law firm, now you can also be the president of your own foundation. You're very special," Catherine observed. "Not bad for a slow-witted ambulance chaser."

The name David chose for the foundation was Follow Your Dream, Inc. The "purpose" section of the incorporation papers stated, "Read the name of the organization, Stupid." David hoped that the foundation could be the mechanism to deal with the complicated business of celebrity, while he concentrated on the last part of his baseball career.

David issued a press release after his strikeout, proclaiming that the dream continued to be intact, but that the interpretation may have been flawed. He would be giving no more interviews until further notice, or his next base hit, whichever came first.

David's next at bat came on the M's road trip at the end of July, during the first game of a twilight double header. In the modern baseball world, double headers were scheduled as a last resort in making up a game that had been rained out, when no other economical alternate date could be found. The only solution then was to play two full games on the same day, taxing both teams' bullpens depth and the players' stamina.

Piniella hoped for two back-to-back pitchers' duels, which would allow him to rest the arms of his relievers for the six remaining games of the road trip. The M's were tied for second place, having slipped two games out of first place at the start of the road trip. David's worry streak had been extended to 12 games and 15 days. The press continued to besiege David for interviews, despite his press release stating that none would be granted until later.

"I know you guys write poorly, use bad

syntax, have horrendous punctuation, and utilize clichés like a mason uses mortar, but until now, I had the naive belief that most, if not all of you wags could read. Re-read the release. No more interviews until later. None, zero, zip, nada, no more. Any questions about what I just said?" Which, of course, was a big mistake. Never ask a reporter a rhetorical question. They won't recognize it.

"Yeah, David, about your last at bat ...."

"AAAAAAAHHHHHH" David screamed, running from the horde of microphones, down a corridor toward the elevator, attempting an escape to his room.

David agreed to speak to organizations, charities, scout meetings, and Rotary clubs, but would accept no questions from the audience after his canned speech. Requests for appearances were almost paralyzing, 20 to 30 per day, on the road or at home. More staff was clearly needed for the foundation to handle the increasing demand.

The first game of the double header started as the sun began to sink into the blistering, cloudless western sky over the Arlington, Texas stadium. It was finally cooling off, actually becoming quite pleasant at 109 degrees. Texas had a peculiar weather pattern—the temperature rose even after the sun went down.

David enjoyed visiting Texas, the Lone Star State, where the women were hot, the food hotter and the stadium playing surface hotter still. He had sat in the bullpen on previous road trips to Texas where, despite doing no exercise during the hot summer nights he lost six pounds (from perspiration, loss of blood from mosquito bites, and drool from poorly spit sunflower seeds). He had to admit, it beat Jenny Craig.

David asked Piniella if he could continue to sit in the bullpen at least during the early innings. There, he could soak his bare feet in a bucket of ice water, to conserve energy and stay cool, just in case he was needed in the later innings. "I could be ready at a moment's notice, Skip. It's really hot here, so I figured ...."

"Do you know a good criminal lawyer, Pasteur?"

"Uh, sure. Oh ... I get it."

"Sit down, Pasteur!"

The first game was a back-and-forth battle, with one team taking the lead then giving it up, only to produce more runs and retake the lead. The game began to smell as if this could be *the* test case game.

The game see-sawed toward the late innings as the temperature plummeted to 103. David sat in the bullpen without his ice bucket, observing the Texas crowd in short sleeves and shorts, sipping beer, oblivious to the heat. A foul ball off the bat of Mariner Keith Mitchell sailed ten rows behind the Mariners' bullpen, and landed on an unoccupied seat. A scramble for the ball began. The chase involved a group of kids, both boys and girls, plus several adults, both men and women. If there had been cats and dogs, they would have joined in as well. This pack of presumably normally intelligent human beings, David reflected, risked life and limb, not to mention permanent and severe injuries, so that they could corral and thereafter possess a four-dollar baseball off the bat of a mid-level ballplayer to whom they had no particular allegiance.

David eyed the continuing drama as the posse, acting as one, not unlike a flock of sheep, scrambled from row to row pursuing the elusive white sphere. Finally, a man in his early 30s grabbed the still-moving ball, just as a nine-year-old boy made his futile attempt for possession. The adult, in his badly sweat-stained T-shirt, held the ball high above his head in triumph, as though he was Salome and it was the head of John the Baptist. When he lowered his arm, the T-shirt guy was surrounded by five glaring youngsters. When the glaring failed to produce the desired result—the ball being voluntarily gifted to one of them—the children began to lobby, then cajole, then argue, then scream at the possessor.

"Times have sure changed," David observed to nobody in particular. It used to be when you lost the foul ball competition, you went back to your seat to compete again. Now the competition just begins when possession is established. "Hey, Mister, I'm a little kid. I have short legs. I almost got it. Come on, Mister. That's not fair! I was here first. I want it. You got more. You can buy more. Please, it's mine. You took it from me. Pleeeeeeeease!"

David thought the kid and his pals of the moment were going to accuse the T-shirt guy of robbery, call the police, then allow him to plea bargain down to giving them the ball and five Cokes. T-shirt stood tall and resolute, told the youngsters to check their parents' marriage certificates, as he was quite certain they didn't precede their birth dates, and started back to his seat, where his wife proudly awaited his sweaty return.

"That happen a lot nowadays?" asked David of Bosio, who sat with him in the bullpen observing American culture unfold.

"All the time. Fair is fair—unless you

lose–then, whatever. The small kids are the worst. I fear for the future of this country".

David said, "Screw the country. I worry about *my* future. I'll worry about the damn country in October."

Bosio laughed while looking toward the dugout. "Uh-oh, Piniella wants you," he warned.

David jumped up and trotted to the dugout, observing for the first time that Greg Pirkl was standing on third base, dusting off his dirty pant leg.

"Is it too much trouble, Mr. Pasteur, to allow me the courtesy of inviting you to assist this ball club with your limited talents?"

"No, of course not, Skip."

"I am so very pleased. Sit down, get loose, and stick your head in the game instead of near your rectum. You're part of this team, kinda."

"Okay, Skip, I'm sorry."

"And," Piniella continued, "don't call me Skip. It doesn't sound right coming from you."

"Oh, okay Sk ... Lou."

Piniella turned away as Dan Wilson squibbed a hit through the hole between first and second, scoring Pirkl from third. Mariners 7, Texas 6.

Two innings later, the game was tied at 9. Piniella had used four pinch hitters, two pinch runners, and was intently looking at his scorecard/roster with available players listed in black ink. An injury to Edgar Martinez in the seventh inning further reduced Piniella's tactical maneuverability. Martinez was pulled from the lineup when his wrist began to swell with post-trauma fluid. Piniella perused his player list. Only one position player remained to be used, aside from two relief pitchers in the bullpen—David "The Milk Man" Pasteur a.k.a. "The Worrier."

Soon it was the top of the tenth. The Mariners' first batter walked, then stole second. Griffey popped out. Amaral dribbled a grounder to second base, causing the second out, but advancing the runner to third base. David was the only player left to pinch hit, but, and this was a huge, enormous "but," David would have to hit and stay in the ball game to play defense in the bottom half of the inning. Not a hopeful set of circumstances. Pasteur would hit for Luis Sojo, a little used-utility player, who had pinch run in an earlier inning and stayed in to play short. Sojo was 0-2 on this hot and muggy evening, and he looked bad in those two plate appearances. On the other hand, Sojo was a real ballplayer, with a good glove, young foot speed, and an athletes body which possessed all its hair and had a fully functioning prostate. David would bat and then play—where? Left field. It would be the least vulnerable defensive position—unless of course it wasn't.

Piniella spoke while shaking his head at the roster taped to the wall. "Pasteur, grab a bat. Get a hit. Don't worry about last time. Stay loose. Go get 'em, Milk Man."

Showtime, David thought, or more realistically, Truth or Consequences. It was time to find out about the rest of his life.

In his previous at bats David had felt no real fear of failure. He did not, and could not, believe the vision was a fraud. He had been fearful of a 90-mile-per-hour fastball hurtling at his head and coming to rest near his stirrup and anvil bones, but not fearful of his gifted skills. But that was then, and this was now, he thought while strapping on his rarely used batting glove. I now have facts that I didn't have at the beginning of this thing. The dream must be wrong. Forget about what Casey said. Forget about the rationalizations she had been helpfully manufacturing. I do not possess 30 consecutive hits, and now I know it. So what else was not true? The answer.... Stop it! he commanded himself. This type of thinking is not conducive to success. These are bad, negative thoughts. Hold it—I'm not some 18-year-old Hare Krishna candidate, out with the bad thoughts in with the good. Just breathe deeply. Okay, good. Deep breaths in ... slow exhale .... Good. Again .... Deep in. Hold it. Good, slow out .... Excellent. Now, that's better. Calm. More air. Bend down, pick up the resin bag .... Tap the handle of the blond wood bat. Good. Relax. Walk toward the batter's box. Calmness. More air. Big breath .... What's that? Huh, strange, a little light-headed. No big deal. Fix it with oxygen, that's what's needed. Focus on the task. Focus with good clean oxygen .... Big breath .... Good .... Funny, I feel more woozy, not less. I wonder ... if ... I'm ... hyper ... venti ....

David opened his eyes and saw 20 other eyes staring back at him, over the shoulder of a guy wearing white.

"Hi," David said. "I guess I'll have two cheese, small fries ...."

"You okay?" said plate umpire Bud Edwards, concern emanating from his stubbly, fleshy face as he peered down into David's.

"One thing ...." David asked.

"What?" said the Texas trainer who was

kneeling over David, taking his pulse and worrying.

"Am I on the ground, and if so, how come?"

"Yes," everyone answered, like a Greek chorus.

The Texas trainer stopped taking David's pulse. "You fainted. Heat stroke or something."

"No," David said, "I've never fainted before, ever."

"Well, you have now."

"Could it be cancer, Doc? You can tell me, I can take it. Is it the big C? Tell me." David did his best Cagney imitation.

The Texas trainer looked at the umpire. "He's fine."

"But give me a minute or two, okay?"

The crowd evaporated from David's sight, revealing the night stars twinkling in the sky.

"Can I get up?" David asked.

"You really should," answered the trainer.

David sat up, feeling normal and rather rested. The trainer checked his pupils and his vital signs, and diagnosed him one, neurotic, and two, hypocapnic—too little carbon dioxide due to number one. David rose to his feet and began to stretch in preparation for his pinch-hitting duties. Piniella took several steps toward David.

"They announced your name, Pasteur, so if you don't hit now, you are out of the game. Sojo is out of the game 'cuz of the announcement as well. He can't be reinserted, so please tell me you can hit and play."

"Lou, I feel fine. I think I just freaked out and forgot how to breathe. It can happen to anyone who has no experience in carrying the weight of the world on his back. I can play."

"You sure?" asked Piniella.

"No," said David.

"Okay, just relax," Piniella advised.

"That's how this damn thing started. Just leave me alone," David said testily.

"Batter up. Let's go gentlemen. This ain't no picnic. In or out. Step in or step out. Let's go," said the home plate umpire, clapping his hands for emphasis.

David was to face Jim "The Aggressor" McGowan, a six-foot three-inch veteran, who had played with several teams, including the Oakland A's. He was a fastball pitcher with the second highest walk ratio to nine innings pitched in all of baseball. This was interesting information when sitting around with the evening sports page, but for Pasteur, it was a totally irrelevant statistic. It was David's belief that no Major League pitcher would dare negligently walk a middle-aged, ambulance chasing pinch hitter. David doubted he would ever see two balls in a row for the rest of his career. He hadn't so far, even before the dream revelation. McGowan had been a starter all his career, but when he signed with the Rangers, they transferred him to a swing man—a spot starter, a sometimes closing pitcher, and as now, a very important pressure-filled, late inning relief stopper.

David stepped into the batter's box, surveyed the environment, saw it to be hostile, and took several practice swings. McGowan looked in for a sign, then stepped off the rubber to give David more time to think about the situation. David figured he'd had more than enough quiet time to think about it when he was flat on his back in La-La Land. He stepped out, looked at the third base coach Sam Perlozzo, saw him flash the sign for a double in the gap between the outfielders, and stepped back into the box to await McGowan's first offering.

McGowan was determined not to give up a hit. Cheap or expensive, it mattered not, especially to someone or something like Pasteur. McGowan decided to educate the upstart "dreamer" with some reality aimed at his head.

McGowan looked in for a fastball sign, gloved hand resting on his bent knee as he observed his catcher's flashing fingers. The fingers spoke curve. McGowan read the digits and disagreed with what they commanded. He shook his red-capped head like a floppy-eared dog ridding itself of an ear tick. The fingers wagged again, requiring a fastball, low and in.

David thought this arcane way of communicating might be effective, but it took too much time for his liking. Two could play the mental 'let's think about it and worry yourself into ineffectiveness' game. He stepped away from the plate to let McGowan think about it, whatever 'it' was. David wasn't sure what he should do after he had called time-out.

Discarding other options, David hefted his male equipment, not because he needed to adjust or rearrange his jock strap, but because that's what ballplayers do. David wanted to send the subtle message to the mound that even though he was a lawyer conversant with the Following Car Doctrine, he could lift "his" with the best of the greats, like Willie Mays, a notorious All-Star hefter. David had often discussed this phenomenon with Casey while sitting in their den watching baseball on the big-screen TV. They wondered what sixth sense ballplayers had which mandated that when the television camera was pointed directly at them, they immediately felt obligated to adjust their underwear, sometimes lingering over their zippers for an inordinate length of time. Casey's theory was that these young men had an inherent fear of leaving their prized possessions somewhere or forgetting them altogether, much like women who feared removing their earrings in the powder room and leaving without them. David never gave this circumstance much thought until now. Having checked his equipment and finding it still attached, he stepped forward into the batter's box.

Once again, McGowan bent at the waist, found his sign from the catcher, nodded his head in agreement, and went into his stretch. He looked at Wilson now on third and threw to the plate. It was a fastball that trailed into the right handed hitting Pasteur.

David could not pick up the pitch out of McGowan's hand, due to a combination of fear, adrenaline, and lack of skill. The hitting background at the Texas stadium was average, the batter standing at the plate was not. David, unable to pick up the pitch, froze. When he finally saw the ball, he noted that it was heading over his left shoulder on the rise. In the microsecond that followed, David knew that his career and most likely his jaw were about to be shattered. He willed himself to move—up, down, left, right—anywhere out of the path of the ball. His mind commanded, but his body disobeyed. His boring, mundane life passed before his petrified eyes, and as it did, he found it in serious need of improvement. If he survived this assassin's fastball, he swore he would do better as a father, a lawyer....

THWACK.

The sound was deafening. David's hands tingled. He stood in disbelief as he realized that his face and head were uninjured. He came out of his deer-in-the-headlights trance to hear the Mariner dugout erupt in screams. David looked down the third base line to see Wilson charging toward him in an all out sprint, shouting, "Run you asshole!" David took this as a sign to move out of the batter's box and head for first. It was only then that David saw the ball moving away from him. It was hooking down the third-base line, like a wounded duck heading home after being shot out of the sky by intoxicated hunters. The ball hung in the heavy Texas air, allowing the left fielder time to streak toward the foul line, where the ball was dropping toward the white chalk line. Chris Copacino, the speedy third-baseman, turned his back to home plate and sprinted toward the fast dropping ball. Copacino looked up over his shoulder, got a bead on the ball, extended his gloved hand as far as it would go, and saw the ball begin to nestle into his cracked brown leather glove. That was the last thing Copacino saw for several minutes. The Ranger left fielder, who also had his eyes totally focused on the blooped ball, collided at full speed with Copacino, knocking Copacino out and the ball to the ground. The left fielder, although still conscious, was grabbing his knee, unable or unwilling to crawl to the ball where it lay unattended in the deep outfield grass, like a forgotten toy.

David, still not sure how the ball had made contact with the bat, rounded second base to see a peculiar scene. Copacino was lying on his stomach, crosswise across the left field foul line. It appeared he was sleeping peacefully, unaware of or unconcerned with the screaming in the stands. The left fielder was sitting ten feet away from the prone Copacino, both hands grabbing his bent knee, like a mother cuddling her child. Twenty-five feet beyond him, toward the left field fence the ball had come to rest. The shortstop ran toward the unattended ball, past his fallen teammates, deciding that since he was not a doctor, he should be a shortstop.

David saw all this, together with the pinwheeling arms of Sam Perlozzo, the M's third-base coach, urging David to get the lead out and his butt down to third. David continued his labored journey toward the base. Ninety feet times three doesn't appear to be a vast distance, unless a 43-year-old is trying to run it. David was gasping for breath when he was signaled to slide. David concluded that the shortstop had gathered the ball from left field and had thrown it in his direction. He flopped into third base, banging his chin in the dirt, ahead of the covering pitcher, McGowan.

"Safe!" yelled the blue clad umpire into David's ear. David asked for time so he could catch his breath and not pass out again.

The busy Rangers' trainer sprinted toward left field to assist the injured players. David sat down on third base, observing the war zone around him.

"What in the name of Yahweh happened just now, Sam? How did I get here?" David asked the coach, who had taken his cap off and was scratching his head in puzzlement.

"You just tripled, Counselor," Perlozzo

said, while watching Copacino come to on the outfield grass.

"Okay. Good. How?"

"You froze, Counselor. I mean like an ice statue. The ball rode up and in—must have hit your bat on its own, 'cuz you sure as hell didn't move that son of a bitch off your shoulder."

"I froze, huh, Sam?"

"I thought it was going into your bloody ear, you know, take one for the team, but I guess you didn't need to."

"Isn't that what they call bat control?" asked David jokingly.

"Don't start with me, Milk Man. I guess your slump is over."

"I can only hope so, Sam. I'm glad it's over—if it's over."

"We're not out of this yet, you know, not by a long shot. They got one more at bat, and you've got to stay in the game. You okay to do it?"

"Yeah, just don't expect me to climb any fences or gun anybody out at home."

"Catch the ball, Counselor. Just catch

what's hit to you."

The top half of the ninth ended with a whimper after the injured were cleared from left field. Copacino was taken to the hospital for X-rays, and the left fielder was able to limp off the field with only moderate assistance. The next Mariner batter struck out, stranding David on third base, setting up David's defensive debut in the Major Leagues.

David jogged out to left field, a ball in his glove, in preparation for warming up his arm. He warmed up what passed for an arm by tossing the ball back and forth with Chris Bosio, still in the bullpen in case he was needed. David had played second base in high school because it was the shortest throw in the infield. Even then, David possessed the weakest arm of any player on the team. He often wondered how two players of the same height and weight, utilizing identical throwing techniques, could achieve totally different results. The speed of David's throw was woefully inadequate for an outfield position. In fact, while he managed to throw the ball from second to first without a bounce most of the time, he had played infield only moderately well back then, 20 years ago. The Texas outfield was about to become an adventure. An adventure witnessed on ESPN.

David continued to play catch until a ball thrown to the bullpen was not returned. David looked around, sure he had missed the return throw, then realized the warm-up ritual was over. It was showtime yet again.

David took his position in left field. The last time David was this close to left field was when he had gone to a game at the Kingdome with his accountant. George Freeman held the peculiar opinion that sitting in the left field bleachers gave a real baseball fan the best view of the game. The perspective was detached, yet one could observe the intricacies and machinations of the entire playing field from this distant point of view. George truly believed that sitting behind the back of the left fielder on a hard aluminum bench was the essence of real baseball for the aficionado. David thought George was truly full of shit.

Now David would be living Freeman's hypothesis, except David would not be relaxing on slabs of scored aluminum in the bleachers, but standing on the field of play. Funny how life turned out, David thought as he waited for the Rangers to come to bat at the bottom of what he hoped would be the last inning of the game. He prayed nothing would be hit at, near, or anywhere around him. It would be best for all if Tim Davis, the Mariners' new closer, could keep the ball from being hit to anywhere close to left field.

The first batter to step in against Davis was a rookie speedster, Pete Andrew, the Rangers' shortstop. A switch hitter, he batted from the right side against Davis. The stadium lights were full on and in total effect. Catching a fly ball during a night game could be an adventure for veteran outfielders playing in an unfamiliar ballpark. For David, the adventure could quickly turn into a nightmare.

David set himself. His feet were evenly spaced, hands on knees, adrenaline pouring into his bloodstream. He felt like a spectator but he wasn't. He was actually *playing* Major League Baseball, not just swinging at Major League pitching.

Andrew hit a three-and-one fastball through the hole between short and third, toward David. David charged the ball as it bounced toward his position. By the time the ball got to David it was moving, but just barely. David stooped over, gloved the quivering ball with his mitt, picked it up cleanly, transferred it from the leather to his bare hand and sent a looping throw back to Fermin at shortstop. David returned to his left field position, secure in the peculiar knowledge that he was now fielding a 1.000. What a confidence builder. He had picked up an imperceptibly moving baseball from the tall left field grass, but had done it with verve and aplomb. And people doubted my abilities, he thought.

The next Ranger hitter popped out to the second baseman, Amaral. One out, one on. Mariners ahead 10-9.

Next up was Jim Liptak, a large, slow-footed catcher and another dead pull hitter. He batted left handed. Davis worked Liptak 0-2, but his next pitch was lined over third base. Dead pull hitter my ass, David thought to himself as he sprinted for the ball. David got to the ball quickly and fielded it cleanly. He looked up toward the infield and to his amazement, but not really, saw Andrew round second in an attempt to get to third on Liptak's hit to left.

He's challenging my arm, that little shit. David thought as he hesitated a brief, sweaty moment, then uncorked a rope toward third baseman Edgar Martinez. Well, perhaps not a rope, more like thin twine. Nonetheless, his throw sailed into the third base area. His throw was off the mark, up the baseline toward second, but generally in the area.

"Shit!" David yelled to himself. He stood still to see how bad the result would be. His throw, off line as it was, still had some zip to it. It took one hard bounce some ten feet from Edgar's glove and hit the sliding Andrew in the jaw, whereupon he dropped like a large stone down a wellshaft. Martinez ran to retrieve the ball, which lay inches from the comatose runner's right ear, picked it up, tagged out the prone Ranger, then threw to first base in an effort to catch Liptak, who had rounded the bag a little too far. As he scrambled back to first base Tino Martinez made the tag. Double play, game over. David would get credit in the record book for an assist, as he had technically and in this case literally thrown "out" the opposing runner.

"Take that!" David shouted to himself as he ran in from left field, skipping like a nine-year-old. Andrew began to stir. Good. He wanted no more guilt.

The Mariners went on to sweep the four-game series in Texas.

The Seattle Mariners had become a real American League contender.

18

The newspaper headlines, the TV shows, and the sports magazines recounted "The Inning of the Living Dead" for weeks. *Sports Illustrated* ran a cover story on the entire Pasteur experience:

> More people were found injured and comatose in one inning of the Mariners-Rangers game last month than were found in sanctioned Las Vegas boxing matches during all of 1992. Players dropped like Japanese soldiers in a John Wayne war movie, and when the dust had settled and the bodies removed, the Mariners,

led by David "the Milk Man" Pasteur, were in first place. They played with the confidence of a team that knew something good and bizarre could always occur, and usually did.

Pasteur has 20 game-winning hits, a Major League record. The Mariners now truly believe that with their pitching staff healthy and more seasoned, along with Pasteur's strange but timely hitting, they can remain in first place. Since the Inning of the Living Dead, the Mariners have won 22 of their last 30 games.

Pasteur is hitting .980. Cardozo, Pasteur's sheepdog, has thrown out the first ball at several home games, all strikes. Stranger still, it hasn't rained in Seattle for over a month. With less than 40 games left to play in the season and the Mariners leading their division by four games, the team could go from last to first, primarily due to the "vision."

The city of Seattle is smelling Pennant. The rest of the country is smelling horoscopes. Not since Nancy Reagan left the White House with a pack of Scorpios trailing her has there been this much attention on the supernatural. Pasteur's bizarre success has rekindled the art of charting rising moons, horoscope readings, crystal ball gazings and lucky charm production. Rabbits everywhere are fearful of losing limbs. The Mariners report receiving two tons of assorted charms, crosses, rodent paws, rooster tails and other lucky paraphernalia per week.

When asked by Bryant Gumbel on the *Today Show* last week if he would play next year, Pasteur said, "I'll sleep on it and get back to you."

Pasteur's newly formed foundation, Follow Your Dream, Inc., reportedly is grossing $100,000 per week, and funding projects across the country, from inner-city Little League playing fields to a team of plastic surgeons working to repair the birth defects of children in South American villages.

Newly appointed vice president for the foundation's baseball division and former Washington State University baseball player, Maria Rodriquez, announced that the foundation would donate $1,000 to the newly formed Blind Very Slow Pitch League of Southern California for every hit the Mariners get for the rest of the season.

As September dawns, the chances that Pasteur can continue his hitting streak are astronomically against him. Yet the man from nowhere can inspire us all. Where dreams are kept, life sometimes follows.

David looked at the cover of the magazine as it lay on his coffee table. It featured a family portrait, with Cardozo dressed in a gypsy outfit, gazing at a crystal sphere the size of a bowling ball. David and the girls were dressed in baseball uniforms. Casey wasn't in the picture. She was currently sitting at a desk surrounded by checks and bank statements. Cardozo lounged in the living room licking himself, which he did very well.

"What the heck are we going to do about your checkbook?" Casey asked, as David lounged on the couch, reading yet another volume of great literature, *Nazi Mistresses of Winston Churchill.*

"Excuse me? I didn't hear. Casey, did you know that Mr. Churchill slept with several women of the Third Reich, who would pass on sensitive information to their SS masters, who controlled them from Dublin?"

"I said, your checking account is out of balance by $14,780. My account is off by $6,000. None of your checks are clearing, and some of mine aren't either. I'm going crazy trying to balance these accounts. If you won't help me, you can explain all this to the IRS when they take you away in chains to spend the rest of your sorry life in prison."

"No, it's true. He had three separate mistresses and, remarkably, they were all working for Himmler. Heidi, the buxom redhead, was the best spanker of the three and might well have been related to Adolf himself."

"David!" Casey screamed, "Will you listen to me? No one is cashing your checks. They don't present them for payment. Did you know this was happening?"

"Kinda."

"Which means?"

"I'll write a check, and they say, 'Thanks, I'm just going to keep this autograph, okay?' and I say 'okay.' So I guess I know the accounts are for schtink."

"But that doesn't explain my checks."

"You're a Pasteur, aren't you?"

"To my regret, yes."

"Well, there you have it. Case closed. Turn over the accounts to the foundation, or give them to George. He'll reconcile them for us. You won't, I can't, and neither of us wants to.

"Are you taking Cardozo for his haircut? Remember, Friday is Cardozo Appreciation Night," David reminded her.

"Yes, but I think it's a real stupid idea," Casey answered, punching buttons on her ten key in total frustration at the accounts. "The PR department is really stretching it for this promotion. Whose dumb idea was this, anyway?"

"Mine. The proceeds go to the Humane Society so the pet *owners* can be sterilized."

"Figures," she said.

"What? If Schotzie in Cincinnati can get all that attention with Marge Schott, for goodness sake, why can't Cardozo get a little media coverage, too?"

"Do you remember before all this happened, when you took Cardozo into the Safeway store with your sunglasses on at night? You walked him up and down the slippery floor as if he was a seeing eye dog. He had all that hair covering his eyes, and you both kept running into the meat counter."

"So what's your point?" David asked as the phone rang.

"My point, David, is you can not be trusted when it comes to that dog. Your judgment is usually suspect, and when it comes to the hairy one ...."

"You were the one who laughed at the clerk when I felt the twenty dollar bill to make sure they weren't cheating us."

"I was so embarrassed."

"Wait till Cardozo night. You're really going to be .... Hello?" David spoke into the phone as he picked it up on the third ring.

"You're filth. Watch your back, you Jew prick." Click.

David replaced the receiver softly and sat back down next to Casey.

"What was that?"

"The Colonel. He's getting crazier every day."

"What this time?"

"Same stuff, but his voice is even more out there than the last few times."

"Should we call the police?"

"Probably, but his words aren't actually threats, at least not legally. It's just obvious to us that he's crazy as a loon. He may even be getting dangerous. Maybe we should hire a .... No, forget it. We've just got to watch the kids ourselves."

"Okay, David. By the way, the Colonel's craziness has nothing to do with baseball, does it?"

"Probably not. He was a fruitcake before, but our fame certainly hasn't made him any more peaceful with his world."

"Are you going to do that TV show with Dr. Joyce Brothers on Dreams, Celebrity and Violence?"

"Yes, we tape it with Roy Firestone next week when we're in L.A. for our last road trip. Why, should I ask her about the Colonel?"

"Why not?" Casey asked.

"Because she's as much a psychologist as I am a baseball player. We both just fell into some gig, and she managed to milk it for everything it was worth. I should milk so well."

"You do."

David continued his role as an active lawyer on a few selected cases. Catherine hired two associates to keep up with the increasing legal work. David dropped into the office several times a week to review critical letters, which had already been mailed, examine important pleadings, which had previously been filed with the court, and of course to dictate documents which Catherine had already dictated.

"You seem to be running this place better than when I ran it," said David, sitting in his office in one of the red studded leather client chairs. Catherine took notes behind the desk that David formerly occupied, in a quieter life.

"When, praytell, did *you* ever run this place?" asked Catherine as she punched up a case on her computer, scrolling expertly through the data.

"There was a time, oh, about eight years

ago when you were out for two weeks with that flu that wiped out small towns and villages. I ran things damn well for those ten days, don't kid yourself. I'm capable of running things, and those days proved it."

"I thought you and Casey took Lindsey to Disneyland then?"

"Yes, that's true, but I ran things from Mr. Toad's Wild Ride, thank you very much."

They both laughed like the best friends they were. Catherine had run every part of the law practice except "impressing" the clients and going to court for the past 20 years. Now she was hiring lawyers, helping to run a foundation, and trying to keep things together until David came back to their business, and consequently back down to Earth.

"What are you going to do about the Muler case, where our client's husband ran into the cow that was walking on the highway with her baby cow?"

"Calf," David said, "not baby cow."

"Sorry. Anyway, the insurance company is taking the position that the two cows had the right of way ...."

"Because they were in the crosswalk?"

David joked.

"Maybe. Who knows? Anyway, the adjuster wrote to us saying they see no liability on their insured's part. Further, the fact that our client's husband has since divorced her because she now has scars on her terribly broken legs is of no consequence."

"I want to try this case. What's the available insurance limit, $100,000?"

"Yes."

"Okay, let's get a trial date and go after the insurance company. I've met the husband. A jury will crucify him. To know him is to hate him."

"Okay," said Catherine. "Now you have to decide what you want to do with the rest of your law practice, because you might just be out until October."

They looked at each other and said at the same time, "Who knew?" They giggled.

⚾ ⚾ ⚾

David's last road trip to L.A. turned into a media circus. The Mariners, now in first place, were the talk of the baseball world. And of course, the movie people were scrambling for David's attention, not to mention the talk shows, producers, book agents, and other assorted carrion.

"Your story is a great made-for-TV movie, Davey Boy. It's simple yet bizarre, vivid yet deeply clouded. It speaks to the child in all of us."

"And your point?"

"My point, Davey Boy, is this. Sign here and we can option your life. Also, I know this up-and-coming starlet who used to be a contortionist. She loves ballplayers."

"My life is already optioned to my family. Goodbye and please stop calling."

Gee, a contortionist, David thought. Perhaps I spoke too soon. Well, maybe I'll take just one meeting. Maybe she's able to scratch her forehead with her foot.

David now took batting practice regularly, in the vain hope that he could improve his hitting. The quantity of his hits was, of course, impossible to improve upon, but David hoped he could improve their *quality*. One reporter measured all of David's hits, put them back to back, and mathematically concluded that his hits had traveled, in total, about as far as those of a myopic Little Leaguer who stepped in a bucket. David worked with Romero, the batting coach, hitting only off the tee in conjunction with the pitching machine, hour after hour and day after day, honing what few skills he had.

David and Romero also viewed films of the great hitters, observing their hitting mechanics in a vain attempt to emulate their success. Romero then videotaped David's swing and compared it to the great swings of baseball lore the visual difference was staggering. However, the statistical results were remarkably similar. One day in early September, Romero spoke bluntly to his protegé.

"Pasteur, we've been working for months now, and I gotta give you a ton of credit for all the hard work and perseverance you put in day after day. But I gotta say to ya, ya can't make a pig's ass into nothin' but a pig's ass, and Pasteur, you're just a pork butt, now and forever."

They were sitting on the ground near the batting cage, sipping a Miller Lite, after completing another 150 swings in the bowels of the Kingdome, a place that could house the Phantom of the Opera comfortably.

"Let me get this straight. You are now convinced that batting practice will do me absolutely no further good, and furthermore, it can't help the team win our Pennant drive."

"Yep."

"A *total* waste of time."

"Yep."

"I should quit."

"Yep."

"I cannot improve my swing?"

"Yep."

"Any hope of improvement?"

"Nope."

"You make it sound hopeless."

"Yep."

After that discouraging conversation, David no longer took batting practice. This gave him more free time, especially on road trips, to spend in the community working on behalf of the foundation.

David spent one particular afternoon during the L.A. road trip at the children's ward of St. John's Hospital in Santa Monica. A camera crew from *Entertainment Tonight* followed him on this excursion. The show was doing a special segment on community volunteerism among sports figures. David had grown to dislike entourages, as they were cumbersome, a waste of time, and called too much attention to the simple act of visiting sick kids in the hope of bolstering their spirits. Yet this was, after all, show biz.

The three black and white stretch limos pulled up to the tall, mirrored glass entrance, disgorging the multitude of hangers on, makeup and camera people, David, and, of course, Mary Hart. The group swept into the hospital with the fanfare of Clinton arriving to board Air Force One for a hair cut. They all packed into a too-small elevator, where David stood hard against Hart. She wore a tight leather skirt and a low-cut ruffled white blouse. A squash blossom necklace dangled in her cleavage. She had a smile not altogether sincere, but so bright that most people forgot to notice that it never quite reached her eyes. She wore perfume that was part gardenia and part brothel. She was very friendly toward David. David liked that.

"Now David, just pretend that the crew and I are not here. Act naturally. Just dial into the kids, who are really looking forward to seeing you. We set all this up in advance, scouted the sick ones. There's one little girl who is gravely ill. She told my staff some interesting stuff. She knows all your stats and has baseball-playing brothers."

"Not much to memorize, stat wise. Short

career. Short guy."

"I think you're cute, for a short guy," Hart said, attempting to flirt as the elevator rose to the children's ward on the fifth floor. The door finally slid open and the crowd bustled out, moving and chattering restlessly. They walked briskly to the end of the polished hallway, to a ward festooned with silver and multicolored balloons, streamers, and happy faces painted on the yellow walls.

Before this year, David had never been in a hospital that catered to children, or even into a children's ward. He wondered how the nurses and doctors could go to work each day, knowing that their days and nights would be filled with broken little bodies, encased in plaster and wrapped in tubes. David would do all he could do to make the children's lives, and those of their care takers, if not a little easier, then at least more fun for this moment. David had been told that for days after a visit, the small patients would be in great spirits, much more manageable, and in some cases, fevers would actually drop precipitously. Happy people make for healthier people.

David spent several hours in the children's ward, talking, joking and basically hanging out with the staff and patients. Toward the end of the visit, Hart directed David to the room of a 12-year-old girl named Andrea, who possessed the blackest hair and blackest eyes he had ever seen. If she wasn't an exceptionally beautiful little girl, she would have reminded David of a Newfoundland puppy. She'd been given a private room for the last six months, not due to the wealth of her family or the generosity of her insurance company, but because she had an infectious disease and no immune system. David and one camera person gowned up, placed blue surgical masks over their mouths, and entered Andrea's room. She was sitting up in bed wearing a black robe with red piping. Shiny medical equipment stood ominously off to one side.

"I understand this is Princess Di's room, and I was wondering if I could meet her."

"Thank you for coming, Mr. Pasteur."

"Dave. You have to call me Dave."

"You can call me Ms. Regal," she joked.

"Good name for a princess."

"I'm not though. I'm just sick."

"Yes, I know. I hate hospitals myself, and I guess you've been in here too long. Want to leave?"

"Boy, do I. Can you get me out of

here?"

"Wish I could. What else can I do?"

"Are you really a lawyer, Dave?"

"Yes."

"I always wanted to be a lawyer."

"Why did you want to be a lawyer?"

"So I could right the wrongs I see, but now I want to be a baseball player or a doctor."

"Doctors are better. Less travel and you do more good than hitting a baseball. You like baseball?"

"All my brothers play. I play softball. My brothers say you're a fluke."

"A fluke? Well, what do you think?"

"I'm not sure. I have some real problems with your dream."

"Want an autograph?"

"Not particularly."

"Oh. Then what can I do for you?"

"Do you know who Babe Ruth is?"

"Was," said David. "Of course I do."

"So you know about when he went to the hospital and a sick kid said hit me a home run and he did and the kid got better, so I thought that since I'm a sick kid, and, well, you know ...."

"Please don't ask me for a home run!"

"No, of course not. I told you, I know baseball."

"Okay, what then?"

She sat in her narrow bed, pensive, wearing a furrow in her small forehead as she examined her fingernails like a secretary after a manicure.

"I think my brothers are wrong," she finally said.

"You mean about that fluke thing?"

"Yeah. So what I want is for you to hit that stupid ball like a *real* ballplayer. You know, like everybody else. A real hit, maybe a line drive? What do you think? You do that, and I'll get better, just like that other story, okay?"

"Holy moly, Andrea, I'm no Babe Ruth."

"No kiddin'" the cameraman blurted out, engaging in a total breach of professional etiquette.

They both looked at the cameraman, oblivious to his presence until his editorial interruption.

"Sorry, couldn't help myself."

David and Andrea looked at each other and started to giggle, then laugh, and then dissolved into hysterics. The cameraman joined in the laughter, his shoulder-mounted camera shaking in response. The three people in the small room continued to laugh until Mary Hart stood in the doorway shaking her head, attempting to understand what the hell was so funny. She looked at her watch and began tapping her foot. This was TV and time equaled deadlines. Laughing was not in the script.

The three finally caught their collective breaths, but by now they had the giggles so badly that every little thing set them off into renewed peals of laughter, replete with watery eyes.

"Okay, here's the deal, Andrea. Forget about line drives, Babe Ruth, flukes, and brothers. You get better, and I promise to pay for college. Any college, anywhere. You want to go to law school or med school, I pay for that, too. Your brothers want to see me hit a line drive, they can buy their own tickets and hold their own breaths. Deal?"

"Seriously? College? I never thought I could ...."

"Absolutely. I'm a lawyer, and lawyers always tell the truth. You get better, which I know you will, and you're in school for as long as you want—my treat, for real, as an officer of the court. You can trust me."

That really made the camera bounce.

David arrived at the ballpark after drafting an educational contract on a hospital lunch napkin in Andrea's room.

"I want you to know, Andrea, that even though this is written on a napkin, in pencil, with many of the words misspelled, it is an enforceable agreement. Besides, our deal is on film," David said, pointing to the cameraman, "and I can't very well deny that we have a deal, right? There's proof, in the camera."

"Right," she said.

"But you have do your part."

"I know. I'll get better. And then I'm going to cost you a lot of money."

"I know you will, Andrea, and then we'll laugh and point at your brothers."

With laughter that touched her black eyes, she deftly high-fived David's outstretched hand.

David called Maria Rodriquez back in Seattle from the clubhouse phone and asked her to send a real contract to Andrea, with copies to her parents. He also asked her to call Andrea's doctors to see if they needed anything regarding the medical finances, but first she should call Andrea's parents and alert them to the reality of David's visit and his serious offer. Otherwise, her parents would no doubt believe that their little girl had gone septic and crazy in the same day.

David lay on a training table across from Amaral in the visitor's locker room, receiving heat therapy for his left leg. Amaral had been having the season of his dreams. A "magical season," really, but no one ever mentioned words like magical after the Xavier press conference. Everyone else in the world wrote about it endlessly, but there was an unspoken agreement among team members not to indulge in conversation about the "dream." They did, however, indulge in unrelenting barbs about which awards David would actually collect at the end of the season.

David "The Milk Man" Pasteur was being mentioned for many awards, including Rookie of the Year, Most Valuable Player,

Comeback Player of the Year—David's last softball season, all agreed, was a disappointment,—and of course *Baseball Digest*'s coveted Most Unlikely to Succeed award, as well as *Baseball Review*'s Who's That? award.

"How's the leg, Rich?" asked David, while doing his daily three sit-ups.

"It's nothing, David, but I can tell you, if I happen to break my back and my head gets severed from my body, I'm still playing through the pain. I'm not going to let nothing—that's nothing—interfere with the rest of this season. They will have to drag me out of here."

"Good to hear it. But if it should happen, let me handle the case," David joked. "I've only handled one missing body part case, and that was a hand. A head, that's a major league separation. I would enjoy that. I love the sound of that word—decapitation."

Amaral chuckled and scratched his bottom. The two had become close personal friends over the season, and Rich liked to keep David around so he wouldn't feel so old in a clubhouse full of children who shaved.

"Phone call, Counselor," said the clubhouse manager, a spry, crew-cut gentleman in slacks and an Angels cap worn the proper way.

"Thanks," David said, finishing the last of his three sit-ups, grabbing a towel, and wiping the beginnings of perspiration from the tip of his nose. He walked across the cold floor to the wall phone, where the receiver hung twirling on its tangled cord, attached to the cinderblock wall.

"Pasteur."

"David, I found you! I've left messages everywhere," Casey said, short of breath.

"Casey, what's the matter?"

"Cardozo ...."

"Hey, how is my perfect, black-nosed puppy?"

"He's been poisoned."

"C'mon ...."

"No, it's true, I'm not joking. The girls are nuts, crying, scared. Hell, I'm scared, but I'm ...."

"How do you know?"

"The vet said so."

"How does he know?" David queried.

"I don't know. Ask him. But you have

to come home."

"The Colonel?"

"Who else?"

"Accident? Maybe it's not poison, and if it is, maybe he got loose and found some ... I don't know, bad meat, rat poison."

"No, it wasn't, and you know it."

"Okay, okay. But I've got a game in 90 minutes. We're in a Pennant race. I can't just leave for Cardozo. What could I do anyway? I'm not a vet. I'm not even a priest." Casey refused to acknowledge David's attempt at levity. "How serious? Does he really need a priest, Casey?"

"I think he might," she whimpered. "The vet said he'll do everything, but ...."

"Damn it."

"We need you home ... 'cause you're ... please ...."

David tried to be reasonable and logic this out. "If I was still a lawyer and in trial, say, out of town, you wouldn't ask me to drop everything and come home, would you?"

"But you're not, are you?"

"No, but ...."

"I think you should come home. We need you here. Now. You do what you want, but I promised the girls I'd call you. They don't understand any of this. They want their Daddy."

"Well, I don't understand it either," said David, shaking his head and at the same time attempting to sort out the proper thing to do. He began to list the pros and cons of his upcoming decision, attempting to rationally and intelligently make a snap judgment without any facts.

"Well?" Casey asked.

"I don't know what to do, Casey. I love that beast, but baseball has been very good to Cardozo. He would understand if he understood English."

No response from Casey.

"I'll do what's right. I'll call you back."

"Bye." Click. She was pissed.

David slammed the phone back into its cradle. He remembered a phrase from his college ethics course, or maybe it was a line he'd read in the men's room at a college bar, something to the effect that if you *really* didn't want to do something, it was probably the right thing to do. I hated that stupid class,

David thought as he walked to Piniella's office and knocked on the door

19

David came downstairs from putting his two small people to bed. They were not hysterical, but scared and bewildered. He tried to explain, but he couldn't. He attempted to console them and couldn't do that either. This Daddy stuff was not so easy sometimes. Earlier, he had called the vet at his home. The vet was a Mariner fan, who was listening to the game on the radio in the background. Cardozo was in intensive care, and doing poorly.

"Mr. Pasteur, it's poison. Not much doubt. We did a lot of lab work. It's probably arsenic. Cardozo's very ill. The good news is that he's not too old, he's big and strong, and your wife got him here pretty quickly."

"Will he make it, Doctor?"

"It's too soon to tell. It's still touch and go."

"You calling from Seattle, Mr. Pasteur?"

"Yeah, why?"

"Oh, I thought you would still be in Anaheim with the team."

"I flew back for this. Just got in. I thought I'd call."

"Oh. Well, it's 3-1, seventh inning. I'm a big fan."

"Thanks, Doc. Look, I know you'll do everything you can. I don't want him to suffer, even though he's made me suffer all these years. Seriously though, he's really a part of this family, and ...."

"Mr. Pasteur, I'll do everything I can. I'll bring in other people if they can do something I can't. Cardozo is rather a celebrity pooch around here, and I'm not planning to lose him on my watch if I can at all help it. Besides, this town needs your head into baseball, not on sick puppies."

"Thanks, Doc. Nice of you to say so. If there's anything I can do ...."

"Find out who did this. You'd be surprised how many pets get poisoned every year. Find this guy. It makes me sick to see this kind of thing, and unfortunately, I see a lot of it. I'm usually helpless by the time they get to me."

"I think I know who did this one."

"Well, good. Call the police, make a report, and have them call me for medical confirmation."

"I don't think it's going to be like that."

"Excuse me?" responded the vet.

"Forget it. Tell me this one thing. How likely is it that Cardozo found a stash of poison and just devoured it, no malice intended, pure accident?"

"Not very likely. It was put into his food. Someone wanted this dog dead."

"I thought so. Call us with good news, bad news. Heck, call us if there's no news."

"I will. One last question."

"Sure."

"You any relation to ...."

"No. I'd still be trying to get the royalties off that rabies invention if I was."

The vet laughed, said he'd call, and hung up to return to listen to his radio, where the Pasteur-less Mariners were struggling in the late innings. They lost in the ninth.

David stood in front of the Colonel's house, at 11 o'clock at night. He wore dark sweats, high top tennis shoes, and a baseball cap worn backwards, and carried a thick-handled 30-ounce baseball bat. He stood before the Colonel's large picture window on the militarily manicured lawn, leaning on the bat like it was a walking stick and waiting for God knows what. David thought about the man inside, a man who was obviously spiraling out of control.

David knew that the Colonel had his own demons. He also knew that mental health counseling, or in-patient incarceration would do the Colonel a world of good. Medications had come a long way in stabilizing personality disorders and in particular, people's problems with anger. That was all well and good, David thought, but those modalities took time, bureaucracy, and the Colonel's cooperation. David's way didn't.

David watched as the curtains parted to reveal the dark silhouette of a man, and then fall back to full dark. The Colonel's two brass carriage lights came on suddenly, casting brightness onto the porch and spilling light toward the front lawn, where David continued to stand, waiting as if at a bus stop. The front door, heavy and ornate, creaked open an inch at a time. It was finally flung fully open, revealing the Colonel, wearing spit-polished combat boots, the sort that pretty young grunge-band groupies wore in fashionable Northwest dance clubs. David didn't want to give the Colonel any credit, but he had to admit that the laced up boots looked better on the Colonel than they did on young girls dancing to Pearl Jam. The Colonel's fashion statement was completed with fatigue pants and a bright white tank T-shirt, with dogtags dangling on his elderly, graying chest. The only thing that wasn't military issue was the glass pint bottle of some brown liquid that the Colonel held in his left hand as he pointed at David with his right.

"What you want, Soldier?"

David sauntered over from the lawn to stand on the cement walkway, and leaned upon his shiny bat, in a laconic fashion. He heard the question, but did not reply.

"You hear me? You're on my property. I'll call the cops! Get off here. I own all this," he said, waving his arm in a sweeping motion, as if he was presenting the plantation of Tara to David's view.

"What are you drinking, Colonel?"

"None of your business. How's your dog, you Jew bastard?" He cackled as he took a gulp from the pint.

That was of course what David had been waiting for, confirmation. It wasn't enough for a court of law, but he wasn't a prosecutor tonight—he was the judge. David gripped the bat gingerly with one hand and dragged it up the walkway, bouncing its tip nonchalantly on the cement, making a hollow sound.

"What you got there, a Major League hockey stick, eh?" the Colonel cackled again. "Is that how you punished that mutt?" The Colonel took another short swig from his bottle, observing David as he slowly continued toward his open front door a lawyer with a bat walking toward his barracks.

David strolled past the Colonel, who stood in the doorway, brushing against his shoulder as he passed. The Colonel was too stunned to resist David's entry.

David stood surveying the living room, very neat, all possessions precisely set in a particular place. A large mirror hung over the mantelpiece. Lining the room were photos of the Colonel, in various stages of his past military career—as a drill instructor; with some sort of parachute thing strapped around his body; loading an artillery shell. A china chest full of military memorabilia stood in a corner of the neat but darkly brooding room.

"Get out of here. You're trespassing," he hissed.

"No, Colonel. I'm doing more than trespassing, you jar-headed asshole." And with that, David set himself as he was taught, shifted his weight evenly, spotted the stationary target and swung. The lamp, made of some sort of stone material, was belted deep into the dining room. Next up: the china cabinet. Then the framed mantle pictures, perfect swings, perfect results. He was on a roll, he felt good. Loose, easy swings. David's next target was the large mirror. One swing, and it was history.

David stopped to catch his breath and looked around at the destruction. As he did so, his anger dissipated. At the same time, he thought of the Colonel. He had not tried to stop David at all. The obvious thought that ex-military personnel might like and therefore keep firearms had not occurred to David until just that moment. Big firearms, with large barrels. Huge bullets. David had a bat. David liked the Colonel's end of this deal better. The

Colonel was nowhere to be seen. David, now armed with a bat and insight, went searching for him.

David wandered throughout the house, looking for the missing Colonel, searching as if he were a detective on *America's Most Wanted*, but unlike the TV cops, without a real weapon of his own. Not that they gave weapons training in Bar Mitzvah class. David hated guns. As David searched, he thought he heard a distant moan. He followed the sound to a door off the kitchen, a room as immaculate as the others, with sparkling white appliances and a polished floor.

The door was slightly ajar and David stood to the side, like he had seen Sergeant Friday do. He slowly slid the door open, half expecting to feel a bullet slam into his soft middle-aged body at any moment. The door stuck halfway open, preventing David from seeing fully into the darkened room. This unexpected event caused his heartbeat to soar into the low 400s.

David listened for more sounds. Go home, his mind screamed. Just leave, go home, pretend you weren't an incredibly stupid person who had no self-control and just destroyed some poor guy's home because he killed your dog. Well, maybe not destroyed, but he had certainly committed a felony. Make that another felony. What the hell is this season doing to me? he thought. A meek and mild little lawyer? Later. I'll think about these issues later. Right now, think about this moaning sound and decide if there's a gun around someplace that's pointed at me.

David took a deep breath and scooted toward the opening. He peered into the dimly lit laundry room and saw the pistol on the floor. A big pistol. Of course, all pistols are large when you have never seen them outside of a sporting goods store, in a glass case, locked.

The dull gray metal weapon rested near the door, but there was no hand in sight. He heard another sound, barely human. David forced the door open further and sprang into the opening. There he saw the Colonel in a tight fetal ball, moaning, his hands clenched into fists closed tight against his chest. David kicked the gun away as he had seen on the TV cop shows, and bent over the Colonel. David was no doctor, but the Colonel was clearly not doing well. Neither were David or Cardozo. It was all very confusing.

When the 911 response team finally left, David walked Casey back home through the neighborhood gawkers, who had gathered to see the source of the flashing red lights.

David told the police who interviewed him that his foundation would pay for any medical bills that might not be covered by the Colonel's insurance. His story was simple. He had been out walking in the night air when he strolled by his neighbor's house. He heard a frightful noise of breaking glass and investigated, discovering the Colonel breaking up his own home. David intervened and subdued his crazed neighbor, who then went catatonic. David called 911. Pretty simple. Mostly believable. No one asked any deep, penetrating questions, except to inquire as to why he wasn't in Anaheim helping the Mariners chase the Pennant.

"Bad shoulder, Officer Lewis. They're saving me for the kick finish. I'm too old for a long season."

"That's great. Do you think we can win it all? Is it really possible?"

"The possibilities are endless, even though the season isn't. Thanks for responding so soon, Officer."

"No problem, Mr. Pasteur. By the way, would you mind ... I mean could I ... I mean, would it be too much trouble ... my boy ...."

"What's his name? I'll tell him how great and helpful his dad is."

The Mariners were swept in Anaheim over the weekend without David. Meanwhile, the second place Rangers were tearing up the opposition, winning eight of ten games, including seven straight against the American League West. The M's were now just two games ahead of the Rangers. The two teams were to meet in a four-game series in Seattle, the last series of the regular season. Everyone prayed that the series would not decide the division title, but rather only provide a warm-up for the M's first championship in franchise history. However, as the month of September unfolded, it was not to be. The M's were two games above .500 through the rest of September, which was good, but not good enough. The boys from Texas played even better. Much better. The Rangers, since acquiring a young pitcher from the Mariners in the early part of the season, were able to bolster their pitching rotation to such a degree that the team ERA went from over 4 to below 3.0. This, then, allowed the Rangers to utilize their big power hitters and team speed to maximum potential. They led the league in home runs and doubles, and were second in runs scored per game.

Xavier Washington's arrogant personality and loner qualities did not lessen when he was traded to Texas, but in the rough-and-tumble Texas town, Xavier's "get out of my face" attitude was, if not embraced, at least accepted by the writers and fans. Washington had pitched well but erratically since his arrival in his new city. There were stories circulating around Dallas about his late-night extracurricular activities, but no reporter was terribly interested in delving too closely into such rumors during the September Pennant drive. As long as Xavier threw over the plate, reporters looked the other way.

As the season wound down, the Mariners began to fall victim to that terrible disease of never having been "there" before—pressureitis. Defensively steady players made errors. Runners were left on third base in late innings, causing Piniella to lose more hair and gain additional useless pounds from anxious overeating. The M's, a young and inexperienced team at the start of the season, were still young, but now had experience, at everything except how to deal with national attention and the collapse of their league lead.

The late season stumble focused more attention and placed ever-increasing pressure on David and Casey. The pressure was well stated in a syndicated column authored by

Pete Parker, the *Seattle Times* reporter:

> What is it like to go from obscurity to the height of visibility, dragging an entire region of America on your sore, middle-aged back toward a first-time Pennant? Answer: Terrifying. David Pasteur now has only six hits left and perhaps as many as 21 games remaining (four in the regular season, maybe ten league championship games, and, dare we actually mention it, seven World Series games). The pressure on The Milk Man and his publicity-shy family is enormous. Mickey Mantle was an unknown in comparison.
>
> The Texas Rangers now come to town to attempt to end the impossible dream, which started many months ago when David awoke from a restful night in the Arizona desert. As the Rangers drive into our city and past the Space Needle, the number of hits Pasteur has obtained will wink at them from atop the landmark. A dramatic end to a spectacular season.

Xavier "You Worship Devils and

have Sold Your Children to the Slavery of Hell" Washington will be accompanying his new team, of milk white purity, into the Devil's Den in an attempt to derail the dream. It still could turn into a nightmare. Amaral is in a slump. Griffey is not producing in the clutch. Edgar Martinez is still dinged up. Buhner has been unable to hit the long ball as he had in previous months. The pitching staff has been seen in lawyers' offices throughout Puget Sound, filing for non-support against their teammates, who have been unable to produce runs since September.

Perhaps it's too much pressure, or perhaps this young team is not yet ready. What is certain is that this last series will make or break the Mariners for the year. When the dust settles, one team will remain standing. The Mariners need to win two out of the four games to get into the Series. If you believe in the 30-hit theory, and if the M's need Pasteur's hits to win their division, then what's left for the Championship games? With only six Pasteur hits left, this obviously means the M's need to win without Pasteur. This town is beyond thirsty for the sweet taste of victory. It's been too long. This season is too magical. Here comes the season, so take out your good luck charms, spare no incantation, dismiss no tradition, fail not to engage in your particular rituals. The M's need it all, and the Rangers are on the horizon. Abracadabra!

David and Casey drove home from the Kingdome in silence. There was not much to say after their 9-1 loss to the Rangers in the third game of the four-game series. The M's were now tied for first place, with one final game to play. The Mariners easily won the first game, negating the need for a Pasteur hit. It had been downhill from there. The teams base running was atrocious. The relief pitching was non-existent. David had used two of his hits in the losing effort, and now had only four hits left. Of course, if the M's could not win their last regular season game, there would be no use in hoarding the alleged remaining hits for future games that might never be. Uncashed checks were worthless. It now came down to nine innings. Nine innings of a dream, nine innings left in a career. Nine innings of celebrity left.

"How are you doing?" asked Casey, as she weaved her car through traffic on the way to her mother's house, where their two children had been deposited earlier so Casey could worry alone in the upper deck of the Kingdome. Casey had lately decided not to accept the company of Cyrus at home games, but to sit alone among the sellout crowds, totally anonymous, creating her own stomach acid in her own public privacy. Before the dream had invaded her life, she enjoyed sitting in her own seat, among strangers, enjoying the play before her, unbothered by her husband's commentary and would-be managerial suggestions. Now, this was even more true. Casey needed her privacy desperately.

Casey maneuvered the car up the steep hill, with its view of downtown, in Saint Esther's neighborhood. Esther generally kept the girls until their overachieving father and their privacy-starved mother came to gather them up.

"Hi, Mom. Any problems?" Casey asked her mother, the designated sitter.

"Yes."

"Oh, what happened?"

"We lost, of course! I'm just sick. I can't

sleep, I'm so worried. David," she said, "how can everyone fall apart at the same time? I mean, can you believe this? You can't do it *all*. They have to help some. I'm so disappointed. My ladies at the nursing home where I volunteer can't sleep either, they're terribly worried. Who's starting tomorrow?"

"Ask Piniella." David laughed. "I'm just, well, you know, who I am," David said.

"Well," she said, "I know that you're doing your best, but what's going on with ...."

"Mom, please. Not you, too? We'll be fine, and if we're not, heck, we're not."

""I know *you'll* do fine. I am absolutely confident you guys will win tomorrow. My heart says so. And if you don't win, well, it must be for the best."

"Are you Jewish? Casey, your mom's a yenta. You know, bring home a 98 on your report card and she says 'what, not a 100?' You bring home a 42 and she says 'so, what's the big deal? No one is good at everything. Not to worry, eat something, you're too thin!'"

Esther laughed and kissed her daughter goodnight and good luck. She handed over Lindsey and Lauren, wrapped sleeping in big fuzzy blankets. Each parent took a child to the car, laying them into the back seat for the short ride to their own home.

"You're awfully quiet, David. You okay?"

"Yeah. I'm fine. I'd just like to sleep all the way through the night sometime soon. I wake up exhausted."

"I know. Soon. This will be over soon, and then ...."

"We have to win tomorrow. We just have to. I ...."

"You're whining."

"I know, so what? I get to whine. I'm old enough, I'm entitled. Cyrus sent us a huge fruit basket today, with a cute note."

"What did it say?"

"Thanks, regardless."

"He's a class act."

"So are you."

"Thanks."

When Xavier Washington was called from the bullpen to relieve the Rangers starter, Mike Rennie, the sellout crowd rose to their feet and booed lustily. Xavier strolled toward the mound, apparently unaffected by the negative noise cascading down upon his wiry frame.

The M's had battled back from what looked like a 5-0 defeat, the first run coming when the Ranger back-up catcher, a veteran of 26 years in the Major Leagues, sat on M's starter Greg Hibbard's hanging curve and drove the ball 415 feet straight to center field, where it disappeared into the bleachers. Later in the game, Texas scratched out two more runs and led by five.

The Mariners' hitting continued to be unproductive until the sixth inning, when the team finally found their stroke and manufactured two runs on three hits. Then, in the seventh inning, the M's scored again on a home run from Jay Buhner, with two runners on base. The game was now tied, 5-5.

Casey sat in Cyrus' box, counter to her own wishes for anonymity. Instead, Casey's face hung out for the TV cameras to inspect at their will, and inspect they did. The cameras played constantly on Casey's tightly drawn face with every up and down nuance of the game, as Cyrus exhorted his team to "Score more runs, dammit."

Xavier ambled to the mound, to ringing denunciations of his manhood, parenthood, and religious affiliation. His warm-up tosses completed, he stood calmly on the green carpet behind the mound, pulling on his cap. Clearly, the biggest two innings in Mariner history were about to unfold. Just as clearly, Casey was going to need CPR, but only after completing the act of projectile vomiting. She hated this tension.

The first M's batter Washington faced was the lead-off hitter, Felix Fermin, who had not come close to a hit all evening. Fermin spent a full four minutes fouling off pitches, until Xavier finally threw ball four to the speedy shortstop.

The next hitter, Amaral, bunted the first pitch. The ball bounced short of the mound. Washington's only choice was to throw to first, allowing Fermin to advance to second. There was now one out in the eighth, a speedster on second base, and Griffey coming to the plate. This season, unlike his previous seasons, Griffey was not connecting with the ball when there were men in scoring position. In fact, his year to date average with men on base was only a disappointing .225.

Xavier threw all his pitches low and outside, until Griffey pulled a soft two hopper to second base, rushing his swing with adrenaline and impatience. Fermin flopped safely at third as Griffey headed back to the dugout. Two outs. Game tied. Runner on third.

Edgar Martinez, the 1992 American League batting champion, had been injured in the stretch drive with a pulled hamstring. He had faltered at the plate and his base running was hampered as well. Despite the injury, Edgar was hitting a solid .302 and making good contact during most plate appearances. He was slated to bat next.

Piniella sat in the middle of the crazed M's dugout. Tension was thick, voices loud with apprehension. Piniella sat staring at the cement between his large black shoes as Martinez settled into the batter's box.

Piniella gave a sign to the third base coach, who relayed it to Edgar. Martinez obediently stepped away from the plate as time was called.

"Counselor, let's try and use one of the four left," he said in a soft and well-modulated tone.

"I'm hitting for a batting champion?"

"You deaf?"

"Just petrified."

"If he tries to hit you, let him."

"Easy for you to say."

Edgar walked back to the dugout, past David. They both stopped between the dugout and home plate as David's name was called throughout the Kingdome.

"Now batting for Edgar Martinez, David PAAASTEUUUUR!"

And here it was. One of those baseball moments that people throughout sports come to expect every so many years. Bobby Thompson's home run, Kirk Gibson's home run, Carlton Fisk's home run, and now the potential for a Pasteur ... something.

The TV cameras all turned toward Casey, sitting along the third-base line, and memorialized her unheard words, "Oh shit!"

Dave Niehaus, the play-by-play announcer for the Mariners, summed up the situation over the radio air waves.

"So it comes down to this—my, oh my! What a game, what a season. Bottom of the 8th inning, two out, runner on third base, just 90 feet away from the go-ahead run in the last game of the regular season for the championship of the Western Division of the American League. Now the personal battle comes down to David "The Milk Man" Pasteur and his ex-teammate, ex-roommate, who reportedly disliked each other on sight many months ago when they first met. David has never spoken of those early events. Of course, the entire world knows about the 30-hit season, and what Xavier Washington thought about it as well.

"So here we go, young against old, yet both are neophytes, unaccustomed to the pressure, both in their very first season. Mix in bad blood and we have real big league drama. Oh, and here comes Jim Hendry, the grizzled five-year veteran manager out to talk with his young pitcher. You gotta think in this situation that walking Pasteur has to be considered. Hendry is probably saying to throw fastballs, just throw strikes, but still, you gotta think about walking him and pitching to Buhner, who has already hit one home run today, but not against the pitcher who's out there now.

"Here comes the home plate umpire to break up the conference, but in a situation like this, Bud Edwards will give Hendry more than the normal time to discuss this critical situation with his young pitcher."

Hendry, standing on the mound, was very brief with his instructions to Washington. "This ain't personal, but if you fall behind, walk him."

"But .... " Xavier attempted to argue.

"Got it? I don't believe in this vision

shit, and I can't explain it, but I don't have to try and explain nothin', so walk him and I'll bring in Sweeney to pitch to Buhner."

"But he's a... ah... you know, he's a damn *lawyer*. I mean, he ain't shit."

"One ball, then put him on. End of discussion. Got it?"

Hendry jogged back to his dugout. The Kingdome came alive as never before in the history of the ball club.

Esther, sitting with her daughter and Cyrus, stood and led a section sitting in the stands near her in a group cheer. Casey hated that.

Washington was seething. This was *his* moment. No asshole manager was going to dictate how he used *his* talent. A Jew lawyer with a dream. "Bullshit, take a peek at this, you shyster dick," Xavier said to himself, lips moving.

He looked in for his sign, waved off the first, second and third signs. They settled on a forkball, low and away.

"Ball one!" shouted Edwards, from behind his mask.

Hendry held up four fingers indicating to

the catcher an intentional walk.

"Crap!" Washington stormed at the umpire. "Everybody is trying to screw me." He tried to calm himself. "Now I'm supposed to walk him? Bullshit, I ain't gonna be known as the first guy to run from Pasteur's deal. Walk a civilian? No way. Not me."

His next windup was conducted in such a way as to leave no doubt that he was not planning to issue an intentional walk to this particular batter. Mark Matthews, the veteran catcher read Xavier's intent and quickly crouched behind the plate in anticipation of Xavier's second pitch. Hendry, whose foot was on the top step of the dugout, watching intently, simply could not believe what he was seeing. The arrogant little shit was disobeying his direct order. Hendry started out of the dugout, yelling a terrible insult toward the mound as the ball was released from Washington's hand.

David swung. Not at the ball, exactly, but at a spot over the plate. David had studied Xavier's pitching tendencies on video tape. He had never envisioned this scenario, but he had hoped that he might find some common ground discussing pitching when a friendship between the two was at least possible. Based on David's taped studies, intuition, and pure guesswork, he had swung at a location that he believed the ball was likely to intersect. It did.

At the same time Washington released his pitch, the young arrogant thrower heard a terrible scream of protest emanating from his manager's throat and automatically turned his head toward the awful sound. Xavier never saw the ball bounce on the front slope of the mound, and certainly never saw it carom skyward toward his groin. He also didn't feel the ball hit him. He did, however, have a vague recollection of his body pitching forward in the direction of home plate, falling directly on top of the fair ball as if it were a grenade and he was auditioning for the Congressional Medal of Honor.

The ball didn't explode.

But Hendry did.

He stood outside the dugout, still in foul territory, screaming at Washington to stop hatching the bloody ball like some prone, writhing bird. The Texas shortstop, Jon Borth ran to the mound, searching the immediate area attempting to locate the ball as he had lost sight of it from his position in the field after it struck his teammate. The shortstop searched frantically until he heard Hendry scream, "It's *under* the son of a bitch!"

"What?"

"Under him, dammit! Dig it out of 'em!"

The slightly built and lightly muscled shortstop threw his glove to the grass, bent down on both knees, placed his hands under the incapacitated pitcher and flipped him onto his back, like a visiting nurse, only less gently. There it was, a baseball, come to life, reborn once again. Borth, still on his knees and gloveless, grabbed the ball and rose to his feet. He proudly held up his newly found treasure to his manager, like a five-year-old with a freshly discovered Easter egg. Hendry however, was still screaming on the sidelines.

"I found it!" Borth yelled, smug for just a moment, forgetting that the ball he held was still live and that play continued.

David scampered to second base, easily scoring Fermin, unaware of the hatching that was taking place on the mound. He stood at second breathing hard, observing the scene. He looked at Washington still cupping his privates. He saw the shortstop holding his trophy on high. He observed the third baseman standing next to his shortstop, having run over to assist in the search for the hidden ball. He saw third base, gleaming white in the Kingdome lights, beckoning.

Wait, his brain commanded, what's happening here? The crowd noise was deafening. David looked beyond the third base coaching box, past Perlozzo standing near it, and into the owner's box in the stands to see Casey and Esther screaming. Screaming and pointing. Why pointing? What's wrong with this picture?

Oh, I get it. If the shortstop and the third baseman are standing near each other in the center of the infield, then third base isn't covered. RUN!

David took off on his own initiative, head down, churning for the extra base. Borth saw David's movement out of the corner of his eye and suddenly realized he was totally out of position, and he still held the ball. He ran toward third. The race was on.

David slid into the base head first. Borth ran toward the bag, diving at the sliding lawyer. He fell atop Pasteur, just as David's fingers brushed the canvas base. The two players lay tangled together in the dirt of the Kingdome infield, face to face, cheek to jowl.

"Hi," David chirped at the dazed infielder. "This is fun, huh?"

"Safe!" yelled the umpire, observing the tangled players from his vantage point above the sprawl.

David's gutsy maneuver turned out to be

crucial to the entire season. The next M's batter drove David in from third on a bunt single.

The Mariners held onto their lead through the top of the ninth. The season for the Texas Rangers was over.

20

DREAM TO END TODAY?
7TH GAME TO DECIDE IT ALL

AP Seattle. Today ends one of the most bizarre baseball seasons ever played since the game was first invented back in some cow pasture in Cooperstown, New York.

The Mariners and the Los Angeles Dodgers meet today in the Emerald City to decide the championship of baseball. Both teams have traveled such a long way since April, but no team has traveled as peculiar a path as that of the Seattle Mariners to this seventh game of the World Series.

The M's are out of Pasteur hits, having exhausted them all in the previous games. Pasteur's 30th hit in the bottom of the eighth inning in game five of the Series was his first "legitimate" Major League safety, a bases-loaded, one-out line drive over second base, scoring two runs to win the game and even the series at three games each. It was also his last hit, if one subscribes to the vision theory.

David Pasteur has, in one season, achieved a statistical legacy that will never be equaled, beginning with a batting average of 30 for 31, and a batting percentage of .9666. (Of course 666 is a number fraught with demonic significance.) The Mariners needed each and every one of Pasteur's squibs, squabs, chalk-flying bloopers, wind-blown drops, and who will ever forget The Milk Man's 11th inning "hit" to tie the third game of the Series. The slow dribbler to second base looked like a routine ground ball, which would have ended the inning and given the Dodgers a 3-0 game advantage. But Dodgers second baseman, Russ Engle, dropped the ball while making the backhand transfer to his throwing hand, and the run scored from third base. The official scorer was soundly booed by the Kingdome crowd after he flashed the hit sign.

The crowd, screaming for an error to be ruled, reasoned an error ruling would have "given" Pasteur another hit, as he would have been credited with only 28. When the official scorer, Pete Parker, sports columnist for the Seattle Times, was asked after the game why he had ruled the play a hit, he responded forcefully, "That's how I saw it. Pasteur's speed has increased over the season, and in my opinion, he would have beaten the throw even if the ball hadn't been dropped making the transfer. As to the ludicrous idea that I could affect Pasteur's future hitting by my ruling is preposterous. I don't subscribe to this dream thing. The Mariners have nine innings to win the series tomorrow, and I hope they do. But that was a hit, and I called it a hit."

The starting pitchers for tonight's game will be announced at noon. Pasteur's use as a pinch hitter or role player will await the lineup card that Mariners manager Lou Piniella will submit.

The Seattle Mariners have beaten long odds to get to this game. Coming this close and not completing the impossible dream would be a pity. Pasteur has refused all interviews until after tonight's game. After Series game six, he stated, "I can't imagine anything that hasn't already been said, asked, analyzed, reviewed and questioned to death. I shall therefore remain mute until the last ball is caught."

The question, then, may come down to the Pasteur factor, which is only fitting. Will the Mariners need Pasteur's magic, and does Pasteur, if called upon, have any magic left? All questions will be answered tonight. Will it be lucky sevens, or snake eyes?

David and Casey lay in bed in the early Saturday afternoon before the seventh night game of the World Series. The girls were at their friend's house, being baby-sat by parents who were terribly disappointed that no tickets were coming their way.

"I'm taking your kids for the entire night and missing the event of the decade. Does that make any sense?"

"Yes, Bob, it makes sense," David replied.

"Davey Boy, you got any hits left? You can tell me. Do you? Can you win it? Can you? *You've* got to know. I'll put some green down in Vegas for both of us."

"Goodbye, Bob."

Cardozo, now a vegetarian, left his position on the floor, jumped up onto the king-sized bed, and began to lick Casey's toes, which were exposed to the afternoon sun as it poured through the Pasteurs' bedroom window.

"How are you feeling, Counselor?" Casey asked, resting her head on his rising and falling chest.

"Okay."

"Nervous?"

"No."

"Depressed?"

"A little."

"Suicidal?"

"Maybe."

"Want more?"

"Baseball or sex?"

"Either."

"Yes, both please."

"Who says it's over? Isn't it possible ...."

"Don't start with me, Casey. I'm done with playing. It was beyond great, but now I'm just a spectator in a Mariners uniform, taking up space on the home team bench."

"Maybe you do have one more hit. Maybe you don't need Dumbo's feather. Maybe your last hit was really an error."

"No, it's over."

"When are you going to the ball park today?"

"I don't know. Probably around three. I'm going to take batting practice today against a real live pitcher. The team is holding the

First and Last Annual Milk Man Memorial Batting Practice competition. There's a $1,000 pot. The bet is that I won't see the ball, I won't touch the ball, I won't get ...."

The doorbell rang. Cardozo withdrew his pink tongue from Casey's toes and jumped off the bed to investigate the ringing.

"Someone has to get the door," observed Casey.

"I'm naked. You go."

"So what am I?"

"Oh, excuse me. I thought you were wearing a wrinkled raincoat ...."

She pelted him with a pillow.

The couple then played rock-scissors-paper. David lost. A bad omen. He put on a robe and opened the front door.

Sitting on the doorstep, a giant bouquet of flowers greeted him. A small white card was attached to one white rose. The card read, "That was a very effective way to get my attention. Thanks. Col. Robert Powell P.S. Send the bills for your dog to me. I'm mortified about what happened."

The network command truck bustled with activity as it sat parked by the Kingdome gate in preparation for the upcoming broadcast. David walked past the truck, into the players' gate, and through the clubhouse door. The clubhouse atmosphere was filled with tension—no rough housing, no jokes, no press until after the game. David, however, was not tense. In his mind, his season was over. His mission now was to keep this club, his club, loose. The Mariners played poorly when they played tight. The club was just too inexperienced to rise easily to the occasion of big games. They just hadn't had enough practice in coping with the pressure. Of course, the large, unspoken issue that permeated the club house was the knowledge that the Milk Man was out of hits, like a gunslinger with no more bullets in his gun. That certain knowledge that Pasteur was empty had a melancholy effect on the team's pre-game preparations. David had anticipated this level of team fear and had prepared for it the only way he could. He had sized up the club house chemistry, and decided to become the crazy chemist Pasteur without benefit of a Bunsen burner. Moving from the clubhouse to the trainer's room to the equipment room, he gathered his teammates into the center of the locker room and spoke.

"Loosen up, guys. This is just a baseball

game. It's not like your puppy died. And to prove that it's difficult to kill dreams and puppies, especially when they are blessed by the karma of the M's, I give you, your favorite good luck charm, your beloved mascot, your...."

The locker room door flew open revealing Cardozo, who ran into the center of the room, wearing a full Mariners uniform, including two shiny pairs of baseball shoes, a baseball cap, flip-up sun glasses, and a warm-up jacket. David slipped a cassette into a tape player, cranked the volume up to "disintegrate" and allowed "Doctor, Doctor, give me the news ..." to pour forth from the small but powerful speakers. David requested Cardozo's accompaniment in tripping the light fantastic. Cardozo agreed. David bowed to his partner, dramatically unlaced Cardozo's front pair of shoes and, grasping his two paws firmly in hand, led the drooling dog around the makeshift dance floor, boogeying to the bass guitar of some get down all-American rock-n-roll. The team members began to clap and smile. The dog began to how—it was his favorite song—and Piniella came bolting out of his office to investigate the racket.

What he saw astounded him—a loose, jovial, "what the hell, this is fun" clubhouse full of players who were clapping and laughing to the beat of Cardozo's furry swaying hips.

Cardozo and David made a fabulous couple. It was later agreed that in the future, Cardozo should lead. Piniella could not help himself. He started to smile, then chuckle, then guffaw.

What an unbelievable season, Piniella thought, turning back to his office. And it's almost over—dang.

21

The seventh game of the World Series began with George Will throwing out the game ball. The new Baseball Commissioner was very pleased with the small market success of the Mariners this season. The large vs. small market debate was *the* issue of the early '90s, and one which Will was uniquely able to oversee.

The Mariners took the field to begin the seventh game. Randy Johnson, the M's first 20-game winner in club history, would start, after only three day's rest. Piniella figured that there was no tomorrow, and Johnson was the team's go to pitcher, so Piniella went to him.

The Kingdome's sellout crowd started making noise early. When Johnson took the mound, the noise increased. When he struck out the side in the first inning, the crowd went into a screaming frenzy.

The game began to turn into a baseball classic in the bottom of the first inning, when two Dodger outfielders made three spectacular catches, robbing the Mariners' first three batters of a single, a double, and a home run, respectively. The game sped along, with both teams displaying athletic talent that would be remembered for years—runners stretching singles into doubles, two runners thrown out at home plate, two sliding triples, three spectacular double plays, infielders diving for balls with fantastic results. It was a season-long highlight film compressed into one game. By the end of the seventh inning the score stood at 2-2, and both starting pitchers were totally and irrevocably gassed. The game and the series would be decided by both teams' respective bullpens.

In the top of the eighth inning, Chris Bosio came in to relieve Johnson. Bosio had been used as a starter all season long, but now he was being asked to get the team to the top of the ninth inning, where the Mariners' closer would then get the ball and hopefully get the job done, as well.

Bosio was not sharp. Generally a control pitcher, with excellent location, he walked the

Dodgers' lead-off hitter on four straight pitches not even close to reserve catcher Bill Hasselman's target. Piniella paced the dugout. David looked for Cardozo to kick. Bosio then fell behind the Dodgers' second baseman, Chris Bernard, a young man who had been called up from Albuquerque in late August, and who had been performing exceptionally well. He hit Bosio's next pitch over first base on a line. The ball caromed into the right field corner, where it bounced around like a pinball, allowing the runner to score all the way from first base. Piniella came out to the mound, spoke to Bosio for a short time, snapped the ball back from Bosio's hand, and brought in another relief pitcher, Bobby Ayala, who desperately needed to get somebody out. The pressure began to tell as Ayala also was unable to find the plate, and when he did, his offerings got tattooed. Only good luck and a diving play by Amaral, who smothered a hard hit ground ball behind second base, prevented the damage from being mortal. Nevertheless, when the side retired, the Los Angeles Dodgers were leading by three runs. The M's had two more at-bats left in their season. They had to get busy immediately, or begin a long unwanted vacation as losers.

The Mariners evened the score in their half of the 8th inning, when Edgar Martinez hit a three-run homer, with two outs to bring Seattle to an hysterical and historical 5-5 tie.

Casey, sitting with Esther, Susan, Denise, and Cyrus, looked at her seatmates' demeanor. She concluded they looked like inmates on death row who had access to hallucinogens, knowing death was near, but too spaced-out to be appropriately scared. Casey was more calm than at any time since her early Arizona days. The season was almost over. David was a bookend in the team dugout, an interested observer who could play no active part in the outcome of this game, except to lend support as a vocal cheerleader. She saw David pacing in the dugout, shouting insults to the Dodgers and encouragement to his teammates. He was having a very good time on this, his last day as a professional ballplayer, and Casey no longer had to worry about her husband's performance. She even thought he looked cute in his too-tight uniform.

The ninth inning began with the Kingdome crowd coming to their feet as the team took to the field for maybe the last time this season.

Mac Suzuki, the M's closer this night, was so filled with adrenaline that his first pitch was a fastball, clocked at 98 miles per hour. Unfortunately, it hit the backstop on the fly for ball one. The catcher came out to the mound and quietly said, "For God's sake, get a grip. You gotta stay loose. I'm tempted to bring that damn dog back out here for a dance."

Suzuki laughed in Japanese, then settled down and threw strikes the rest of the inning, sending the Dodgers down in order.

Bottom of the ninth inning, seventh game of the World Series. Score tied. Three outs left for the Mariners. Hollywood couldn't have scripted it better.

Yet another standing ovation was observed by the millions watching on television and around the world. What everyone wondered was, where was The Milk Man? Would he be used? Could he be used? And would it make a lick of difference if he was used? The ninth hole hitter for the M's was Mike Blowers, the designated hitter for this most important game. Blowers swung at the Dodgers' pitcher's first offering and bounced a grounder between third and short for a lead off single. Fermin, the Seattle shortstop, bunted Blowers to second for a perfectly executed sacrifice. Eric Anthony, the swift-footed left fielder, was having a terrible series, hitting .120 with no runs batted in. He worked the count full then struck out on a slider well above his head.

Two out. Runner on second base.

Piniella looked down the bench, locked eyes with David, then smiled a smile of despair, shaking his head slowly like Cardozo answering a direct question. The American League Gold Glove 2nd Baseman of the Year, Rich Amaral, stepped up to the plate, saw a pitch he liked, and spanked a hanging curve into left field for a short single. Blowers could only advance as far as third base. The crowd began to chant—Milk Man! Milk Man! The crowd noise grew and grew, like the pool of acid in Piniella's stomach.

Piniella now stood up in the dugout. Keith Mitchell, sitting next to David, was summoned to pinch hit against Mac MacEwan, the Dodgers' ace closer, who had allowed only five hits in relief during all of September.

Mitchell, in his last Major League at-bat the season, stood in against the well-traveled closer. For the next five excruciating minutes, Mitchell fouled off pitch after pitch after pitch. McEwen threw 12 pitches—all strikes, except four—and walked Mitchell to load the bases, with two outs.

The capacity crowd now rose to their feet once again, swaying in unison, as an inner-city church choir might do on Sunday morning, chanting for the magic of The Milk Man.

Piniella walked slowly down the dugout to stand in front of David Pasteur, now sitting at the far end of the bench, examining his shoe tops. David looked up at Piniella's craggy, jowly face and smiled warmly.

"Hiya, Lou. What's up?" David said, very much wondering why Piniella was not managing the team instead of passing the time of day with him.

"You, I think." Beat. Beat.

"Excuse me!" David blurted.

"I'm dead serious, David. You're up."

Griffey, who sat next to David, didn't move. The polite thing to do would have been to leave the two individuals to their private discussion and walk to the other end of the bench. Not on your life, Griffey thought. I'm listening to every inflection of every word. He sat still as a statue, eavesdropping.

"Perhaps I need to summarize," David said quietly, then shouted, "I don't got no more hits, okay? It's just me now! Can't you count? I can. Thirty minus 30 things is zero."

"You got us here—you take us home."

"I'm calling Cyrus." David whined like a child complaining to his mom. "You've lost your mind."

The umpire, now standing near the Mariners' dugout, demanded that any decision Piniella was going to make should be made this instant. "Get a move on here," he commanded.

Piniella and David paid him no mind, their attention totally focused on each other, both glaring into each others' face.

"Lou, I'm not here to tell you how to manage, but are you NUTS?"

Piniella shrugged, turned his back on David and signaled the lineup change to the umpire, which was announced to the world.

David looked at Griffey for help, then Buhner, who shrugged his shoulders and said, "What the hell. Figure something out when you get up there."

"That's your advice?" David barked.

"Hey, you asked," Buhner reasoned.

"But I'm just an attorney."

"Not until this one last at-bat you ain't. Stop whining." Buhner smiled. "Hit it outta here–go get 'em!"

David examined his options as he slowly selected his bat out of the rack. It wasn't

Shakespeare exactly, but the question was similar—to hit or not to hit. Of course, David *wanted* to hit. More accurately, he wanted to get a hit, not just another at-bat and then fail. He forced himself to select his bat, now renamed the Milk Man Model by the manufacturer, Louisville Slugger, Inc. of Louisville Kentucky. The Foundation would receive a royalty for years to come for its use, and David would receive free bats for the rest of his life, which was not a terribly useful item for a trial lawyer—but free was free.

So it had come down to the destiny of the dream, a fitting end, David thought. Preordained, pre-determined, pre-menstrual .... No, no, concentrate for God's sake, feel the moment, feel the fear .... Be the ball ....

Judge Burns sat in his large, barely heated home, with his larger wife, watching a six-inch television in his kitchen while his wife waddled about, building him a six-story sandwich, chock-full of cholesterol. The judge watched the small screen while David's name was announced as the Mariners' pinch hitter. His wife of 25 years, who always wore a flowered muumuu, asked, "Isn't that the lawyer fellow who was rude and disrespectful to you at that girl's trial?"

"Indeed it was, Gertrude. More mayonnaise, please. And the higher court, I'm pleased to say, affirmed my decision. More cheese please, Dear. Of course, I wish David the best of luck at this at bat for the community's sake, but when he comes in front of me again I'll delight in crushing him like the pissant he is. More horseradish please, Gertrude." Burns looked down upon the Formica countertop to see his normal pool of sweat begin to form, despite the house temperature hovering around 57 degrees.

When David's picture was flashed onto the screen, coming out of the dugout, the judge reconsidered his prior opinion. "On the other hand, I hope the cocky son of a bitch strikes out. More ham please."

Traci was sitting up in her bed, naked, her luxurious hair cascading down to her shoulders. As David's fame increased, and as the season progressed, Traci had received store-wide attention, then chain-wide attention for selling Pasteur his first Major League wooden bat. She was promoted to assistant manager soon after the bat sale. She then, on her own initiative, asked David, who remembered her as the helpful retail clerk she was, to come to her store for an in-store promotion, which David readily agreed to do. After that coup, Traci rose to store manager, presiding over 30 employees, and began to date the owner's son, who lay snoring beside her in a wooded cabin on Orcas Island in the San Juans.

"Wake up, Stewart! How can you sleep through this? C'mon! David's up—he's coming to bat. Piniella actually put him in! Wake up you jerk."

"You wore me out, Honey," he said, turning away from the set. "It's just another baseball game. I'm beat."

"You're worthless!" she screamed. "A defining moment in the sport and I'm a part of it on some level, and what do you do? You sleep! Well, I'm done with you, starting now!"

She threw back the bed covers, slipped on a robe, pulled the plug out of the wall and gathered up the TV set. She carried the television out to the guest bedroom, slammed and locked the door, turned the game back on and settled in to see her man meet history. As for the jerk next door, "He's outta here," she concluded.

Cardozo's vet sat among his 25 guests crammed into his wood-paneled basement. He had been offered two tickets for early series games by David, but was unable to attend. No one could get tickets to the seventh game. The Lt. Governor had trouble getting tickets, so he was watching in the good doctor's basement with his other friends and neighbors. There was a framed picture of Cardozo in a baseball cap on the fireplace mantel. Dr. Singer let it be known to all his friends, acquaintances, co-workers, and peers that he alone was almost totally responsible for the Mariners' success in the baseball season about to end. His logic was somewhat strained. Cardozo was the linchpin of the Pasteur family. Cardozo had been poisoned. David could do nothing but worry until Cardozo was saved. He had saved Cardozo. David was able to continue to hit. Without Singers' cutting edge medical skills, Cardozo would have been dog meat and David would have been paralyzed with grief, thus unable to adequately perform. The simple conclusion was that Dr. Singer, DVM, was a substantial cog in the Mariners' well-oiled winning machine, and without his assistance, David would not be walking toward home plate in this memorable moment. Dr. Singer was quite vocal as to this fact and shared it with his guests throughout the game until the assembled guests told the good doctor to put a sock in it and turn up the television.

Leigh Stanton sat at the Golden Gopher club in Minneapolis, with her short-time boyfriend, Robert Steen, assistant to the mayor. David's abrupt departure from her apartment on that summer evening had rocked Leigh badly. She had never been rejected before. Never. And to be rejected after her assets had been so nicely put on display in that private and exposed moment took hours to overcome. Leigh was not the type of modern female to dwell on the past, but instead, she kept her eyes firmly on the future. The Golden Gopher club in downtown Minneapolis was packed with politicos and powerful businessmen, all eyes glued to a bar-sized television screen on this October night.

"Now hitting, number 30, David Pasteur." The stadium announcer's voice was carried over the airwaves to Leigh Stanton's perfect ears, one of which was being attended to by Mr. Steen's tongue.

"C'mon David!" she yelled to the screen. "Stop that!" she commanded her date. "I want to hear all of this."

"Oh, that's right, you met him once,"

Bob Steen said, replacing his pink tongue where it belonged.

"I did more than meet him, Bob. I spent an unbearably delightful evening with him. He is so cute, funny, and a devoted family man."

"He said no, did he?" Steen teased.

"Don't be crude. It wasn't like that," she flared, "just watch the game. As a matter of fact, he offered me a position with his law firm when I graduate. I'm considering it."

The Colonel sat in the dayroom of the VA Hospital psych ward with 20 other patients. The color television bolted to the wall displayed The Milk Man strolling toward home plate. The Colonel, still dressed in his blue bathrobe, moved closer to the set. His chin showed gray stubble, his once closely cropped hair disheveled. A person observing the Colonel for the first time would think him depressed and forlorn. He was, however, happier and more contented than he had been in years.

When first admitted to the hospital, the staff had performed a full and detailed medical workup, revealing the Colonel's blood chemistry to be completely unbalanced. This had led, in turn, to the Colonel's mental imbalances. Throughout the next several weeks, the medical staff tuned up all his systems, fed him balanced meals, weaned him off alcohol, and medicated him with anti-depressants.

He now sat with his new pals, cheering the Mariners. "You guys know he's my neighbor. Great guy. He has two gorgeous little girls."

"Go on," said a one-legged Korean War vet, holding onto his aluminum IV stand. "You don't know squat."

"Listen, you jarhead. I tell you, he is a personal acquaintance. Knew him when he was still a lawyer. When I get out of this hotel, we are going furniture shopping together.

"C'mon David!" he screamed at the wall, "I've seen your swing, it's a thing of beauty. Stroke that sucker, neighbor!"

Tom Schwanz sat in his living room, his baby girl dressed in Mariner diapers, bouncing on his bony knee. He had settled the Powers case within a month of losing the motion for the IME. His oldest son had taken Pasteur's autograph and had it framed, and it now hung over his bed.

"I still can't believe Pasteur is in a baseball uniform. I mean, he looks as bad in his uniform now as he did in his office."

"Dad," Schwanz's son cautioned, "stop it. The Milk Man looks great, he is great, and he'll win this game. You just wait and see. Don't bad-mouth your friend. I thought you liked him."

"Well, I do, it's just that ... I mean ... he's *me*. *I'm* a better athlete, *I'm* a better lawyer, but *I'm* the one sitting in a house with a feces-making drooler watching *him* in the World bloody Series. I just can't believe it. Hit it out, you pudgeball you!" Tom yelled, cackling.

Andrea Regal was apoplectic. She had been screaming nonstop for the last three hours, while her two brothers, both Dodgers' fans, watched their sister go crazy. She looked great. They were finishing their fourth tub of buttered popcorn.

"Now you just watch my lawyer smash it. He is the best, better than Babe Ruth."

"Oh, please," the boys screamed in unison, truly amazed at their sister's stupidity. "Just cuz he says you can go to Santa Monica City College and he'll pay for parking don't make him Babe Ruth."

"Except for his stomach," the younger brother added, giggling and slapping his knees.

"Harvard, Yale, Cal Western State—anywhere I want to go, you fathead. Can't you read?" Andrea said as she shook the framed education contract in her brother's face. "Oh, I forgot. You can't read, can you. C'mon, David, pop it again, like you promised! Line drive!"

Mac MacEwan, the Dodgers' efficient closer, stood on the back side of the mound, rubbing a crease into a new ball while observing David tap his bat handle with tacky black pitch. MacEwan was tense. At 31, he was at the top of his game, with a great command of his repertoire of five pitches. His current ERA was well below 2.0. He had recorded 34 saves this season, as well as seven wins. The only game he had lost all season was due to a bad pitch, extra-inning home run he had given up to M. L. Jacobs of the San Francisco Giants, way back in April. MacEwan was very confident. Only one thing concerned him. He had never pitched to a lawyer before.

Mac was well aware of Pasteur's phenomenal season his string of miscues, flares, parachutes, and swinging bunts. MacEwan was taking nothing for granted. He wore his lucky socks, in addition to his lucky jock strap. He warmed up in his ritualistic way, prepared to win the World Series by retiring this strange one-season legend. MacEwan's fastball was popping, his curve ball breaking. He was exactly where he wanted to be—in control of his team's fate. Put out this fire, and get his team to extra innings.

Larry Smith came out from behind home plate to make sure of their signs and to assure that no miscommunication would occur. Smith was in his second season with the Dodgers. He was known as a superb offensive catcher, in the mold and tradition of Roy Campanella or Johnny Rosboro, but without the defensive abilities of those two predecessors. Smith could call an excellent game for his pitcher, but sometimes had a tendency to rush to the ball when receiving a pitch in his crouch and when setting his feet in preparation for a throw to second base. Smith spoke intently to MacEwan, staring at the pitcher's chest.

"Okay, Mac, here we go. We're going straight fastballs, probably a curve to waste.

Remember, he's just a lawyer."

"What's that mean?"

"I don't know, but he don't either. You okay, Mac man?"

"Yeah, I'm ready. Let's do it."

"Okay, let's go after this fat little turd."

Smith pounded his catcher's mitt against his shin guards, adjusted his face mask and crouched behind the plate, signaling for a fastball, low and outside.

With two outs and bases loaded, David stepped up to the plate. He placed himself hard against where the now obliterated chalk line had formerly indicated the back of the batter's box.

He had settled himself into the front portion of the batter's box during his previous 31 at bats in order to beat a late-breaking curve. He now took up residence in the furthest portion of the batter's box, the area farthest away from MacEwan and closest to the umpire's chest protector. He staked out this new geographic position for a well thought out reason. He had never stood there before, and it might be fun. No use getting into a rut on one's last at bat, David thought as he dug a toe hold with his right foot in the dirt surrounding home plate.

It was strangely quiet in David's head as he peered out toward the pitcher's mound. The crowd noise was deafening in the Kingdome, but David was in an entirely different space, where the environment was serene, peaceful, yet filled with purpose.

David quickly went through all he had attempted to learn from Romero, who now sat next to Piniella, spitting onto the dugout floor in nervous anticipation. After failing to recall even one batting tip, David just waited—waited to see and then hit the ball.

MacEwan threw a blur. David knew he had .4167 of a second to see, react, swing, and connect with the erratic fastball propelled down the middle of the plate. His swing took 2.5 seconds. It was charitably called "a tad late" by one television announcer broadcasting the game. "He looks like an uncoordinated lawyer with a serious perception-reaction problem," another radio announcer intoned.

"Strike one," spoke the umpire, a needless redundancy to David's swing and miss.

MacEwan's second fastball danced like a jitterbug. David swung high, the ball went low. David spun awkwardly in a 360-degree circle of the truly clumsy, falling to one knee and pulling a muscle in his left butt cheek. David thought he looked beyond foolish. He knew he felt foolish. I looked better in spring training the first time I hit against a machine, he thought. Actually he had not.

"Strike two," said the umpire.

"I know that!" David snapped.

David stepped out of the box to take inventory of himself one last time. It was a very short review. He had no confidence in his ability, he felt awkward, looked worse, and now his ass hurt.

David cursed Piniella.

David cursed the dream.

David cursed his lack of ability.

Then he just cursed.

The peaceful and serene headspace that David had carried to the plate totally evaporated when he spun like an unbalanced top and stumbled like a jerk. His sweat had stained and soaked his white uniform in an instant after his flop. The crowd noise invaded his awareness. His hands shook, and he wanted to empty his bladder desperately.

David arranged himself once again in the farthest portion of the right-handed batter's box, again dug a toe hold with his back right foot, and waited for MacEwan's next humiliation.

The pitch from MacEwan's three-quarter sidearm delivery came toward the plate in what appeared to David to be slow motion. The baseball rotated slowly from side to side, and, improbably, he could see all of it! He could actually see the red seams as they spun, indicating a slow curve. Romero's lectures were true—the great hitters could see the seams of a pitched baseball and thus were able to read and adjust to the pitch. Now, in this one improbable, glorious moment, so could David.

He set himself, waiting for the ball to cross into his hitting zone. David took a small step backward with his right foot in preparation for striding fully into the pitch and slightly lowered his bat to make contact. He shifted his weight onto his front foot, pivoted his hips in perfect synchronization with his hands. It was all coming together—the hours of work paying off—the dream happening. The ball looked huge as it slowly came toward the middle of the plate. His swing was perfect, smooth, and powerfully controlled. Microseconds later, MacEwan's slow curve nestled directly into Smith's catcher's mitt.

No words were uttered for several seconds by anyone. Pasteur, anxious to hit the ball, had swung late, as usual. Smith, equally anxious to catch the ball, had rushed his catch, moving himself and his glove into David's path. The plate umpire, Bud Edwards, made a hand gesture, a seldom used hand gesture *never* before seen in World Series play—the sign for catcher interference—Pasteur was sent to first base, all runners advanced 90 feet. The Game was over. The Series was over. The Mariners had WON.

Cardozo snored contentedly on David's side of the bed. The dog slept hard, unaware of the cold December rain which pelted the Pasteurs' bedroom window, their electric blanket cranked to womb temperature. Casey was deeply asleep dreaming private dreams in a contented fetal position. David lay beside her, a smirk on his stubbly face. Seven weeks had passed since his bat struck Larry Smith's catcher's mitt, giving the Mariners the victory in the seventh game of the World Series. His season was now truly over, his lawyer life ready to begin again. Except last night ... last night....

"Casey, are you awake?"

No answer came from the sleeping form.

"Casey, Sweetheart, are you up?" he said, while driving an index finger into the side of his wife's neck. "Honey, listen ...."

"Whaaat ... I'm sleeping," she finally responded.

"Honey, last night—I had a dream ...."

"NOOOOO!" Casey screamed, now fully awake.

"Yeah, you see, I was at half court, with three seconds left in the game ...."

The rest was drowned out as Casey's pillow found its mark.